<u>The Client</u>

A novel by: Jessica Gadziala

The Client

\-

PROLOGUE

Wasp - Past

"You're a traitor," I grumbled, fingers toying with the fringe edges of the white woven blanket hanging off the side of the couch in Raven's new living room.

"I'm not a traitor!" she objected, scoffing, bright blue eyes dancing as her red-tinted lips curved into a smile.

Raven was the perfectly put-together yin to my wild and messy yang.

Even at seven in the morning, she had her gleaming black hair perfectly styled down her back, her blue eyes lined, her lips painted. Everything from the ice blue color of her silk tank to the white slacks that neither clung nor sagged too much to her high heeled sandals to the simple solo silver bangle on her wrist spoke of carefully curated class. Which was exactly what Raven had been her entire life.

Why she'd adopted knotty-haired, chipped-nail-paint, hole-in-her-jeans me was completely beyond me.

Opposites attract, and all that, I guess.

"You are only supposed to fall into a rich guy's dicksand temporarily," I told her.

"Dicksand?" she repeated, and I felt my lips curving up because it never failed to amuse me to hear her cool confident, ladylike voice say curse words. Though, most of the time, it was only when she was repeating something I said.

"Yes, his dicksand. Like when you meet a guy and he's giving it to you good, and he's pretty to look at, so you get obsessed with him, and he becomes your everything. It's supposed to be a temporary thing, falling into someone's dicksand."

"I didn't fall into his dicksand. I fell in love. I know, I know," she said when I made a hissing noise. "You don't believe in love. But it exists."

"It's not that I don't believe in it. It's that I think it is a chemical reaction. A fleeting one, at that. And women are usually the ones fucked over in the fall out of it. You've worked with me forever. You know how it goes."

"But what if it lasts?"

"It doesn't."

"But what if it *does*. Shouldn't I be willing to take that chance?"

"You're *my* soulmate, damnit," I reminded her, smiling.

"I am," she agreed, nodding. "And we love each other as much as two platonic friends with no interest in girl-on-girl sex can. We both need men still, though. We always have."

"For a night. To get that good dicking. That's it."

"He's a good man, Wasp," she told me, sitting down across from me, crossing her ankles, reaching up to mess with her hair. Raven was not, as a rule, a fiddler. She didn't muss her hair or tap her fingers or shake her leg. She was always the image of perfect put-togetherness. But she was fiddling, drawing my gaze up, seeing the wistful, far away look in her eyes.

She really was in love.

And he really was a good man.

I was happy for her.

Truly, I was.

But my heart was breaking a little for my loss as well. As selfish and silly as that sounded.

Raven and I had never been parted for more than a weekend since we were little kids. And as soon as we were adults, we hopped in a converted school bus, and lived on the road together for years.

Until we made a pit stop in Navesink Bank.

And she fell in love with one of its residents.

I had figured it was a fling, something to last the summer. Or even a year.

But that ring on her finger said she was never coming back on the road with me.

"I reserve the right to run a background check or have him followed at any point during your marriage," I insisted, making her laugh, a big white smile on display.

"I think Roman has come to expect that from you ever since you showed up in his office and threatened to castrate him with his letter opener."

"I didn't threaten to castrate him," I insisted, shaking my head.

"Yes, you did! He told me."

"Then he has a very bad memory. I threatened to jam the letter opener up his urethra," I recalled, making Raven snort.

"You did not."

"It had a better visual," I told her, shrugging.

"It's memorable, for sure. He had the good sense to look mildly certain that you weren't being facetious."

"If he breaks your heart, he will learn really quickly how serious I am," I told her.

I had one friend in the entire world.

I would happily seriously injure a man for her.

"I rest easy at night knowing you have my back," she told me. "And he loses a little sleep knowing that too," she added, smiling.

"You're happy, right?" I asked, needing to hear those words. They'd be the ones that would make a clean cut of the tie that had held us so closely all those years.

"I am blissfully happy," she clarified.

Snip.

I felt myself tumbling away, falling endlessly, wondering how I would ever feel grounded again.

Because that was what Raven was.

She was the anchor to my out of control boat.

She was the soft place to land when I jumped out of a plane without a parachute.

Raven was the calm to my chaos.

Without her there, I couldn't imagine what life was going to be like.

But I was going to find out, wasn't I?

"I'm happy for you then too," I told her, meaning it with everything I had.

"I was thinking—" she started, pressing her lips together, unsure if she should continue.

"About?"

"About what you are going to do now."

"I'm going to do what I always do. Hop in the skoolie. Make some men pay for the shit they thought they could get away with. And then get paid for that."

"I know. It's a passion of yours. But... I don't like the idea of you doing it alone, you know? For safety reasons."

That had crossed my mind as well. I might have been wild and a bit reckless, but I wasn't stupid. I understood just how risky the job we—and now I—did was. Pissing off men could lead to all sorts of sticky situations. And I wasn't too fond of the idea of ending up in a shallow grave in the woods somewhere, getting dug up and eaten by scavengers.

I wasn't sure how I would continue to do my job—and do it safely—but I was about to figure that out.

"You know me, Raven. Nothing can hurt me," I reminded her.

"Sting first, ask questions later, right, Wasp?" Roman's voice asked, coming in through the kitchen in his gray suit, looking stupidly handsome and happy. I could see what Raven saw in him. He walked up behind Raven, placing his hands on her shoulders, leaning down to press a kiss to the top of her head. And she damn near melted. Hell, my ice-cold heart thawed a bit.

"That's right," I agreed, nodding.

To that, he gave me what I could only call a brotherly smile. One that was amused, concerned, and exasperated all at once. I knew that smile. Because I had two brothers of my own. Reeve and Cyrus, who worried about me more than they needed to.

"I forgot my gym bag," he told us. "I'll be out of your hair in two minutes," he added, rushing off toward the stairs.

"Stop looking at his ass."

"Look, if a man is going to steal away my best friend in the world, I just want to make sure he has all the goods, okay? Trust me, it's not like that. He's asexual to me. You know we've never had the same taste in men anyway."

"That's true. One of the tenants of our friendship."

"Exactly. No bitchy in-fighting because you like them tall, dark, and handsome."

"And you like them silent and good in bed."

"Those are the only good kinds of men," I insisted, getting another laugh out of her.

"Seriously, though, Wasp. Maybe it's time to retire. I'm sure you could find a new passion in life."

It was the easier solution.

The problem was, I wasn't as confident as Raven was that I could find something else to do with my life that I would find halfway as exciting, as fulfilling, as what I did now. Just the idea of staying in one place made my throat feel a little tight. The idea of having to go to a nine-to-five where I had to wear *flat shoes* all day? That sounded downright torturous.

"I'm not done yet," I told her, shrugging. "I will know when I'm done. And, let's face it, there is a time stamp on this career anyway. No man is going to fall for a wrinkly, droopy-boobed version of me. So I am going to keep going while I'm in my prime. Socking some money away. Maybe investing some of it, so I can have a nest egg. And then retire when I get too droopy-butted to reel them in anymore."

"I thought your boobs were going to droop."

"Oh, they will. Everything is going to droop, Raven. We need to learn to accept that now. We will appreciate our bodies more if we do. Anyway, yeah. I know I can't do this forever. But I have a little bit left in me. But I promise that I will find ways to make sure I keep myself safe on jobs. Okay? Don't worry about me."

"I'm always going to worry about you. Even if I know you can take care of yourself."

"Psh. Give it a year or two. You'll have a baby on your hip and one on the way. You'll forget all about worrying about me."

"You know that's not true."

"I like the idea of you having a couple of little Ravens running around. Then I get to drop in, be the cool, crazy aunt. Corrupt them in an untold number of ways, then take off again to let you deal with the aftermath."

"I trust you are one-hundred percent capable of being that evil," she agreed. "But we haven't really... discussed that yet."

"What? Why? That shit is important. Hey, Cassanova!" I called as I heard feet on the stairs again.

"Yeah?" he asked, brows raised.

"Do you want crotch gremlins?"

"Is that... is that another kind of threat?" he asked, brows scrunching, looking over at Raven for help as she tried to hold in a laugh.

"She means children," Raven clarified.

"Oh. Yeah. Of course. I'm really close to my niece and nephew. I would love a few of my own. Why? Are you plotting ways to turn them against me for stealing Rebecca away from you?" he asked, smirking. And right then and there, I knew he was worthy of her.

"He calls you by your government name?" I asked, grimacing. "Ew."

"You're the only person who calls me Raven," she reminded me.

We'd given each other nicknames when we were kids, deciding our real names weren't cool enough.

She was Raven because of her beautiful hair.

I was Wasp.

Because I could sting once.

And then keep on stinging.

"Alright, ladies. I'm out. Are you sticking around for a while, Wasp?"

"And have to be constantly nauseated by your lovey-doveyness?" I asked, smiling. "No. I have a job, actually. I'm heading out after I leave here."

"I know you have a busy calendar, but we expect you at the wedding," he reminded me.

"The wedding? I will be here the night before to give Raven a bachelorette party she will never forget. It will make the antics in that *Hangover* movie seem tame."

"I don't doubt that in the least," he agreed, nodding. "So long as you have her at the church the next morning. And conscious enough to say her vows, I have no problem with that. I have to get back. Love you, Beccs," he called, eyes warm. "Fear you, Wasp," he added, giving me a salute before heading out.

"Okay. Fine," I admitted. "He's perfect."

"He is, isn't he?" she agreed, hearts in her eyes. "I'm excited to start a life with him."

I would never tell her this.

But I was terrified to start a life on my own.

But there was no denying that was exactly what I was going to need to do.

For better or worse.

ONE

Wasp

"So what is it that you do, Wendy?" the man at the bar asked me, using the name I used for all my marks. Wendy was a sweet, accessible girl-next-door, or an uber-hot red-headed sex goddess when necessary as well. She was a woman of all cloths.

What is it that I do, Kenny—whose real name I happen to know is Matthew?

I make men fall in love with me. Then I cut their legs out from under them.

And you're next on the chopping block.

"I'm a kindergarten teacher," I told him, knowing from his wife that he liked the good girls, the ones he thought he could corrupt. Like she had once been.

That was why I kept my natural blonde hair color, but tamed it more, kept the makeup to a minimum, put on a sweet, unassuming floral sundress with a little white sweater just for the extra kick to the nuts.

He was an easy mark.

I had been in this for years.

I could spot them a mile away.

The *I never lived up to my full potential as a human being, so I am going to live out my childish teenage fantasies of being a stud while I have a loving wife and a handful of kids at home* guys.

They were butter.

I was a hot knife.

And I didn't even need him to fall in love with me.

The wife knew he'd been screwing around for the better part of a year, but her PI had never been able to get a good enough angle to prove it. I was just the bait. Who happened to have a room facing the parking lot on the first floor. Where the PI was waiting in his car with a good camera.

They didn't need much.

Him naked.

Me with some of my clothes off.

Make it look really compromising.

I could cut out before it went beyond a little kissing and boob and ass grabbing.

And collect a nice little paycheck to stick into my savings.

I'd learned to get a little more serious about socking money away, about properly investing in my future, when Raven married Roman, and I came face-to-face with the reality of a retirement plan that didn't include the two of us getting a nice little apartment in a busy city, having the time of our lives living the good life.

Also, without Raven, that meant I needed a hell of a lot more money to be able to pull off that plan without her input.

So as much as I loved the long con of making a man fall for me, these shorter ones were paying me more and faster these days.

It would be shocking to the normal woman to know just how many 'devoted husbands' ended up fucking around behind their wives' backs.

Not me, of course.

I was just jaded enough to pretty much think the vast majority of them were trash who couldn't be trusted.

That said, I knew a man or two in my business who had some choice things to say about the female population too.

In short, we were all mostly assholes.

Which sucked for the good ones.

But, thankfully, people like me existed to make them pay for what they did.

Kenny/Matthew practically had to work to keep the drool in his mouth. I could see the image playing across his eyes.

Us in a room.

A ruler on the nightstand.

Him 'teaching' me to say all the dirty words he wanted to hear.

I wouldn't begrudge anyone their fetish. But you took that shit home. You worked them out in the bed with the woman you swore your future to.

Asshole.

But the smile I gave him was warm enough to toy with my own eyes.

"I have so much respect for teachers," he claimed.

I imagined he did. Since he had three children and a handful of teachers who taught them. I couldn't help but wonder how many of them he had fantasized over during parent-teacher conferences.

"It's hard, but rewarding work," I agreed, toying with the rosé I had ordered. I didn't drink on a job as a rule. You never wanted to lose your response time if something went south. You always had to be prepared to act if it became necessary. Alcohol made it difficult.

Luckily, Kenny/Matthew was probably just taking it as more of my good-girl persona.

If he only knew how *not good* I was.

He would run screaming.

It was one more drink for him and twenty more minutes of banal get-to-know-you talk at the bar before I was saying I was tired, before he was using that as an in to get himself back to my room.

And then clothes came off.

Hands grabbed.

I could practically hear the pictures getting snapped.

And then, the getaway plan.

"Oh my God. Oh. My. God," I gasped, yanking away, clutching hands to my bra-clad breasts, eyes wild.

"What's the matter, honey?"

Ugh.

Honey.

He called his wife that.

"I can't do this!" I declared, reaching for my dress, holding it to my chest. "What was I thinking? I don't do this. I'm a relationship kind of girl," I insisted, backing toward the door. I was going to need to leave the shoes. Given that they were ugly tan kitten heels I didn't like anyway, it was no loss.

"No. Wait. Come back here," he demanded, reaching for me.

"No! No. I can't. I'm so sorry. Really, you're a nice guy. I just can't. I can't."

With that, I flew out the door, knowing he wouldn't follow since he was naked.

I was most of the way there, too, but I luckily hadn't known any shame in my life.

"What? You've never seen tits before?" I snapped at the guy I passed in the hallway, making him jerk his head in the other direction as I rounded the corner, slipped into my dress, then made my way barefooted out of the building.

"Did you get it?" I asked as I walked past the PI.

"Got more than we need."

"Great. Tell the client I will see her in half an hour," I told him, making my way down the street where I'd parked my skoolie—converted school bus house.

A couple hours.

A couple grand.

Fair trade, in my humble opinion.

And, luckily, my living expenses were low. The big money had been the up-front cash to convert the old school bus into a house on wheels. Once that was done, it was really just gas, insurance, phone, and various streaming services to keep me entertained while on boring cases in an areas where I couldn't get out in the fresh air.

I'd painted the offensive yellow and black vehicle a crisp white. Then I'd gutted and rebuilt the whole inside. It was one of my proudest projects to date.

People didn't generally see me as a handyman sort, what with my penchant for ankle-breaking heels and a complete inability to take instructions from anyone.

Luckily, online videos were a perfect resource that didn't talk back or condescend to me.

And so, I rolled up my sleeves. And I built my home. From the rustic farm wood floors, to the white cabinets that lined the left side—along with a farmhouse sink, a hot plate, and a mini-fridge—to the built-in padded booth that took up the left side, that Raven had once used as a bed. I'd been the one to decide to lift the full bed in the far back to make more storage for clothing as well as a water tank to feed into the minuscule shower. I'd done the research on composting toilets. I'd figured out the electrical. Every inch of my home had my blood, sweat, tears, and frustrated rage in it.

I loved it more than was probably appropriate for an inanimate object.

I dropped down in the driver's seat, taking a deep breath, reaching for my phone, shooting a text to Raven.

We'd made a deal.

I texted her before a job, telling her my expected timeframe. And then I texted her afterward. If it went beyond an acceptable margin of error—and having worked alongside me all the years she did, she knew what that would be—she reserved the right to call the local police and report it. Or, in lieu of them helping, call my brothers so they could get someone on it. Being outlaw bikers with a lot of connections in the criminal world, they could have someone on my case in an hour tops, if it ever came to that.

It didn't matter that it had been years. Or that she did, indeed, have a couple little Ravens running around—along with a little Roman—she still insisted on the texts.

And for just a couple moments, I didn't feel quite so alone anymore.

I wasn't someone prone to loneliness.

I liked being alone. I was solitary by nature. I found most people tended to get on my nerves after a while. That said, my alone had always included my brothers when I was young. Then Raven.

This alone? This was a different kind.

I had no one to run to after a hilarious twist to a job, to laugh with, to drink with, to blow paychecks with at local shops.

I didn't like the idea of the job getting old. Or this lifestyle getting old. All I ever wanted to do was travel, to snatch up every memory I could, to see every important sight, to live deeply, yet temporarily in every location I visited.

But it had been over a decade now.

I'd seen every state. Been to every large—and many small—attractions. I'd sampled every regional cuisine from Georgia peaches and Southern barbecue to New York pizza and Jersey bagels, and whatever weird hybrid concoctions they were always coming up with over on the west coast. I'd seen sunrises in California and sunsets in Connecticut. I'd experienced hurricanes and tornadoes and the whole other kind of natural disaster known as the humid summers of Florida.

But, well, I'd seen it all.

I didn't remember the last time I felt excited when I got a job in a different state, rushing to plan a trip to hit places I was stoked to see.

Like everything, even realized dreams can become mundane after a while.

My phone rang in my hand, making me jolt. Seeing Raven's name, I answered.

"What's the matter?" she asked, to the sound of a baby whining in the background. Little Roman was a notoriously fussy newborn, and was proving every bit as demanding a toddler.

He wants to live on my boob, she'd told me one night, sounding half-asleep. *Well, he is a boy*, I'd quipped, making a laugh move through her.

"Nothing," I said, shaking my head even though she couldn't see me.

"You sent an entire text without eggplant or middle finger emojis. Something is up."

"We can't forget my favorite emoji. I couldn't live without the facepalm. "And nothing is wrong."

"I know you better than that. You sound off. Don't make me Facetime you to confirm my suspicions. I'm a complete wreck. No one wants to see that."

"Your 'wreck' is most people's 'good day.'"

"Wasp..."

"I don't know. I'm bored. And not excited about anything," I admitted, because she was my safe space, because I could trust her with that small bit of vulnerability.

"Come home," she demanded automatically, worry slipping into her voice, knowing I was never someone prone to dark moods.

"I am home," I reminded her.

"You know what I mean. Come to Navesink Bank. I would love to see you. The kids too. And your brothers. Their kids. We all miss you so much. It's been forever."

"It's been two months since my last visit."

"And that is forever."

"I'm okay. Really. I think I just need to get out of California for a while. Everyone is too happy. It's pissing me off."

To that, I got a snorting laugh. "You're ridiculous. Well, point Wanda in this direction. I'm not saying you have to come here, but if you end up here, we'd be happy to have you."

"Wanda and I were thinking of somewhere gloomier. Like that place in that god-awful vampire movie you made me watch."

"Forks?" she asked.

"Yeah. The place where it is so rainy and moody that vampires can walk around without *sparkling*. Or, you know, bursting into flames like the non-lame *Buffy*-era vampires did."

"I know that there is no out-stubborning you, but if the mood keeps up, please come home. We can binge-watch old TV shows and reminisce."

"You have three children. Binging is out of the question."

"Not if I pawn them off on friends or family. I can always make time for you. You know that."

She could.

But that didn't mean it was easy for her to do so.

She had her life.

I had mine.

Our paths tended to connect for a couple hours every few months. Or longer over the winter since Wanda didn't like living in cold conditions in the harsher months, not having that great of insulation or the kind of heating system that would work round-the-clock.

"I promise if I am in some downward spiral, I will come home. I'm probably just in need of some fun. I've been on back-to-back jobs for months."

"The infidelity business is always booming."

"Speaking of—"

"Don't worry. Roman is still having nightmares about your Christmas morning threat to string him up by his balls if he cheats on me."

"By a string of Christmas lights. Don't forget the best part."

"Yes, of course. A festive threat."

"Gotta keep it fresh." Even if we both knew Roman was not the cheating sort. If you could count on anything in the world, it was that the sun would rise, the tax man would find you, and Roman was one-thousand-percent head-over-heels for his wife.

"Okay. If you promise you're alright, I will leave you alone. I know you need to move Wanda."

"Yeah. We are not very inconspicuous parked a block from the hotel," I agreed. "Kiss the kids for me."

"You suck for teaching them that song, by the way. Now I have to sing it to them every night."

"*'Goodnight, Demonslayer'* is classic Voltaire. And a very good message for kids, in my humble opinion."

"I love you. Thirty-five Louboutin pumps."

"Love you back two-thousand bags of Fritos."

"Goodnight."

"'Night."

Feeling marginally better after a talk with her, I turned over Wanda, and headed toward the meeting place with the client, collecting my check, going back to the hotel to check out, and then went straight out of town. Out of state.

The sun was rising when I finally pulled over into a camping ground, pulled the curtains on all of the windows, put the massive wooden plank down across the door to prevent any access, climbed into my bed, and passed out.

I woke up startled and groggy, not sure what day it was or what town I was in.

Flopping over in my bed, I fumbled for my phone finding it tucked under the pillows, opening it to see what time it was, and where I was currently parked.

Satisfied with that, I opened up my email, ready to spend a moment or two scrolling through the junk, deleting it so I wouldn't have to pay for yet more storage.

I didn't expect any work emails.

Usually, there were a couple day—or even week—gaps between when I finished one job, and when I had another lined up.

There it was, though, demanding attention.

If nothing else, work provided a distraction from my uncharacteristically sour mood.

Opening it, I found something a little unexpected. Not the desperate preamble full of hurt and anger and bitterness.

But, rather, a name. Followed by instructions to search his online presence.

Curious, I did so before finishing the email, wondering who the hell this Fenway Arlington guy was if this client was talking about him as though he was somebody.

I found a ton of social media accounts full of pretty views, epic parties, beautiful women on yachts and at poolsides.

Rich guy aesthetic, that was how you would describe his social media presence.

Rich of the old money, born-rich sort.

Rich was rich, but rich couldn't afford yachts. They couldn't flex that hard.

Wealthy was a category of its own, one this man belonged squarely in.

There weren't any good, close pictures of the man himself, just a hint of a seemingly handsome profile, the outline of a very nice suit, his legs.

No up-close selfies to see if he had also won the genetic—along with socioeconomic—lottery.

Interested, I clicked back over to the email.

There is a cool hundred-grand in it for you if you can do the impossible.

If you can make Fenway Arlington fall in love with you.

Perhaps I should have been suspicious of that sort of money. But then again, I knew what bitterness did to a woman. It could make them go to any lengths to get payback.

If Fenway Arlington was crazy wealthy, it wasn't a huge leap to imagine some of the shoulders he rubbed against—and the women he bedded and broke the hearts of—were wealthy as well.

You will want to make sure you have your passport, the email added. *Fenway is currently getting into trouble in Paris for the third time this year. I will offer five grand up-front as good faith money if you agree to the job.*

Five grand was nothing to sneeze at.

And on top of it all, I got to see a brand new sight.

I didn't, as a rule, do international jobs. There was a lot of risk there. Different laws. It was touchy.

That said, there was nothing illegal at all in making a man fall in love with you. Then breaking his heart. Certainly not in France, anyway.

I had a passport.

It only had one stamp in it, from a post-high school trip with Raven down to the Bahamas to let off some steam and drink legally while we were still technically illegal.

It looked like I was about to get another one.

Excitement bubbled in my belly, little champagne fizzles of anticipation, as I typed out a response before climbing out of bed, not even bothering to change, just turning Wanda in the direction of the east coast.

Raven was getting her wish.

I was coming to visit.

But only so that I could park Wanda in her driveway while I took off.

I would just tell her I was taking a vacation. I didn't need her worrying about international jobs. She had enough on her plate.

Besides, this would be cake.

I mean, how hard could it possibly be to make Fenway Arlington fall in love with me?

TWO

Fenway

Paris was getting old.

After about three weeks, I'd been to every party worth going to, visited every old friend I'd ever made, dined several beautiful, but wholly uninteresting women.

It was about time to move on.

To go where, I wasn't sure.

Somewhere hot and sunny.

I hadn't taken my yacht anywhere since dropping Miller off in Greece.

I was sure it missed me.

"You're not paying attention," one of the girls at the table told me, pouting.

She was right. I wasn't. Because I was done here. And once I was done, my mind couldn't seem to focus on anything other than the next natural high to chase. The next city to get lost in. The foods. The parties. The old friends. The new ones I would meet.

Maybe the international incident I might create.

My old friends back over at Quinton Baird & Associates hadn't heard from me in a while. We were overdue for a reunion too.

If I could find a woman to create a scandal with, that is.

The women at my table were all the same. Beautiful, eager, accommodating.

Unchallenging.

People who met me generally thought I liked everything light and fun and easy.

Which was true in many ways.

But not when it came to the kind of women who caught my attention for more than a night.

No.

Those women always had something extra.

Even if that 'extra' was simply that I couldn't have them.

Because they were married to Russian mob bosses.

That was a fun one.

Cost me an almost painful amount to fix that one. But it had been worth it in the end.

Besides, women forced into unhappy marriages with assholes who treated them like dirt deserved a little fun too.

The woman across from me—with the pouting lips, not used to being ignored when she was accustomed to always being the most beautiful woman in the room—wasn't a challenge. If I crooked a finger, she would follow along. Just your average, every day fortune-chaser, one who was willing to secure it on her back or knees.

And while I admired someone who knew what they wanted and pursued it ceaselessly, it was too easy. And easy was boring.

But, I decided as my eyes started to scan the bar, easy might be all I could find my last night in this particular city.

I was about to drop some money on the table, and invite all of them back to my suite for a hot tub party and too much champagne.

Then there she was.

There was something about the air in a room when the kind of woman I was after stepped into it.

It got thicker and slower, buttery smooth and demanding attention.

My gaze followed the vibe, finding the source of it.

From the looks of things, I wasn't the only one who noticed the charge in the air. Because every man in the vicinity's eyes were on her.

This ravishing creature in a backless black dress that dipped to the smallest part of her lower back, with her icepick heels, long, wavy blonde hair, perfectly symmetrical, delicate face with her intelligent, cold, blue-green eyes.

She walked through the crowd like a queen making her way to a throne, chin parallel to the floor, shoulders back, gait sure, hips swinging just the right amount.

Fucking perfect.

Perfect.

"Ladies," I said as the woman in question moved to sit at the bar, ordering a drink from the dumbstruck bartender. "Have another couple rounds and a ride home on me," I told them, reaching into my wallet, tossing a wad of cash on the table.

I imagined there was a mix of delight at the amount dropped there to be split, as well as the disappointment at knowing it was all they were going to get from me.

But I couldn't be bothered watching all of that play out.

Not when the woman had her elbow on the bar, her slender arm lifted to hold her face in her hand.

Bored.

Well, I could certainly help her out there, couldn't I?

Moving away from the VIP section, I made my way down the stairs as the first brave man approached. Young and cocky, he moved in aggressively, leaning into her space, getting an ice-cold sideways glance. Even from a distance, I could see her only response to him before turning her attention to the back bar.

"No."

Strike one.

It wasn't long before the next man moved in. Older. Somewhere around middle age, handsome enough even if he was losing a battle with sweets judging by a bit of a hangover waistline. But that suit he had on was designer. The watch on his wrist cost a cool ten grand.

If she was after a rich husband or sugar daddy, this would be her choice.

She didn't bother glancing his way as he started his spiel, just let him finish his preamble before shaking her head at him as well.

Interesting.

A beautiful woman dressed like she was, alone at a bar. They were typically there for a reason. Usually, that reason was a man.

But she didn't check her phone or look toward the door, didn't glance at the clock on the wall to her left.

It didn't seem like she was waiting for a significant other.

All the more intriguing.

I hung back, letting the next guy try his luck. But the moron didn't even bother to take off his wedding ring when he went up to her.

That seemed to get her attention when he waved his hand to gesticulate.

Her head turned slowly, eyes keen, a predator sizing up her prey.

I couldn't make out the words or the tone when she spoke, but the frigidness of her expression sent a chill through me from a solid twenty feet away.

The man shriveled before her, shoulders curling in, chin dipping toward his chest.

By the time she was done speaking, he looked suitably chastened, rushing off. Not to rejoin his friends across the room, but straight out the front door. I imagined home to his loving, unsuspecting wife.

"Now how is he going to go home and offer his wife his balls if you have them in your pocket?" I asked, moving in beside her, facing forward, nodding at the bartender who already knew my drink. I'd been to this bar many times over the years.

"That sounds like his problem," she told me. And for an ice queen, that voice was all milk and honey, sweet and smooth. I couldn't help but wonder what it sounded like when it was moaning.

But one thing at a time.

"If you're not waiting for your man, and you won't entertain any of the ones who are coming up to you, what are you doing here?"

"Can't a woman enjoy a drink alone at a bar?"

"Sure she can."

"And how do you know I'm not waiting for a man? Have you been watching me?" she asked, half turning her head toward me, cold gaze doing a slow sweep. I wasn't sure I'd ever felt as exposed before as I did right then.

"Yes," I admitted, figuring it would be useless to lie. "It's your own fault, though. You are very watchable." Something about that seemed to rub her the wrong way. When her head faced forward again, I could have sworn her eyes rolled. "It has been a long time since I saw someone dress three men down that quickly," I added, not ready to give in just yet, even if my usual charms appeared to be failing me.

"It hasn't been long since three men have deserved it," she shot back.

"Oh, we can't all be that bad," I told her, smile pulling up.

"Like you?" she asked, giving me her attention once again. "With the boyish smile and the bone structure that speaks of good breeding and the nice suit, but the casual lack of tie and undone two buttons? You're one of the good ones? With the harem of girls still mooning over you from half a bar away?"

"So I wasn't the only one doing some watching," I concluded, feeling like I had a leg to stand on now, making my grin go from boyish to cocky. "It was me you were waiting for, wasn't it? Had your heart set on me from the moment you walked in the door. Don't worry, you wouldn't be the first to fall head-over-heels in love with me at first sight," I teased, watching as one of her brows arched up slowly.

"I wonder what it must say about a man who needs the attention of every woman in a bar?" she mused, speaking to the bartender who looked uncomfortable being put on the spot, seeming to sense her jab was at me, and not wanting to risk his tip.

"I think it says he knows that it takes many women to fill the space of the *one* right woman."

"I'm not the right woman."

"You don't know what kind of right woman I am looking for."

"Open legs, closed mouth, most likely."

"See, now that is where you're wrong. I like mouths open too. Oh, don't look at everything under that cynical lens of yours," I suggested when her lip curled at my wording, misunderstanding my meaning.

"It is the only lens I have, Mr.—"

"Arlington. Fenway Arlington."

"Fenway Arlington," she repeated, and I have to admit that I liked the way my name sounded on her lips. "Does anyone in the world have quite as pretentious a name as you do, Mr. Arlington?"

"Well, I have a cousin named Love."

"Their actual name? On their birth certificate?" she clarified, disbelieving.

"On their birth certificate. And all her monogrammed baby blankets."

"Alright. Love wins."

"May I ask your name?" I asked. "Or should I just continue to call you Ice Queen in my head?"

"Wasp."

"Wasp?" I repeated, and it was my turn not to believe. "That has to be your bar name."

"My bar name?"

"The name you give random men at bars because you don't like the familiarity of them calling you by your actual name."

There was a moment of bewildered interest before she banked it down.

"I don't have a bar name. My name is Wasp."

"Don't worry, Wasp," I told her, letting it drop there, knowing she would ask for more.

"Worry about what?" she asked, unable to help herself.

My gaze slid in her direction, holding hers for a long moment.

"I don't mind getting stung," I told her, dropping some more cash on the bar, getting up, and walking out.

Wasp, and I was still not convinced that was her actual name, needed to be left hanging. She needed to be on the hook. She wasn't the kind of woman you could seal a deal with in one night. And if she was, I wouldn't have been nearly as interested.

Chances were, if she was at that bar, then she was staying at the hotel across the street.

Which meant we had to serendipitously on-purpose happen to cross paths again.

I shook my head at my driver, deciding to walk back to my own hotel.

Suddenly, the city that had become so dull to me, everything dimmer and less exciting than when I first arrived, had burst back to life.

Lights blazed.

Music blasted.

Lovers kissed on corners.

Everything pulsed, begging to be experienced.

Maybe I wasn't quite so done with Paris after all.

I mean, I couldn't just leave a woman like her all alone in the city of love, now, could I?

THREE

Wasp

Paris was everything I thought it might be. And more. And less.

I had experienced that phenomenon more times than I could count over the years. When I built up my expectations to towering skyscrapers that nothing could measure up to.

There was also something to be said for the fact that I was experiencing it on my own. There was something about sharing a travel experience with someone else that made it even more special.

To have someone to point out things to.
Did you see that?
Do you hear that?
Oh, my God, get a picture of that.
I think we need to treat ourselves.
Alone, I was both the sense of wonder and the voice of reason. So I didn't stop for that third pastry on my walk from my hotel to the corner store where I needed to pick up some fashion

tape to be able to put on the dress I was going to wear to meet Fenway Arlington.

Meet.

But I'd had my eyes on him for two days leading up to the actual meet-cute.

I needed to study him, since the client who hired me had been oddly tight-lipped about everything in her emails.

I was used to women pouring their hearts out to me about their situations, everything from how they and their spouse met right up to when they suspected he was cheating. I knew the names and ages of children, physical descriptions of the porn stars they knew their spouses preferred. I knew their daily schedules and what their favorite drinks were.

But with Fenway's case, all I got was a couple of cryptic messages claiming he was someone who had caused many international incidents because of women that had needed to be kept out of the society pages by a professional "fixer." And then I was told how he needed to be brought to his knees by a woman, so he could learn the repercussions of his lifestyle.

That was a cold kind of revenge, if you asked me, but I understood that even more than I did the hot, raw, exposed-nerve sort of revenge that most women typically approached me with.

Cold was natural to me.

And after watching the warmth that was Fenway Arlington—and all the women who flocked around him, pretty little trust fund bunnies—I knew that my natural cold, maybe even amped up a bit, was exactly what was going to set me apart, make me intriguing.

Pair that with a dress that exposed more than it covered up, not even bothering to put flower petals on my nipples under the slinky material, and I was pretty much catnip to his tomcat self.

He'd been an easy enough man to find, even in a city as bustling as this one.

He was a man of wealth which meant he would flock toward places that had VIP sections and top-shelf everything. Which narrowed things down a bit.

Then once I found him, uglied down in oversized clothes, glasses, and a hat for good measure, he was easy to pick out of a crowd.

There was a magnetism about him that made you notice him immediately, even if you somehow missed his ridiculously good looks.

It was almost obnoxious to be both breathtakingly handsome, fit, stylish, and immeasurably wealthy all at once.

That said, obnoxious was a trait that did seem to come to him naturally at times.

I'd followed him to a few establishments over the course of those first two nights of surveillance work.

He was always the one getting loud, starting trouble, urging others to get into some as well.

He was over-the-top, generous, and completely unconcerned with social mores or actual laws.

A part of me had worried that, even if I did catch his eye, that his attention span was too short to be able to run a long con on him.

Then there he was.

And then he was gone.

Leaving *me* hanging.

Me.

No one left me hanging.

No one.

That was not how it worked.

I hanged everyone else out to dry.

Not the other way around.

I threw back the rest of my drink, got off the stool, and made my way toward the door, heels tapping so hard against the floor in my agitation that I was surprised they didn't snap.

He thought he was playing me, I decided as I made my way into the elevator in my hotel. He thought that by schmoozing then rushing off, that he was going to have me salivating after him. He thought he had the upper hand.

Well.

He was just going to have to learn, wasn't he?

No one got the upper hand over me.

Certainly not in the game of cat and mouse that was intrigue and interest and sexual chemistry.

Oh, no.

I just had to ramp it up the next time I saw him. And I would see him again. No way was I going to turn down the life-changing kind of money that was being offered to me just because I was pissed off that this man-child thought he could out-intrigue me.

"I told you not to call me," I grumbled at my phone to Raven, knowing it was barely six in the morning back in Navesink Bank, that she was going out of her way to check in on me so early in the morning.

"You know I have to worry about you."

"There's nothing to worry about," I assured her.

"You are working an international job. There is plenty to worry about."

She'd broken me when I'd dropped off Wanda. Don't ask me how she managed it, but she'd gotten the truth about the trip out of me. Then she'd promptly started fretting about it.

"It's a very safe job," I assured her. "Really. The client is like a puppy dog. All tail-wagging and lapping tongue, no brain."

"How do you know about his lapping tongue?" she asked, tone teasing.

"Oh, ew. No. Gross."

"So he's ugly?"

"No. He's actually stunning. But that is beside the point."

I wasn't necessarily morally opposed to sleeping with a mark. In fact, there were not many things my moral code was against. But I didn't want it to go that way. It gave some of the power away. The women held all the power up to the moment that backs hit mattresses. After that, in many situations, she ended up on the losing side. It was bad business.

Sure, sometimes, there was some fumbling and making out. But I always saw it more as acting than anything else.

Certainly nothing went as far as oral sex.

And I planned to keep it that way.

Men were easier to lead around when they were thinking with their unsatisfied dicks. They were malleable as little boys. As eager to please as well.

You wanted him salivating, dying for one touch, one taste.

And then you wanted to keep denying him.

Until he was so overwhelmed with sex hormones that he was tricked into thinking he was madly in love.

Then, well, he would offer you absolutely anything in the world to get you.

Which was precisely when you ripped the floor out from underneath him.

It worked like a charm.

Every single time.

It would work on Fenway Arlington as well, once he knew that he wasn't in charge here. "I was just teasing. I'm half-delirious from lack of sleep. The kids all caught some sort of stomach bug. It's been... rough over here. But Roman and I seem to be immune, so I took the night shift, and he is going to take the day so I can sleep."

"You poor thing. I can't imagine."

I really couldn't, either.

I'd never been responsible for any living thing. My brother had once bought me an air plant as a skoolie-warming present when I finally moved in full-time. I killed it. An air plant. Something that practically lived on air alone and a couple spritzes of water every now and again.

I kept myself alive. Sometimes, barely. That was about as good as I could do.

Raven, and anyone who managed to keep children and loads of pets or even a whole bunch of finicky houseplants alive, amazed me.

"It's times like these that make us seriously think about Roman getting a little snip snip. But then they get well and do something really sweet, and your uterus does this little squeeze..."

"A squeezy uterus sounds like a medical condition."

To that, a choked laugh escaped her, warm and happy to my ear even half a world away.

"I know it sounds weird. I never understood it until Roman and I were together for a while. But then all a sudden, you see a sweet baby, and you get the squeeze."

"I'm pretty sure my uterus doesn't squeeze. I see babies and I think of dirty diapers and spit up and a sporadic sleep schedule."

"Yeah, but you're not with anyone."

"And I never will be," I reminded her.

Raven used to take that claim at face-value, acknowledging that not everyone was meant for long-term relationships, that some were happier alone.

But marriage and a happy home life had turned her into a hopeless romantic who not-so-secretly had her heart set on me finding the right man who would get me to settle down. And then maybe I could have a couple kids, and we could raise them together.

It was a cute image, I will admit.

Except I never saw any of that in my future.

"You know me, the only thing that brings me joy is destroying a man."

I could practically hear the eye roll she was giving me. "Alright. Fine. So how is this man-destruction going?"

"He threw a kink in the works," I admitted because I was comfortable admitting flaws to exactly one person in the world, and she was it.

"Did someone get the better of you?" she gasped, as shocked as I was still feeling. "A *man* got the better of you?"

"It kills me to admit it, but yes. Yes, he did. He approached, talked, and left in this infuriatingly cocky way. Like he knew he was getting the upper hand."

"So now, of course, you must make him pay."

"Naturally."

"I know you need to stay up all night to plan this man's demise, but try to get some sleep. And keep your wits about you. I will check in before bed and when I wake up again. Text me if anything feels weird. I can't be there quickly, but I can be there."

"You're the best, but everything is going to go fine. I underestimated my opponent. It won't happen again."

"I believe you," she agreed. "Alright. The coffee pot is crooking its sexy little finger at me. I have to go. I love you."

"Love you too," I agreed, hanging up, dropping down on the foot of my all-white bed, bending forward to undo the straps on my heels.

On a sigh, I fell backward on the bed, staring up at the ceiling fan, wondering what my next move would be, what his reaction to it might be.

Typically, very little thought actually went into a job.

I had the opposite sex figured out by my sophomore year.

There were three motivators for them.

Sex.

Food.

And whatever it was that made them feel manly. Being good at football. Kicking ass at some war game on their gaming console. Knowing more about obscure slasher movies than anyone else. Whatever it was that gave them superiority.

Sex was easy.

Food could be bought and re-plated.

And in my personal experience, that third one, that was one of the most powerful of them all.

It was why comic book guys nearly jizzed their pants when they came across a good-looking girl who shared their passion. Why men put a ring on the finger of the girl whose favorite season was football.

They wanted you to like what they liked. But not know more about it than they did.

This little character quirk also explained the existence of chameleon women. You know the ones. With each and every relationship they have with a man, they become someone else. More specifically, they become exactly what that man wants them to be. The girl who once hated sports suddenly wore jerseys around all the time and just had to be home to watch the game. The one who couldn't stomach watching even a small bit of fictional gore suddenly excited for the next fight night. The girl who had always been a hardcore cotton candy pop fan getting gothed out and hitting metal shows because she had a thing for a bass player in a local band.

Clearly, these women were lacking in self-confidence. But that being said, one could learn a lot from them. Because their methods worked. They worked every time, if they deployed them correctly.

The problem was, Fenway Arlington didn't seem to have a niche that could be exploited.

He seemed to do—and enjoy—it all. From VIP sections and fancy champagne to dive bars with live music.

I guess one could call him an experience chaser. He was always looking for the next exciting thing.

That meant that it was now my job to find things to do and see and experience in Paris that he'd somehow never done before.

Decision made, I shucked off the dress, donning jeans and a tee, then making my way back out of the hotel, hitting the streets, talking to local late teen and early-twenty-somethings, figuring out what was hot, what was new, what might be just interesting enough to pique Fenway's interest.

Then I would lead him there.

And then to the next place.

Until he just had to know where I was getting my information. Until he was itching for the next fix of something he'd never tried before.

That accomplished, I made my way to my hotel, passing out fully clothed, starfished across the king-sized bed.

I woke up to the sun streaming in through the blinds I'd forgotten to close the night before, foggy from jet lag, lingering dreams tugging at the edges of my consciousness.

Hands digging into skin.

Lips pressed into the dip of the neck, between the breasts, in my hipbone hollows, lower.

And whose head did those lips belong on?

Freaking Fenway Arlington.

"Damnit, Raven," I hissed to my empty room.

I really hadn't needed those ideas implanted in my subconscious. Though, clearly, the underlying sexual frustration had absolutely nothing to do with Fenway himself, but rather the fact that I wasn't even sure how long it had been since I'd known the touch of a man.

Four months?

God, longer?

I was pretty sure it was longer.

No wonder I was having sex dreams.

Well, that was just going to have to wait until this job was over. It was too important. I didn't need any distractions. Not even of the one-night-stand variety.

Annoyed at my mind, my body, and Fenway Arlington, for no other reason than he partook in that sex dream, I rushed through a shower, putting painstaking care into my outfit in case the man in question was snooping around even this early in the day. I sought those pastries I'd denied myself the day before, grabbing a coffee to go with them, and took my breakfast to a local park, avoiding the typical tourist traps in favor of something more honest.

Even as I sat there, though, I felt an unwelcome loneliness settling onto my shoulders, making them slump, weighing me down.

It was especially strange given how accustomed I had become to my own company, how comfortable I was with silence, with private experiences that I would never be able to properly share with someone who hadn't been there to share them with me.

"How nice of you to secure our picnic spot, darling," a newly familiar voice called a second before dropping down beside me on the grass, an actual real-life picnic basket set down in front of him.

My gaze took in his outfit first—a pair of dark wash jeans and a white linen button-up shirt.

It was almost startling to see him not wearing a suit, given that every glimpse of him on his social media included that very outfit of choice.

My head craned up to take in his face, half hidden by designer shades, and I found myself oddly disappointed not to see his light brown eyes.

But only because not seeing them made it harder to read him, of course. No other explanation made any kind of sense.

"What the hell are you doing here?"

"Is that any way to talk to your tour guide?" he asked, pulling open the basket. "One who brought some very nice champagne?"

"I don't need a tour guide," I insisted. "And it is eleven in the morning," I said to the champagne.

"Is it? Huh," he said, tucking the bottle away, coming back with a thermos instead. "Then coffee it is. You look like you need a refill. No, no. I insist," he brushed me off when I tried to object.

"Why are you stalking me?" I asked, taking the coffee, but setting it on my side.

You never took a sip of something you didn't prepare yourself, or watch being prepared. That was basic Girl Safety 101.

"Stalking is a judgmental word. I like to think of it as research from a distance."

"And yet here you are. Brushing my shoulder," I told him as he moved to sit, giving me absolutely no space, but I was too stubborn to move away first. I had a feeling he was banking on that.

"See, Wasp, I was up all night. Tossing and turning, unable to rest easy knowing that you clearly did not come to appreciate how wonderfully charming—and not to mention devilishly good-looking—I am."

"So you followed me."

"Yes," he agreed, nodding. "But I brought snacks," he added, lifting the picnic basket as proof.

"Snacks make it right?"

"Snacks make everything right," he insisted, tone mock-serious, face grave.

"You're ridiculous."

"-Ly charming."

"What?"

"Your sentence trailed off. Clearly, you intended to say I am 'ridiculously charming.'"

"You're something, that's for sure," I told him, shaking my head.

"You can't tell me you're not at least a little curious about what I have in here."

"With your current creep-level, I wouldn't be surprised if it was the severed head of your previous victim."

"Hmm," he said, shuffling through the contents. With the lid lifted, I couldn't see anything within. "Nope. No severed heads. Or other body parts. But we have three different kinds of cheese, crackers, croissants, and grapes."

While I was not someone who begrudged themselves a minor sweet treat every now and again, I should have known that it had been a bad idea first thing in the morning on an empty stomach. The cheese and bread might help me feel less queasy about my earlier indulgence.

Besides, it was all about the give and take with this sort of job. You had to let them think they had you every now and again.

"What kind of cheese?"

"Well, let's see," he said, reaching in to pull out hunks of cheeses on actual porcelain plates.

"Did you... did you steal the place settings from your hotel?"

"I was in a rush."

"They didn't chase you down about it?"

"They will charge my room."

"Oh, right. They are likely used to your antics by now."

"How do you know I have had any antics?"

"Because you are stalking me and trying to schmooze me with stolen food. And you're acting like none of this is a big deal."

"Oh, Wasp, darling, that is where you are wrong. I am taking schmoozing you very seriously. Reblochon?" he asked, holding a wedge of cheese up to my lips.

I hated being fed like I was a child. It disgusted me. Yet... my lips parted, allowing him to press the small wedge within.

"Yeah, that might be more of an acquired taste," he agreed when my lips twisted. "Come on, have some champagne like a real French woman."

Choking down the cheese, I scraped my tongue against the roof of my mouth. "I'm pretty sure the French don't drink champagne in the morning, Mr. Arlington."

"No?" he asked, turning to a man walking down near his side.

"My good sir," he called, getting the middle-aged man's attention. "Would you care for a glass of champagne?" he asked, waving the bottle at the stranger who let out a rapid string of French. I made exactly no words out save for *American*.

Unfazed, Fenway slipped into flawless French right back.

"Voir cette belle femme?" he asked, making the man stop, turn, and look over at me before giving Fenway a nod. "J'essaie de l'impressionner. Aidez-moi ici."

To that, the man's lips quirked up, and he gave Fenway a nod.

"Oh my God, how do you have champagne flutes in there? Are those real glass?" I asked when he reached into the basket again, producing three flutes.

"They attach to the lid," he told me, shrugging, as if this was something everyone knew about picnic baskets. Hell, I actually picnicked more often than I ate inside my skoolie, and I didn't even own a picnic basket. "See? he asked when he popped the champagne, gave it to the man, and he gulped it down before handing back the flute, giving Fenway a knowing look, then heading on his way.

"What did you say to him?" I demanded, small-eyeing him as he poured me a glass, making my mouth water.

See, what Fenway didn't know—couldn't possibly know—was that I was a sucker for champagne. I could drink down a glass of wine if need be, but I would always prefer something with bubbles if I could have it. I also typically liked it pink like that old movie I saw as a kid that I thought was so classy and cool. You know, the one with the socialite in training and the playboy who met on the boat and went to Italy together? Such a classic.

"I was honest," he told me, holding out the flute. "I told him that I was trying to impress a beautiful woman, and asked for his help doing so. What?" he asked when I felt my lip curl. "What could I have possibly said?" he asked, shaking his head as I moved to stand, grabbing my coffee cup, turning to walk away.

I had been falling for it.

For just a moment there.

That charm he kept mentioning.

He had it. In spades. And it was convincing.

Convincing enough to start to fool an actual, real-life conwoman.

Then he had to go and ruin it.

Of course, I was happy for it to be ruined. It wasn't like I was enjoying it. This was a job, after all.

But I was annoyed at myself for getting a little wrapped up in the moment. In the scene.

Of course he was just like all the rest.

They all were the same.

Different faces, different names, same toxic personality traits, same disappointing infatuation with superficial things.

New, sparkly, and symmetrical.

That was what guys like Fenway—and I was becoming increasingly convinced, all guys—were after.

I trudged back to the hotel, annoyed at myself for getting worked up. This was the same old, same old. There was nothing new or unexpected to get frustrated over. It was certainly nothing to screw up a job over.

Then again, no one said it was screwed up. The plan was always to leave abruptly, always leave them wanting more, always needing to continue the chase. It was no fun for them once they caught you.

So maybe this outburst worked in my favor.

I would just start again later. Get dressed up nicely. Make a show of doing some window shopping, getting seen in case he was in the area. Then making my way to the destination, something I hoped Fenway hadn't experienced yet.

Then things would be back on track.

Or as on track as they could be when that freaking annoying boyish smile of his kept flashing across my vision.

What the hell was that about?

FOUR

Fenway

I'd had women turn me down before. When you hit on most of the ones you crossed paths with, chances were, you would know rejection more than a few times. No matter how rich you were. No matter if you were born with good genes.

That said, I'd never had someone abruptly jump to their feet and rush away when we'd been in the middle of a seemingly amicable conversation.

My penchant for screwing up on epic, possibly life-ending scale aside, I was not a glutton for punishment. And I respected a woman's right to turn me away.

Normally, I took that on the chin, and moved onto the next.

Why, then, was I changed into a suit and lingering around her neighborhood 'for coffee' when there was a much better cafe closer to my hotel, you might be wondering?

Yeah, well, I was wondering that as well.

Yet there I was.

Like a lost puppy looking for its owner.

There were other streets to walk down.

Planes to catch.

Yachts to board.

Sights to be seen.

Yet there was no denying the only one that seemed important right that moment was any one with her in it.

Absurd and over the top?

Absolutely.

Though no one would ever call me boring and sensible anyway, so maybe it wasn't as out of character as it felt.

There was an awkwardness, an uncertainty, building in my stomach as I walked down the street for the fourth time, my third coffee sparking off of fried nerve endings.

I was about to give up hope, go drown this uncomfortable sense of self-actualization in one-too-many drinks at the closest bar, maybe take a woman back to my hotel to try to drive out images of my ornery mystery woman.

And then there she was.

Like a kick to the gut in a cerulean blue silk dress that flirted with lines of propriety with the shortness of the hem, the way the bodice hung a bit loose, allowing it to drape just low enough to make it clear she couldn't be wearing a bra with something like that on.

I'd somehow missed her long legs in both my previous perusals of her body. The first night, I'd been focused on her bare back, her almost other-worldly stunning face. The next time, I'd been distracted by her hair, by the way her brows reacted to everything she heard or said.

But long they were, slightly tanned, toned without being bulky, made to look even longer by the six-inch heels on her feet.

Her hair was left down as she seemingly always wore it, flirting with her shoulders, kicking up at the ends with the breeze.

I let her make her way halfway down the street before rushing across, coming up behind her, grabbing her hand, then swinging it between us as I fell into step with her.

"Seriously?" she asked, not sounding surprised by my sudden appearance, and not pulling her hand right away either.

"You almost left without me, darling."

"I almost escaped you, creeper," she shot back, letting me swing our arms two more times before yanking her hand from mine, curling it into a fist so I couldn't claim it again.

"So where are you taking me?" I asked, clasping my hands behind my back.

"Straight to the police station, possibly."

"No. You're far too enamored with me to do something cruel like that."

"Don't you have a private jet to catch or something?"

"I have not a care in the world. Save for the overwhelming sadness I feel over your rejection."

"Somehow, I think you will survive," she told me, rolling her eyes. "I have plans tonight. So go pester some other woman."

"Oh, my darling Wasp, you are the only woman I want to pester, though."

"Gee. Whatever did I do to get so lucky?" she quipped.

Ignoring that, I pressed on. "Where are we having our second date?"

"We haven't had a first date."

"Sure we did. We had cheese and champagne. Rubbed shoulders with the locals. It was absolutely a date."

"I am going to the theater," she informed me. "You are not invited."

"You know what I like about theaters?"

"I don't want to know."

"They are public places. Two people who happen to be there—not on a date—can still somehow end up sitting side-by-side and enjoying the experience together. The woman might even take solace in a sympathetic shoulder should the movie break her heart."

"Nothing breaks my heart," she told me, giving me brief eye contact.

"I don't doubt that. Fine. Maybe the movie will be terrifying, and you will need to hide your face in my suit fabric."

"I don't scare all that easily."

"What if I get scared, then?"

"It's not a scary movie they are showing tonight. It is your average, everyday drama."

"Sounds splendid."

"Splendid?" she shot back, brow raising.

"Yes, splendid."

"No one says the word 'splendid'."

"Oh, but I do."

"Of course you do," she said, turning down a side street.

We fell into companionable silence. Her, because she didn't seem inclined to speak to me, and me, because I didn't want to screw things up before we got to the theater.

"I've never heard of this place," I admitted when we stood out front, looking up at the neon red sign.

Le Brady.

"Not the best tour guide, after all," she told me, moving inside, leaving me to follow behind. Which I did. Gladly.

The inside was what you might expect from any typical arthouse theater anywhere in the world. A small, long room with only maybe fifty to seventy-five very tightly-packed seats. These, in red, staring at the projection screen

It was empty when we moved inside. Tuesday nights weren't a big going-out night for locals, and this place wasn't on any of the tourist type articles on places to visit.

I'd toured this city countless times since I turned eighteen. I'd never even looked twice at the building.

"It's nice to find new places in old cities," I told her. "That's why I like visiting New York. Every time you go, it can be brand new."

"Because hundreds of people have lost their businesses," she insisted.

"That's one way to look at it."

"You can't possibly be optimistic all the time," she told me.

"Why not? There are plenty of things to be optimistic about."

"The earth melting? Wealth disparity? Turtles with straws stuck up their noses? Destruction of the rain forest? Racism?"

"Beautiful countries, beautiful women, beautiful music, great food."

"It is important to be realistic."

"Yes," I agreed, nodding. "But it is just as important to see some good in life too. Otherwise, what the hell is the point of it all?" To that, she had nothing to say. "You know what?" I asked, pausing, making her ask.

"What?"

"I think you're not nearly as jaded as you pretend to be. I think you just want me to think you are, so I lose interest."

"Why are you so interested? In a city full of other women. Why me?"

"Why not you? I think we could have some fun. If you would let yourself."

"What kind of fun?"

"Come with me, and you can find out," I suggested.

"We are watching a movie."

"After."

"Go where with you?"

"Hop on a plane, then on a yacht."

"You can't be serious."

"Rarely, but in this one instance, I happen to be. Pack your things. Meet me at the private airstrip."

With that, I stood, shrugging out of my jacket, draping it over her arms that were pebbling with goosebumps, turning, and leaving.

It was a risky move, I knew, to leave it like that.

But sometimes in life, you had to take a gamble. And me? I liked my hand.

People didn't fight so hard to push you away without ever truly making a stand unless they were interested, just denying it to you, and likely themselves.

Why?

I had no idea.

I couldn't claim to be someone afflicted with such reservations. When I wanted something, I went after it with everything I had. Until I lost interest, or moved onto the next thing, of course.

Apparently, Wasp was someone who denied herself the things she wanted. To what end? Possibly to always be the one holding the reins, always the one with all the power.

But where the hell was the fun in that?

If she showed up—when she showed up—I would make it my mission to shake her up a bit, show her a good time, get some of that ice chipped away.

Sure of the situation, I went back to my room, making the necessary calls as my assistant, Alvy, carefully tucked away my belongings, slapping my hand away if I tried to help because 'remember what happened last time?'

In truth, I didn't.

But they made it sound grave enough for me to drop down in the chair by the sliding doors to watch the city one last time.

"So, what's her name?" Alvy asked, carefully rolling one of my suits in their hands.

Alvy had been with me for going on three years. Which was a lot of staying power for someone who typically had their personal assistants rage-quit after a few months, no matter how handsomely I offered to pay them to stay on.

Alvy was short and slight with close-cropped medium-brown hair, and knowing brown-black eyes. They dressed as they lived, non-binary, sometimes in jeans and a flannel, other times in a nicely tailored suit that was neither masculine nor feminine in design. Today, they wore a pair of black skinny jeans, a white and gray button-up three-quarter length sleeved shirt, and Chucks that had to have been custom made with a pattern of green frogs on the outside and a bright purple tongue and laces.

"Wasp," I told Alvy, shrugging.

"She wouldn't give you her real name, but you are chartering a private jet to take her out to your yacht?" Alvy asked, brow arching up as they went into the bathroom to grab my shaving kit, tucking it into one of my suitcases.

"She doesn't *like* me, Alvy," I told them pressing a hand to my heart. "Can you imagine?"

"Judging by the three-hour rant phone call I got from your previous assistant when I first started, yes, yes, I can imagine."

"Michel had very strong feelings on proper REM cycles. Feelings I clearly do not share. That's why we work so well, Al, I never sleep. You are an insomniac. It's a perfect relationship."

"Did she tell you that she was going to come?"

"Not in so many words."

"Did she say it in any words? In sign language? In Morse Code?" Alvy asked, smirking.

"Her eyes told me she was coming."

"Oh, for Christ's sake," Alvy scoffed, reaching for their phone.

"Who are you calling?"

"The pilot."

"For what?"

"To warn him that you will likely need to make a last-minute flight plan change to somewhere less romantic, and more party-focused when she stands you up." With that, they moved out into the kitchen area to do just that while brewing a new pot of coffee, being a fiend themselves, and knowing I was always up for a cup. "Okay, so what is it about this one?" Alvy asked, handing me my coffee a few moments later.

"Hm?"

"Is she the daughter of a drug kingpin? A princess of a small country? A retired movie star. In her sixties?"

"That was one time," I insisted, smiling at the memory. "And she was a hell of a time."

"Until she slashed your tires when she found out you moved onto the woman who was playing her in the remake of her classic movie."

"Don't be ridiculous," I said, lips twitching. "A movie under twenty years old can't be considered a classic."

"I was the one who had to handle the tire replacement and the press," Alvy reminded me.

"I believe I got you an I'm sorry gift for that."

"You bought me a ten-thousand-dollar living room set."

"That sounds nice of me."

"I don't have a home," Alvy told me, rolling their eyes.

"Well, why not? Do I not pay you enough?" I asked.

"If you paid me anymore, I'd have to start moving money offshore," Alvy told me. "The issue isn't that I need more money. It is that it is pointless to get a home when I am literally never there to spend time in it."

"So? I have a home. I have... six? Is it six?"

"It's eleven," Alvy told me. "Though three of those are family estates, not fully yours."

"Where are the extra two houses?"

"Let me preface this with saying that if you don't know the cities and countries of your residencies, it might be smart to unload them. The most recent was a lodge in Colorado."

'That doesn't count. That is a business."

"A business with a six-thousand square foot home for the owner. That you keep fully staffed, but never visit."

"How could I visit when I forgot it existed?" I shot back, smiling. "Maybe we should arrange to have someone rent it out. Or do one of those house shares there. Would that make it less ostentatious of me to keep it in my portfolio?"

"Slightly," Alvy agreed. "And the other one is the condo above your favorite bar in Boston. So you can just drag your drunk ass up the stairs and pass out."

"That seems like a solid investment. Anyway. I have houses that I clearly never visit. You could have one."

"I could. But I don't want one. Not until I can move into it full-time."

"It sounds like you plan on leaving me one day, Alvy," I observed.

"I am eventually going to burn out."

"How shall I go on without you?" I asked dramatically, making their eyes roll.

"You'll find a way. You always do."

"My suits will likely always be wrinkled."

"You can hire someone to be your personal clothing steamer."

'This is true," I agreed. "And they likely won't lecture me about my choices in women."

"I wouldn't either. If you chose one who was a good option for once."

"Oh, they have all been very good."

"For the pocketbooks of those you employ to fix your messes, I suppose that is true. I will have the art you purchased shipped back to the main estate," Alvy said, waving at the canvases.

"That should do. We should visit the estate sometime this year. Pick the pieces to distribute to other places. It must be getting rather crowded by now."

"You have purchased one-hundred-and-twelve paintings so far this year, so I imagine that is true."

"Pencil it into the schedule."

"Will do," Alvy agreed, zipping my suitcases, then turning their attention to their phone. "Your flight attendant, Joy, wants to know if there is anything she needs to pick up for you and your guest?"

"What can I get that would impress a woman who appears wholly unimpressed by me as a whole?"

"A free trip back home."

"Well, that won't work. You're supposed to be on my team here, Alvy."

"Does she eat? Or is she like that poor girl last year who I caught nibbling on napkins to stay full without gaining any weight?"

"She eats. But not French cheeses."

"That really narrows it down," Alvy said, snorting. "I will tell her to get things to impress a woman. She can figure that out."

"What would I do without you, Alvy?"

"Employ that team of fixers of yours a lot more often than you already do."

"I miss them. It's been over a year since I've needed to hire them for anything, hasn't it?"

"Don't."

"Don't what?"

"Create a problem as an excuse to see them. Some people have barbecues or host dinner parties."

"Well, I can't do that now, can I?"

"Why not?"

"First, I'd have to pick a home. Second, Miller made it very clear that if I step foot in Navesink Bank again, she is going to pay me back for that pig whoopsie."

"Really, you didn't think to check to make sure it was a pet, not a farm pig?"

"I blame you."

"Of course you do."

"You abandoned me that summer."

"I took my mandatory three-week vacation."

"What moron made a mandatory three-week vacation rule?"

"That moron would be you."

"Oh, right. Good corporate policies are one of my many positive traits," I told them, smirking.

"It somewhat makes up for all your personal failings," Alvy agreed, shooting me a smile, eyes dancing.

"Are you ready for some fun in the sun, Alvy?"

"I am ready to watch this woman eviscerate you," they shot back.

"Don't be so keen. You'd be the one having to deal with the mess," I told them, rising out of my chair, making my way toward the door, finding myself uncharacteristically anxious about the plan.

This anxiety only intensified as I waited there beside the private jet.

For twenty minutes.

Thirty. Forty-five.

"She's cutting it close," Josh, the pilot, commented, rocking on his heels.

"Yes, she is," I agreed, stomach tightening.

I'd been so sure.

"Don't worry, Mr. Arlington," he said, clapping a hand on my shoulder. "You know some women. Late for their own funerals, they'll be."

With that, he moved back inside, heading into the cabin, anxious to get moving.

While I was just anxious.

I'd never experienced it before.

I couldn't say I was a fan.

Feeling sweaty with a hammering heart and a flip-flopping stomach with the lingering sense of insecurity and embarrassment. Definitely not something I wanted to experience again.

"Should I tell Josh to change the flight plan?" Alvy asked, checking their phone, confirming what I already knew.

She didn't make it.

She wasn't coming.

I was losing my edge.

"Well, I'll be damned," Alvy said, making my gaze lift from the tarmac, following their gaze to the approaching car.

Relief washed through me in a wave, leaving the uncomfortable anxiety in a puddle at my feet.

The car pulled to a stop, the driver climbing out, opening the back door.

I watched with bated breath as a set of long, tan legs slid out, heels hitting the pavement.

Then, the rest of her body emerged.

In a skintight black tank-top that showed a sliver of stomach, paired with a red and black rose-printed skirt. Of the short variety.

She turned, looking over in our direction, doing a once-over of me, then Alvy, then me again, seeming wholly unimpressed with us both, then finally making her way in our direction.

Slow.

Deliberate.

Knowing that we, the plane, the whole damn world would wait for her if she demanded it do so.

Her gaze slid to Alvy once she was in front of us. "I'm sorry," she told them.

"We don't mind wait—" I started, getting cut off as her gaze slipped to me, cold, sharp.

"I wasn't apologizing to you. I am apologizing to your staff for having to work for you," she informed me, pushing past my shoulder, and making her way into the jet.

"I can see you," I informed Alvy as their grin spread, elated, amused.

"She's going to destroy you," Alvy told me, sounding pleased at the prospect.

"Oh, but how I am going to enjoy the destruction," I told them, turning, making my way into the jet.

I had no idea what to expect.

But I was excited to find out what was to come.

FIVE

Wasp

I had to go.

I mean, not even my innate stubbornness would allow me to screw up a job worth so much. Even if it was stupid as hell.

So stupid, in fact, that I straight-up lied to Raven about what was going on. I never lied to her. Not about important things.

Traveling internationally with a complete stranger fell squarely in the important category.

But I didn't want her to stress out.

I didn't want her talking to my brothers, having some giant issue raised.

Sure, Fenway Arlington was a stranger. And strangers always lent an air of danger. And, yes, he was the rich of the filthy variety, which meant he could pay to have anything done and covered up.

But, really, my instincts said Fenway was a giant puppy dog with a wandering dick and a big ego.

He was harmless as far as I could tell.

So I didn't need my family and friends freaking out because of this job.

If everything went to plan, it would be two or three weeks tops. Then I could be home, investing my newfound small fortune, preparing for earlier-than-planned retirement.

So I had to go.

I was starting to question my decision on the drive from the hotel to the airstrip—in a car that had been sitting outside my hotel waiting for me, because Fenway prepared for everything, it seemed—wondering if I was giving him the upper hand over me.

But one look at the sheer relief I saw on his face when the car pulled up almost late, was all I needed to see to know I was still in control here.

I moved into the jet, trying not to seem impressed. But I was impressed.

I'd flown first class once and felt fancy as hell.

But first class and a private jet were worlds apart when it came to luxury.

The inside of Fenway's jet was bright and welcoming with its sand-colored couches and chairs and the white oak table tops and storage bins.

There was a door opened in the back to a bedroom, the bed itself taking up the entire space, covered in all white bedding. To the side of that was what appeared to be the bathroom. Across from there was a small kitchen space where a woman in a tame gray and white flight attendant outfit stood.

This was Fenway Arlington here.

I half expected the staff to be wearing those dresses and hats straight out of the fifties.

I moved to the couch, settling down in the center of it, making it clear I wanted it all to myself.

Surprisingly, Fenway got the hint, dropping down across from me in a bucket seat with a table in front of him, pretending to ignore me as his assistant brought my luggage inside, and the flight attendant rushed around to make sure everything was just right.

"Fenway," I called, making his head jerk up, turning to look at me.

"Yes, darling?"

Darling.

God.

Could anyone actually pull off that endearment nowadays?

I knew the answer immediately.

Somehow, Fenway could.

"I have two brothers," I told him, lifting my chin. "They are both arms dealers," I added, watching his assistant jolt to a stop in the aisle. "And they are both afraid of *me*," I finished, watching as the facts settled in.

There was the expected surprise, a small flash of worry, but it was all replaced with his signature carefree, boyish smile that made his eyes brighten.

"I do adore a powerful woman," he told me, making my eyes roll.

"Isn't it rude not to introduce me to your assistant?" I asked.

"Alvy is going to spend most of the flight in the cabin."

"To get away from you?" I teased.

"Most likely, yes," he told me as Alvy did, indeed, disappear into the cabin, shutting the door.

"Hey, I don't want to get it wrong. Alvy...—" I started, not sure how to ask, what was PC, how to broach a potentially sensitive topic.

"Alvy is non-binary."

"Which means I should..."

"Use they/them pronouns," he told me. "And don't ask about body parts, or who they like sexually."

"Right," I agreed, nodding. "Because it is ever appropriate to ask someone if they are hiding a penis or vagina in their pants. Or ask if they like to suck dick or eat pussy."

The way I phrased that was a test, wanting to see how he responded to dirty words. As much as porn wanted us all to believe every man liked foul-mouthed women in bed, there were a lot of men who didn't like women who used those kinds of words.

I watched as Fenway's eyes got just a tiny bit bigger, surprised, before they smoldered as he turned, leaning forward like he was going to share a secret with me.

"In case you were wondering," he started, lips curving up devilishly, "I like to eat pussy."

It was my turn to have my eyes widen, to feel the smolder.

Because I hadn't expected him to repeat it.

I don't know why.

His fine breeding, his likely prep school education, the fact that he was so boyish that it was a little hard to imagine very grown man words coming out of his mouth.

Whatever it was, I didn't expect it.

Nor did I expect the impact of the words.

Namely, the tightening between my legs, the deep longing, the way my heartbeat tripped into overdrive.

It wasn't just the word.

Nope.

It was the smooth, confident, sexy way he said it.

I knew right that moment that not only did he like doing it, that he was probably amazing at it too.

Damnit.

"Joy," Fenway called, addressing the flight attendant. "I think our guest could use a *stiff* drink," he called, lips quirked up, making it clear his emphasis was purposeful.

He knew I did want something stiff.

But it damn sure wasn't a drink.

"It's fine," I called. "I'm not thirsty," I added through my cottonmouth.

"Oh," Fenway said, eyes bright, voice low, sexier than it had any right to be, "I think you are thirsty. Should I tell Joy exactly what it is you are thirsty for?" he asked, eyes daring me.

Oh, damn him.

He was not going to be as easy a target as I originally thought.

Who the hell would have thought that superficial, troublesome Fenway Arlington would have layers?

I should have known.

"Pink champagne," I told him, watching as his brows furrowed.

"Pink champagne?"

"Yes. I like pink champagne."

"Like from *An Affair to Remember*?"

"How do you know that movie?"

"Everyone knows that movie."

"I literally know one person who knows that movie," I told him. And Raven only knew it because I made her watch it. She wasn't a classic movie fan; she preferred romantic dramas.

"Those uncultured swine," he said, chuckling. "I enjoy classic movies. My grandmother used to have me watch them with her."

Ugh.

Damn him again.

I certainly didn't plan on having anything in common with the man.

"Who do you like more. Audrey or Katherine Hepburn?" I asked, wanting to prove he wasn't as into it as he was saying.

"They both have their merits. But you have to love Katherine. That was a powerhouse of a woman."

Damn him once more.

I always preferred Katherine. And not just because of her realist forward-thinking, feminist views in real life. I loved her cool confidence in her roles, the elegant way she spoke.

"Clark Gable or Jimmy Stewart?"

"Cary Grant. Obviously."

"Why obviously?"

"*The Philadelphia Story, His Girl Friday, To Catch A Thief, An Affair to Remember.*"

"You have a thing for romance movies," he concluded, making my stomach drop. I never would say that. I would never think that. But faced with my own admission, no other conclusion could be drawn, could it?

"I like all sorts of classic movies. Most of them happen to have a love story attached."

"Fair enough. So, are you not the least bit curious as to where we are heading?"

"I imagined you would inform me eventually."

"Have you ever been to Gianyar?"

"Seeing as I have never heard of that, no."

"It's in Bali. I have a home there. On the beach. Don't worry. You will have your own room. As will Alvy. Everything all above-board."

"Why Bali?" I asked. He had the entire world at his disposal.

"It's beautiful."

"There are other places with more things to do."

"If we get there, and you find yourself bored, we can be in Italy with a day's notice. Or Venice. Amsterdam for some wild fun. I am wholly at your disposal. Use me any way you see fit," he commanded, holding his arms out wide.

"Why would you offer to follow every whim of a virtual stranger?"

"It has been far too long since I've had a travel companion. I've already seen everywhere. It would be interesting to see someone else see it all for the first time."

That was actually rather sweet.

And I really needed not to be endeared to him on this job. I would inevitably feel guilty for scamming him, breaking his heart, and taking a nice sum of money for the trouble.

I needed to get control of things again.

"Don't you ever work? Earn your lavish living?"

"The nice thing about owning many different businesses is you get paid when you are sleeping."

"Don't you want to work for your money?"

"I do work for my money. For a few days a year when there are meetings. When I acquire failing businesses, then make them profitable again. I earn my money, but I don't need to slave away to do so."

"Doesn't jetting off to random parts of the world at a moment's notice seem frivolous to you?" I asked, even if I personally would cut off my left tit—in my personal opinion, my better one—to be able to have that sort of freedom in life.

"Incredibly frivolous," he agreed. "Do you hate me because I'm rich, Wasp?"

This was tricky, wasn't it?

He wasn't supposed to be so blunt. Everything I had learned while researching him pointed to light and silly and over the top. Never serious. Never the type to put you on the spot.

"No," I told him honestly. "My best friend and her husband are filthy rich too."

"So your objection is to me personally."

"My objection is to things—and people—without substance. Surface-level interactions, connections, and experiences are a waste of time."

"Oh, I see," he said, nodding, face grave. "You are asking me to marry you."

'What? Where the hell did you get that?"

"You need deep interaction. I can help you in multiple ways on that front," he told me, tone suggestive, smirk devilish.

"I don't believe in marriage," I informed him, not sure why I felt like I needed to tell him something personal.

"Not even with the right man?"

"There's no such thing."

"As the right man for you? Oh, I think you are selling all of mankind short."

"I think I am selling them just short enough."

"You know what I think, darling?" he asked, giving me what I could only call a soft look.

"Probably not. But something tells me you are going to tell me anyway."

"I think all this cold of yours is hiding something really warm and mushy inside. And you're terrified someone will figure that out."

"Stick to chasing models and buying fancy suits, Fenway," I told him, cool, cold even, trying to cover the churning discomfort of that truth in my stomach. "Psychoanalysis isn't your strong suit."

Unperturbed, Fenway shrugged one of his shoulders, his knowing smile suggesting he knew just how close to the head of the nail he'd hit.

"So would you like that drink now?" he asked.

"Oh, God yes. I will need three just to get through this plane ride," I told him, settling in, wondering how we were going to fill the unforgiving silence in our close quarters.

Luckily, after I got my drink, Fenway offered me mercy, reaching for a remote, making a television pop out of a cabinet, flicking around.

"Here we go," he said, leaning back as he put something on, drawing my attention to the TV.

An Affair to Remember.

I couldn't help but wonder if it was more than the fact that we had discussed the movie. If he was hinting at something. Something about the two of us. About what he thought was going to happen once we got to Bali.

What he didn't know was he was both right and wrong.

It would be an affair of sorts.

And it would be one to remember.

But it would only be real for one of us.

One movie turned into two. And then Fenway immediately put on a third as I shifted uncomfortably around in my seat.

"Fenway?"

"Yes, darling?" he asked, giving me that award-winning smile of his.

"Exactly how long is this plane ride?"

"This leg is about nine and a half hours."

"Leg. Meaning we are laying over somewhere?"

"I have tried to talk Josh into giving up sleep. Alas, he won't cooperate. We need to stop to fuel. Josh catches a little sleep. We can spend that time exploring the airport or getting rooms to rest as well. It would only be about six hours."

"Where are we stopping?"

"Qatar."

"Qatar?" I repeated, the name vaguely familiar.

"Near to Saudi Arabia and the United Arab Emirates. We will be near a sprawling metropolis like New York, only newer and shinier. But the airport itself has entertainment enough to hold our attention for hours. Last I was there, they were running ten art exhibits."

"Ten art exhibits? In an airport?" I asked, sure he was pulling my leg.

"Art exhibits. Prayer rooms. Massage, nails, facials, gyms, showers, and separate male and female sleep rooms."

"We could have an actual vacation in the airport," I mused, shaking my head at the very idea. I thought the airport back in Jersey was fancy with all its little food shops to buy snacks in.

At my comment, something different crossed Fenway's eyes, something soft and sweet, almost, I don't know, whimsical. Could people look whimsical? If they could, that was how he looked right then.

"We can even do some shopping," Fenway offered. "My treat."

"I already have my luggage."

"For Paris, I imagine. Not Bali."

"That's true," I agreed. I didn't even have a swimsuit packed. Or even appropriate shoes for a beach. "But I pay for myself."

"We shall see about that."

"Shall?" I asked, smiling.

"It's the proper word."

"Do you ever notice that a lot of times, 'proper' and 'pretentious' go hand-in-hand?"

"Do you ever notice you get prickly whenever I am being nice?" he shot back, surprising me once again, having previously thought he was the sort to avoid any sort of confrontation. "Who made you believe men are only nice when they plan to screw you over?" he added, tone getting deeper, more serious. In fact, everything about him had switched from lighthearted playboy to a cool, confident, somber man.

I took a breath, leaning forward a bit. "Every single man I have ever met," I told him, telling him mostly the truth. I knew a few good men. My brothers, their friends, Raven's husband. But let's just say they were few and far between. "Though, if it makes you feel any better, it isn't a sexist statement. Most people are kind to you when they want something from you. But men, almost invariably, only want one thing."

"And what do women want?"

"To know where another woman found a dress with sleeves, a pair of heels that don't give them blisters, a bra that doesn't feel like a torture device, for someone to finally recognize their thankless work day in and day out slaving away raising kids and tending house, to be paid the same as their male colleagues, to be able to walk down a street without worrying about predatory hands..."

"And they don't want sex too?" he challenged, brow arching up.

"Oh, we love sex," I told him. "But we don't need to be manipulative to get it."

"You think I am trying to manipulate you into sex?" he asked, tone cold.

"Wining and dining and private jets and airport shopping sprees and Bali vacations. You're trying to tell me you don't expect something out of all of this?" I challenged him.

I don't know what I expected. Maybe one of his flip brush-offs, something silly and dismissive.

I didn't expect for him to unfold from his chair, move across the short aisle, lean over me, and snag my chin in his fingers, angling it up, holding almost unnerving eye contact.

"I don't need to manipulate a woman to get what I want, *darling*," he said, the word coming out more like a curse than an endearment. "What you and I know we both want," he added, his other hand slipping between my thighs, pressing against my panties, dragging a surprised, but undeniably turned-on groan from me. What can I say? I played a good game, but I was a sucker for a man who was alpha in bed. His finger swiped, making my hand slap down on the arm of the couch, fingers digging in. "See?" he asked, releasing my chin, pulling his hand out of my skirt, turning, and going into the cockpit.

Alvy moved out to take the seat Fenway had vacated as I tried to remind my body that it was not part of this scenario, that this was a job, that it didn't matter how hot it was when he turned off the outward mask of light and fun and showed the darker, sexier man beneath, that we could not—under any circumstances—end up in bed.

"It should just be about another hour and a half before we are in Qatar. If you want an escape route, I can arrange it now," Alvy offered, scanning my face, coming to who-knew-what conclusion about the undoubtedly shocked look they found there.

"I honestly don't know what I want," I admitted. "I shouldn't even be here."

"Fenway has that effect on women," Alvy told me, shrugging. "It's that puppy dog side of him he presents to everyone. The enthusiasm can be infectious. And the next thing you know, you're on some mafioso's private vineyard in Italy having dinner across from cold-blooded killers. But then you take a trip to the ladies, get some distance, and the sense seems to return to your head, and you want out."

"Has that actually happened?"

"Would you believe more than once?" Alvy asked, shaking their head.

My gaze moved to the closed cockpit door, imagining the man nestled in the co-pilot seat.

"Yes, yes I can," I admitted, realizing for the first time that this job wasn't going to be as open-and-shut as I first imagined.

"Here," Alvy said, pointing to my phone., "Let me give you my number. If you need out, I'm your person. I am always around. And I know my way out of everywhere at this point."

"God, you make it sound like he runs a cult or something. Oh, Jesus, please tell me he doesn't run a cult."

To that, Alvy chuckled, revealing a deep dimple in one cheek. "You'd think so, what with the magnetism he has. That is usually reserved for the likes of cult leaders. But no. I think Fenway often appeals to everyone's desire to get away from it all at times, to see the world, to drown in luxury. But, eventually, everyone comes to their senses, realizes that those desires aren't what they truly want. They want to go back to their old lives, their old people."

"So the women are always the ones who want out? Fenway doesn't get bored with them?"

Alvy's gaze went to the door, looking at it for a moment before turning back to me.

"Between the two of us, I think Fenway is deeply lonely. I think he chases one high after another, one woman after another, because he thinks that if he keeps himself busy enough, entertained enough, that he can drown all the unpleasant feelings he might have."

"Someone as privileged as he is, why wouldn't he just stop and find what he really desires then?"

"Why are you on a plane with him right now? Why am I? Why does anyone do the things they do that aren't the wisest choices for them? We all have our reasons. Fenway has his too.

But that is his place to talk about them. My advice? Enjoy this while you can. Take what you need from it. Then go back and fix the real problem."

With that, Alvy set to shooting off a rapid-fire text or email, leaving me in silence, pondering their words.

Alvy couldn't have known my real motive for being on this plane. And none of it had to do with my damage, my personal issues, the things that motivated a lot of my decisions in life.

But their words did make one thing infinitely clear.

Fenway, lighthearted, partying, superficial, mega-rich playboy was only part of the whole man. And if I was going to be able to finish this job, I would have to get to know the other sides of him too, the things he masked with the flippant outer layer, the mask he donned to keep anyone from seeing who he truly was.

Because this wouldn't work if all he did was fall in love at surface level.

I had to get deeper; I had to set up camp there. He had to get used to, and enjoy, the invasion. And then he needed to know what it was like to have that ripped away, to feel that emptiness.

It was a slightly more difficult plan, though not impossible.

As I sat there with nothing but my thoughts to keep me company, though, there was no denying a small, infinitesimally small, stirring of guilt in my chest.

A stirring that I promptly squashed right down, trying to remind myself that Fenway had undoubtedly done his fair share of lying and defrauding in his life.

Karma was a belief I held near and dear to my heart.

And, clearly, he had done something wrong to make a woman pay me to break his heart.

I felt marginally better about that as we finally made our descent, as we came to a stop, as the stairs opened, and, finally, Alvy instructed me to go down and wait outside, get some fresh air.

What happened when I did just that was anyone's guess.

But five minutes later, I heard footsteps behind me, then a hand grabbing mine, swinging it as it dragged me forward with it.

"You must be famished," he declared. "Shall we go to one sit-down restaurant, or tour the entire building and create our very own buffet?" he asked, still swinging our arms between our bodies as I rushed to keep up with his pace.

So.

The Fenway representative was back.

I was going to get whiplash if he kept changing it up on me.

"Darling, is everything alright?" he asked, looking over at me.

My back and ass were killing me from sitting still for so long. My feet had taken objection to my shoes five minutes after I had strapped them on. And my stomach was growling so hard that I felt nauseated.

"I was debating my options," I told him instead. No one—especially those of the male persuasion—liked hearing complaints. "What kind of food does the sit-down place serve?"

"I am going to imagine Qatarian."

"I'm not sure I know what that means."

"Me either," he admitted, giving me an uncertain look. "Buffet might be safer."

"Alright, lead the way," I told him, waving my free arm to the massive glass sloping dome building, making his brows pinch as he looked down at me, trying to figure out the mood change.

If he was going to keep me on my toes, I had to keep him on his as well.

"Wait," I said as we got closer to the building. "Shouldn't we wait for Alvy?"

"Alvy is taking a car to the closest hotel to catch some sleep. Josh will sleep here. But for Alvy..."

"Separate male and female rooms for rest," I filled in for him.

"Precisely. Don't worry. We won't leave without Alvy."

With that, he led me into the airport.

Where I promptly became a very obvious tourist, wide-eyed and stopping to gape every dozen or so yards.

Airports in general were massive buildings. This one, though, seemed doubly so. And it wasn't nearly as packed as the airports I had seen in my life. In fact, it probably felt so vast precisely because it was nearly empty.

Even the rows of seats seemed upscale compared to back home with their burnt orange and black leather seats.

"What are you thinking right now?" Fenway asked, leading me up toward an escalator.

"Everything is so *clean*," I admitted. "And not surface clean. Like when you go to an office and the floor is swept and mopped and the garbage isn't overflowing, but if you look closely, the floorboards are grimy and there is dust on the artificial plant on top of the cabinet. Like every inch of this place is clean."

"There is a giant yellow stuffed animal exhibit over there, and you are noticing the cleanliness of the baseboards," Fenway teased, but his smile said he was charmed.

Charmed, I could work with.

Charmed was one step closer to swooning which was one step closer to love.

"What can I say, I marvel at the mundane. So what kind of shopping can we do here once we eat?" I asked.

"The only kind you find in an airport like this," he told me, dragging me toward the food court. "Designer."

Designer clothes meant designer price tags. Normally, I would scoff at that. I didn't need a special tag to make me feel confident in my outfit, validated in my choice. But this job came with a travel and living stipend should I need it. Clothes for the job seemed like a genuine need.

Except, of course, after our bellies were full and we hit the stores, Fenway had somehow gotten to the cashiers at the shops while I was browsing or trying things on. And paid for it all.

Alvy appeared absolutely out of nowhere—I hadn't even seen Fenway use his phone to call them—and took all my bags, disappearing with them.

"Where to next, darling?" Fenway asked, arm dropping across my shoulders, his other waving wide. "The airport is your oyster."

"I think we need coffee," I decided. "And then probably to get back to the plane. It's been hours, hasn't it?"

My eyes certainly thought it had been. I was exhausted. I didn't even know what time it was. All I knew was I was claiming that bed when I got back on that plane.

"It would be more fun to be impractical," he suggested.

"If we don't ever want to make it to Bali," I reminded him. "Did you happen to see the swimsuit I bought for Bali?" I asked, lips curving up, slow and sultry, waiting for the melting thing I knew his eyes would do.

"I did not. Is it very cruel?" he added, smirking.

"Positively torturous," I told him, feeling a strange little giddy sensation inside when he threw his head back and groaned.

"And here I am, a glutton for punishment. Fine, let's go to Bali," he agreed, moving away.

"Um, Fenway?" I called as he kept walking, either expecting me to follow, or completely unaware that I wasn't at his side.

At that, he turned on his heel, head angled to the side. "Yes?"

"Coffee," I reminded him.

"Right. Yes. Coffee. I would have remembered eventually."

"When?" I asked, rolling my eyes. "When we were halfway to Bali?"

"Don't be silly. We're *already* halfway to Bali. Oh, that's a new exhibit," he said, already heading in that direction, a man who was clearly used to the whole world standing still for him.

"You're like a child at an amusement park," I informed him, grabbing his lapel, pulling him along with me.

I should have been annoyed.

Normally, I would be.

It was frustrating when people refused to behave like adults.

Nobody liked a man-child.

Yet as I dragged him through the airport, seeing the goofy grin on his face while I did it, I felt my own lips curving upward, his enthusiasm for life—frivolity and all—was proving infectious.

That was a problem.

But one I told myself that I would think about later.

Then promptly forgot to do so as we got coffee, as we made our way back to the jet, as we boarded, settled in, took off.

I didn't even think about it when I moved off to the bedroom, pulling the pocket door, sealing myself in.

Alone.

But I did not wake up alone.

"Fenway!" I snapped, sensing the presence beside me.

"Darling, shh. I'm trying to sleep here," he informed me, voice groggy, yet somehow playful at the same time.

"Yes, well, that is the problem, isn't it?" I asked, pushing myself upward, slow blinking at the pillows lined between us. "Did you build a pillow wall between us?"

"I did. I couldn't exactly have you trying to have your way with me when I was asleep, now could I?" he asked, giving me a sleepy grin that was a little too intimate, a little too tempting. "I want to be wide awake when you molest me."

A choked laugh escaped me at that as I reached up to push my wild hair out of my face. "Don't worry, Fenway. Your body is safe from me," I told him, lips curving up. "What time is it?"

"Late. Early. Not time to get up yet," he told me.

"How long have I been asleep?"

"Two hours, give or take."

"How long have *you* been asleep?"

"An hour and forty minutes. Give or take," he told me smirking lazily as I settled back down, the siren's call of my pillow proving impossible to ignore.

"You're such a creeper," I told him, rolling onto my side. Facing him. But we weren't going to think about why that was.

He rolled to face me as well, bridging the pillow wall, pulling the top one to position under his head.

"What are you doing?"

"Looking at you."

"Well... don't," I demanded, feeling a completely ridiculous—and unfamiliar—surge of insecurity overtake me.

"You're looking at me too."

"You're in my line of vision," I told him. "There. Happy?" I said, closing my eyes.

I wasn't prepared for the soft glide of his fingertip down the side of my face. So unprepared, in fact, that a shiver worked its way through me. But, thankfully, only on the inside.

My eyes shot open.

"Fenway," I started, hearing a strange thickness to my own voice.

"You're pretty when you sleep. Less guarded," he added. See now.

I hated being called pretty.

I hated every single variation of it.

That was my 'damage,' as Alvy called it. That was my sore spot. That was the place that, when you touched, I hissed and spit and clawed.

I had never felt flattered or tingly or whatever else normal people felt when someone else thought they were attractive.

Why, then, was there a skittering sensation in my belly?

I didn't want to analyze that.

"Think of me like that weird jacks art installment at the airport," I told him, referencing the one he'd tried to reach out to, only to be scolded by a nearby security guard in Arabic. "You can look, but don't touch," I told him, flipping to my other side, giving him my back.

And that was that.

Or so I thought.

My subconscious had other ideas, though, that traitorous bitch.

Because when I woke up again, not only had I scaled the rest of the remaining pillow wall, oh no, I had rolled right on top of Fenway, leg cocked up on his hip, head snuggled in under his neck.

As a rule, I did not spend the night with men.

I always left first, before they could ask me to, before they could brush me off.

I'd heard that old adage about breaking up with them before they broke up with you when I was twelve. I promptly took it to heart, made it a staple practice in my life. So while I didn't do relationships, when I'd do flings, I was always the one to walk away first; I was always the one with the power.

That said, there was no way I could have known that I was a sleep snuggler.

Or how good it would feel to have a strong chest under your cheek, rising and falling gently, soothingly. I couldn't have known how nice it would be to have one arm anchored across my lower back, the other resting on my shoulder.

I felt oddly... smaller. More delicate. And protected.

What the hell was that about?"

"I know you're awake," Fenway's voice called, sounding wide awake.

"You can let me go now," I told him, even if a large part of me was screaming that it wanted to stay just like that, that it liked small and delicate and protected.

But I wasn't small.

I damn sure wasn't delicate.

And I never needed someone else to protect me.

"I don't want to."

"I didn't ask you what you wanted."

"You rolled onto me," he told me. "Climbed me like a cat, more like," he told me, and I could hear the smile in his voice.

"I am a bed hog. You were in my space."

"Hm. Maybe. Explain the soft sighs then."

"What are you talking about?" I asked, planting one arm so I could press up a bit and look down at him.

His lips curved up, cocky, devilish.

Yeah, that smile of his was problematic.

It was entirely too appealing.

Damn him.

"You sleep quiet as a mouse. Even when you toss and turn. Not a peep. Until you scaled the wall, climbed up on me, wiggled around to find the right spot, then let out a couple of soft, sweet little contented sighs."

"I did not."

"How do you know? You were unconscious, darling," he reminded me, reaching up to tuck my hair that had fallen forward behind my ear. "You don't need to feel insecure. As I said, it was sweet."

"I'm not insecure," I insisted, even if a little part of me amended that I never *used to be* insecure. "And no one would ever call me sweet," I added.

"I will. I did. You're sweeter under all that cold and hard. You know what else?"

"No," I said, feeling a heaviness in my chest at the look in his eye, like my body knew what he was going to say before his lips formed the words.

Fenway's hand slid up my spine, fingers spreading out at the back of my neck, a firm, yet gentle pressure. "I bet you taste just as sweet," he told me, hand putting more pressure on my neck, pulling me down.

If asked, I wouldn't be able to truthfully say the movement was all him. Because as much as I would never want to admit it, he only pulled me down to ninety-percent. He wanted me to close the last gap.

I didn't mean to.

I knew I wasn't supposed to.

It was too soon for that.

But I did it.

I sealed my lips over his.

Expecting a sizzle.

There was evidence enough of a small bit of attraction that would lead to a sizzle, even if that wasn't great for the job as a whole.

But it wasn't a sizzle.

It was a spark, a flame, a raging wildfire, ravaging through my system, igniting me from the edges of my hair down to the soles of my feet.

A low, rumbling growl escaped Fenway, vibrating into my body, making my leg shift, knee planting on the other side of him, straddling him. And when my hips sank back down, I could feel his hardness pressing against me, demanding, promising an end to the clawing desire I felt building in my core.

Fenway's teeth snagged my lower lip, dragging a ragged moan from my lips as my hips slid, ground down, felt his cock press against me, turning that wildfire into a towering inferno.

Fenway's hands roamed, gliding over my shoulders, my hips, finally sinking into my ass, dragging me against him once again.

A tremble worked through me, making Fenway fold upward, angling me backward, his hand moving between our bodies, hungry hands scorching a path over my shoulder, down my side, teasing over my ribs, then moving back upward, closing over my breast, tightening.

My lips ripped from him, my upper body arching back, giving him more access. He took it, gladly, his thumb and forefinger grabbing my hardened nipple, twisting to the point of pain, then ever so slightly beyond it, making my thighs clamp to his sides, my hips moving in a circle against him, the pressure building fast. A couple more strokes would be all that I needed.

Except that the jet took that moment to hit a patch of turbulence, catching both of us off-guard, sending me flying backward, head smacking against the closed pocket door, pain exploding across my scalp.

"Shit," Fenway hissed, hands reaching for me, trying to pull me back from my cramped, painful position.

"No, don't," I demanded, rolling away, sliding off the edge of the bed, reaching for the little holes in the door to slide it open.

"Wasp..." Fenway called, voice thick and pleading.

It was tempting.

God, it was tempting.

Which was exactly why I pulled the door, then slid it closed, immediately locking myself in the bathroom, sinking back against the wall.

What the hell was wrong with me?

I literally needed to be whacked in the head to get some sense knocked into me.

That had gone too far.

Not that far, in the grand scheme of things, but too far too soon.

"What the hell is wrong with you?" I demanded my reflection, a reflection that looked like the poster girl for sexual desire. My cheeks and neck and chest were flushed. My lips were swollen, redder than usual. My eyes looked heavy-lidded. My hair was bed-messy.

Clearly, I needed to make sure I didn't have such long dry spells. Especially if I had jobs lined up.

I was horny and needy and he was there.

Sometimes you threw away ideals for pure convenience.

And Fenway Arlington was anything but ideal. To me, at least.

He was over the top and silly and frustrating and lived in his own world by his own rules.

I liked depth.

I craved substance.

I enjoyed people who could navigate on the fringes, but still function in normal society.

I didn't like superficial playboys.

Not even if they enjoyed classic movies.

Not even if they had great taste in food.

Not even if they were the best kisser I'd ever come across.

"Ugh," I grumbled, turning on the water, splashing it on my face, hoping the cold would calm the chaos still raging in my body, the unfulfilled desire that was impossible to ignore.

Okay.

It was okay.

A little bit of sexy times that eventually got taken away from him would only make him want it more. Want me more. Which meant he would be willing to do anything to woo me back into it.

That worked in my favor.

I could spin this.

If my damn body would stop trying to co-op my brain with its stupid demands.

And they were stupid.

Wanting to have sex with Fenway Arlington was likely the dumbest thing I could even think of on a rational level.

Which was precisely why it wasn't going to happen.

Decision made—once again—I tamed my hair, straightened my clothes, worked a kink out of my neck, then made my way back out into the main area of the jet, finding Alvy and Fenway sitting at the table. Joy, the flight attendant, must have moved up into the cockpit.

"Are you okay?" Alvy asked, putting their phone down. "Fenway said the turbulence made you fall out of bed," Alvy added, and I could feel the heat rising on my neck. "You must have really been out to have flown that far off the bed," they added.

"Yeah," I agreed, taking my seat on the couch again, making a slow show of crossing my legs, making sure Fenway's gaze went there, noticed the hike of my skirt. Oh, yeah, I realized as his gaze lifted, eyes blazing, I had him. "I must have been really out of it," I agreed.

"Is that what we are calling it?" Fenway asked, tone dark, daring.

"Yep," I agreed, running a hand through my hair, feeling the smart when my fingers met the little knot on my scalp from the impact. "It won't be happening again," I told him. And maybe myself.

"I think it will. Quite a few times, I would say," Fenway shot back.

"How clumsy do you think she is?" Alvy asked, making the both of us have to press our lips together and break eye contact to keep from laughing.

"How long until we are in Bali?" I asked a moment later.

"Just about an hour," Alvy supplied.

"Anxious to get to my house, are you, darling?" Fenway asked, back to light, teasing.

I was.

I needed a little space.

My own room.

My own bed.

Then things would get back on track, go back to the plan.

Yes, I really was that naive.

And Bali was everything—and nothing—like I had expected.

As it turned out, so was Fenway Arlington.

SIX

Fenway

I wasn't sure I'd ever truly known sexual frustration before in my life. There had always been opportunities to deal with it when it popped up randomly.

Now?

There looked to be no end to it.

Because after that kiss in the bedroom, Wasp was back to cold and distant, not even cracking a smile when I laid the charm on thick, or even when Alvy cracked a particularly biting—and hilarious—joke at my expense.

She was ice personified.

She didn't even start to melt in the sweltering sun as we made our way to our waiting car, as we drove to the house.

In fact, she paid me no attention whatsoever, her gaze stubbornly out the window at her side, watching the sights as we moved past.

It was alright.

I got to watch her watching the sights.

It was a consolation of sorts.

It made everything feel new, seeing it through her eyes instead of my own.

"You can't be serious," she mumbled as we pulled into the drive. "You have a house this big that you, what, visit a few times a year?"

"It's here when I need it, though."

"You could just stay at a hotel."

"I could," I agreed. And maybe, objectively, that was what I should do. Keeping a house you didn't live in—staff and all— was undoubtedly expensive. I didn't know the numbers. I'd have to ask Alvy. All I knew was it wasn't hurting my bottom line. And it kept the staff employed. It wasn't a complete loss if someone benefited from it.

"Do you at least time share it? So other people can actually appreciate its beauty?" she asked, tone accusatory as she climbed out of the car, refusing to take my hand to do so, despite nearly teetering on her heels on the uneven stone drive.

"I do not."

"Well, you should," she decided, taking a deep breath, inspiring me to do the same, the salt water teasing my nostrils, fresh, familiar.

"What do you think, Alvy? Should we time-share it?"

"It is beautiful,"Alvy said. "I can have it arranged."

"Not that you need the money or anything," Wasp went on, turning in a slow circle. "But at least all the energy bills wouldn't be a complete waste."

"Would you like a tour?" I asked as she did yet another turn.

Finally, her gaze settled on the house—the villa—head cocking to the side, taking it in.

It was a two-story home, the first floor of white stucco, the second of terra cotta colored, each level with a covered porch, both in the front and the back, allowing you views of the island to the front and the ocean to the back.

"Okay," she said, turning to face me, eyes unreadable for a moment as she made her way toward me, linking her arm through mine, surprising me enough for my feet to falter when she charged forward, dragging me with her.

I didn't understand her moods, the up and down, the hot and cold, but I had to admit I was more intrigued than ever.

I figured once she was settled in, she might let down the guards a bit, show me more of who was underneath that cold mask of hers.

I had a feeling it would be an amazing woman to behold.

Possibly—dare I even think it—one who wouldn't ever prove predictable, someone who would never get boring.

Someone I might enjoy having around for an extended period of time.

That was a shocking thought, as I hadn't been looking for that. Yet now that it was here, there was no denying I found myself interested in the possibility.

"Wow," Wasp sighed as we moved in the front door, straight into the open concept lower floor, seeing right through the house to the back where the floor-to-ceiling windows showed the back deck and pool area as well as a sliver of the ocean.

The surfaces were deep natural woods, made less oppressive by the abundance of light filtering in through the space.

"Alright, I'll admit it," she said, giving me a wry smile. "I am officially envious of your wealth. I would cut off something vital to be able to wake up to this view every morning."

"Luckily, darling, nothing on your lovely body needs to be severed to be able to enjoy this view. Let me show you to your room," I offered, leading her up to the stairs behind the bottom floor washroom. "This is Alvy's room, if they choose to stay with us," I told her, motioning to the first door. "This is me," I added, walking past the next. "And finally, you," I said, pushing open the door.

The master always had the best view, but hers was nothing to sneeze at, and it was what you immediately noticed when you stepped inside thanks to the floor-to-ceiling windows, white drapes pulled open.

The queen-sized four-poster bed dominated the space, draped all in white. With a massive round box of blood-red roses beside a box of chocolates. And the pink champagne was chilling on the nightstand next to a flute with a stem so thin a strong breeze could snap it.

"Do you treat all your guests to roses and pink champagne?" she asked, sending a sly smile my way as she ran her fingers over the flower petals.

"Don't be silly," I told her, lips curving up. "Most of my guests don't like pink champagne," I added, making a smile brighten her ridiculously beautiful face. "This door leads out onto the back balcony, clearly," I told her, gesturing toward it. "And through here is your bathroom," I continued, walking over to open the door, peeking in, seeing the rose petals floating in the water, the fluffy white robe hanging beside the tub, a pile of bath bombs in a bowl just waiting to be used.

Diann—who was running this house these days—deserved a raise if she pulled out all these stops. I'd asked Alvy simply to make sure the pink champagne was there, not all the rest.

"Do you do everything over-the-top?" Wasp asked, but her eyes were soft as she took in the deep soaking tub, the excessive number of towels stacked at her disposal, the rainfall glass shower, the built-in stereo system in the wall.

"I do," I told her, since it was the truth.

"I'm starting not to hate that," she admitted, shaking her head. "This bathroom is bigger than Wanda," she added.

"I'm sorry, Wanda?" I asked, watching as she shot me a smile.

"My skoolie."

"That is a word I'm afraid I am not familiar with."

"Skoolie. A converted school bus."

"Converted to what, exactly?"

"A home," she told me. "I bought an out of commission school bus, gutted it, and rebuilt it into a home."

"For what purpose?"

"To travel with my best friend."

"Why not travel in a car and stay in hotels?"

"Because not all of us were born into privilege. I'm not hating on you because of it, but most of us aren't that lucky. And we have to make the best out of our circumstances. This was the best for us."

"How long did you travel that way, live that way?"

"A decade or so. Raven crapped out on me a while back. Fell into some guy's dicksand, never resurfacing. She has kids and everything now."

"So you've been traveling on your own too?"

"I hate to break it to you, Fenway, but you don't travel alone. You have Alvy. And the drivers and the pilots and the boat captains."

"Still," I said, shaking my head. "I'm alone." Was that a note of sadness in my voice?

"Solo travel is great," Wasp said, moving past me to go look out at the view. "You always get to pick what you want to eat, where you want to go, what music is on. But it can get—" she paused, trying to find the guts to say the next word. In the end, she failed.

"Lonely," I supplied, finally recognizing the feeling that had made the past two or three years feel so empty, so unfulfilling.

I'd been surrounded by people.

And lonelier than I'd ever felt before.

"I hate that word," she admitted, lip curling up, shooting me a disdainful look over her shoulder.

"But it is the appropriate one, isn't it?"

To that, she sighed, her whole body relaxing with it. "Yes, it's the right word. I miss my best friend. I miss having someone to share things with, to go out hunting at midnight for a restaurant that was open, or making a meal out of convenience store food. I miss singalongs and getting drunk in bars. I like being on my own. I do. But I miss sharing things with someone else too."

That rang true as the most honest—and vulnerable—thing she'd ever said to me.

A strange pang ached across my chest, strong enough for my hand to move there, rubbing my fingertips across it.

"Well," I said, forcing cheer, lightness, wanting to chase the dark out of the room, out of her. "Luckily for you, you now have someone to create makeshift meals with, and get drunk with. Though I must warn you, I am not much of a singer. I will do it loudly. And with great enthusiasm regardless, though."

The sadness slipped from her eyes, replaced by a twinkling I rather liked seeing there.

"Thanks for inviting me here," she told me, glancing away. "It is nice not to be so alone," she added, refusing to look at me, and I was starting to suspect she had a hard time being real and open with someone face to-face.

Relating to that more than she could know, I didn't press it.

"I will let you settle in. We should be having a late dinner tonight."

"Thanks," she said, reaching for the door, moving out onto the balcony, watching the sun start to set.

I went out into the hall, going into my room to shower, change into swim shorts and a white tee, then making my way downstairs, finding Alvy sitting in the kitchen with a woman in her late twenties or early thirties who was chopping vegetables while the two chatted.

Diann, if I remembered correctly. Her mother had been the housekeeper when I'd first bought the place, but she'd been in an accident, hurt her back, and her eldest daughter had stepped into her place.

"Diann," I greeted her, walking over to the bar, pouring myself a scotch. "The guest room was lovely. Thank you for the extra touches."

"Alvy said you were having trouble impressing a woman," Diann said, eyes dancing at my expense. I imagined the two had been joking behind my back. The playboy who had finally met my match. The one woman who wouldn't fall for my charms. The one who refused to take me at face-value. The one who would need more than that from me. And I wasn't sure I could give anyone that.

"She finds herself wholly unimpressed with my personality, my money, and just about everything about me. But she liked the view and the flowers," I told Diann, sitting down a few stools away from Alvy.

"Why her, then?" Diann asked. "If she doesn't like you. Or is that the apple peel?"

"Appeal," I corrected, smiling. Her English was amazing, but she forgot some words. I remember her once calling an octopus a 'sea spider.' "I suppose that is part of it."

"Alvy says she is beautiful."

"Knock-you-upside-the-head, kick-you-in-the-gut, steal-your-breath beautiful," I told her, nodding. "Now if I can only get her to see how devilishly handsome I am," I joked.

"You could try to impress her by being your authentic self," Alvy suggested, getting a brow raise from me.

"Nobody wants to see that. This me is much more fun," I declared, getting off my seat, not comfortable with the line of conversation.

"But what if the fun Fenway isn't what Wasp is after? What if she wants the real you underneath all that?"

That was a valid question.

But the answer seemed simple.

Then she was out of luck.

And then so was I.

But I refused to accept defeat so early in the game.

I was sure I could handle Wasp.

I'd never been more wrong about anything in my life.

And with my fuck-up reputation, that was really saying something.

SEVEN

Wasp

This one of Fenway's many vacation homes was a five-star-resort without any other pesky guests.

Even though there were other houses on the street, the way the backyard was set up secluded the pool and hot tub area in perfect privacy.

Not that I was shy about wearing a bathing suit in public, but it was nice not to have to deal with gawking in case the owners of the other homes were older, leering men.

I'd been telling the truth when I told Fenway my suit would be torturous. It was a red one-piece that dipped nearly to my navel in front, exposed most of my back, and ninety-eight percent of my ass.

I was not a thong bathing suit sort of person. But this one was a pointed choice. I needed him to want me. So much that it was painful. So much so that he was driven half mad by it. Then I would have him. And I could win.

Unfortunately, the weather chose not to cooperate with the plans.

"Monsoon season," Diann had told me when for the third day in a row, I stood at the French doors, staring forlornly out at the pool as well as the beach beyond it.

It had been pouring. The kind of downfalls that offered no respite, not even ten minutes to run out and jump in the pool.

Fenway had been an admirable host, given that half of his entertainment options were blocked by the weather.

We went out to eat.

We watched classic movies.

Night one, my favorites.

Night two, his.

While we didn't overlap any of our favorites, neither of us disagreed with the other's choices.

Alvy had been a silent, sporadic presence, showing up for meal times, then otherwise disappearing entirely, sometimes going out, others simply locking themselves in their room.

I couldn't help but wonder what kind of life it was to chase after a billionaire playboy who changed his mind at a moment's notice, needing all his plans to be changed, requiring excuses to be made, hotels to be booked, luggage to be packed. It didn't seem like Alvy ever got to go home, either. They were an ever-present part of Fenway's extravagant lifestyle. While it seemed like a great job on surface level, what with all their expenses covered, getting to stay in the most beautiful places in the world, brush shoulders with the rich and famous, I also couldn't help but wonder if it must have felt very strange for their life not to belong to them.

Maybe that was why we so infrequently saw Alvy now that their presence wasn't needed. They were trying to get a small bit of privacy, of normalcy while they could.

As beautiful as my room was, I couldn't fathom staying cooped up in it with the rest of the house to explore.

I wasn't much of a cook, but the kitchen was amazing, having every gadget known to mankind—and late night infomercial watchers—tucked away in cabinets. The bar was fully stocked. The television was massive. The couches were like a warm hug.

I'd gotten so used to my cozy—but cramped—living space, I had all but forgotten what it was like to not be able to walk from one end of a home to the other in about ten paces.

As such, I stretched out.

I hogged the best couch.

I slept starfish-wide on the massive bed.

I showered in the rainfall shower and soaked in the deep tub.

I figured that if I was going to do the job, I was going to get something out of it.

Speaking of the job, things had gotten a bit off track somewhere after arrival. We'd fallen into a companionable buddy sort of relationship. All the sexual tension was absent in our interactions, though not absent in my overwrought, desperate system that just didn't want to take no for an answer about sleeping with Fenway.

Being here with him was suddenly very much like having a fun, charming roommate who liked to hang out and watch movies, play card games where they graciously lost their shirt, and talk about little nonsense, superficial conversation.

I was getting nowhere.

And while a part of me was enjoying myself enough not to care, the other knew that I had a lot of money hanging on this. Life-changing money. I couldn't afford to screw it up. Literally.

So when the sun finally decided to chase away the rain clouds on the fourth day after arrival, I made sure I shaved and lotioned every inch of me, slipped into the wickedly cruel bathing suit, and made my way out to the pool a few moments before I knew Fenway would finally come bleary-eyed down to get his morning coffee.

Right from the position where he would stand to pour it, he would get a view of my nearly bare ass as I stood out by the side of the pool.

If I was going to have to get back on track, I had to break out the big guns.

Tits and ass worked when all else failed.

I wasn't above using that to my advantage.

It wasn't long before I heard the sound of the coffee pot beeping.

Two minutes.

Three.

And bingo.

The door was pulling open, and I could simply feel the sizzle of chemistry as Fenway moved out onto the back patio, moving over toward one of the wooden chaise loungers.

"Don't mind me, darling. I am just enjoying this beautiful view this morning," he said, voice deep, sleep-sexy, and just plain sexy-sexy too.

It was working.

"What view is that, Fenway?" I asked, half turning, head cocking down toward my shoulder. "The pool, the ocean, or me?"

"Seen just about every beach in the world. Pools are a dime a dozen. That ass, though? That ass is one of a kind," he told me, lips curving up slowly as he raised his mug, taking a slow sip. Then, without breaking eye contact, pulling half of his bottom lip inside his mouth to clean away the bit of coffee there.

It was like a punch to my aching core.

Everything in me wanted to march over to him, climb on his lap, and have my way with him.

Fuck the job and all.

That was the level of neediness I was experiencing.

For the record, I never said "fuck the job." The job was more than just a paycheck, it was a way of life, it was a mission of sorts. Making men who deserved it pay for their past indiscretions.

"I think you've seen enough," I declared, turning forward, jumping into the pool.

I needed to keep engaging him.

But I needed just as badly to take a cold bath to calm the need coursing through my system.

I surfaced, swimming over to one end of the pool, then taking a few laps. First, because I'd been too sedentary for days. Second, I had eaten my body weight in chocolate since arriving; even after begging Diann to stop buying the boxes, they kept showing up on my bed every evening. And, third, I thought if I exhausted my body enough, it wouldn't have the energy to be so desperate for sex.

I was so focused on my form—made a little anal about it because of a brief stint on the swim team in school, and my natural born competitive nature—I had somehow missed the legs suddenly dangling in the water.

All I knew was I needed a good, deep breath, so I surfaced at the deep end.

Right between Fenway's spread legs.

Eyes level with his crotch.

His lightweight pajama pants were doing absolutely nothing to conceal that he was just as irrationally turned on as I was this morning.

Seeing the problem before it became a whole *issue*, I tried to dip back down in the water, only to have Fenway fold forward, reaching into the water, hands grabbing me at the top of my rib cage at each side, fingers pressing into my barely-concealed breasts.

I damn near came right then and there.

Yep.

That was where I was at.

Boob brushes were doing it for me.

Like we were fumbling, uncertain teenagers.

Fenway froze for a moment, waiting for my eye contact. I didn't want to give it to him, knowing what he would find on my face. Parted lips, wide, hooded eyes.

Undeniable attraction.

But my head lifted; my gaze found his.

Having what he wanted, his hands pressed harder into my wet suit, into my skin beneath, pulling, lifting me out of the water.

I wasn't heavy, but nor was I a waif, either, and I found myself duly impressed by his upper body strength as he kept pulling me up even when he didn't have the assistance of the weightlessness of water to aid him, as he pulled me clear out of the water, higher, until he was lowering me down, allowing instinct to make me spread my legs to the outsides of his, to have my lap drop down onto his.

A choked whimper escaped my lips as my cleft pressed against his hard cock, making a shudder work through me.

My body settled, his hands slid down my sides, curving outward to the flare of my hips, then drifting downward, sinking into the bare flesh of my ass.

I didn't think.

I didn't want to think.

Instead, I wrapped my arms around his shoulders, sealing my lips over his—hard, hungry, demanding.

He gave it right back to me, lips bruising, tongue claiming, teeth nipping.

My hips rocked against his, stoking the desire inside, driving my body upward.

On a low growl, Fenway's lips ripped from mine as his hand left my ass, curling into the hair at the nape of my neck instead, twisting, pulling, arching me backward as his lips met my neck, my throat, down between the V of my breasts, then up again, making my nipples harden, making my hips do another greedy rock against his cock.

Fenway's other hand moved between us, grabbing the strap of my swimsuit, dragging it downward, exposing one breast, then the other.

Using his hand in my hair, he arched me back further, jutting my breasts toward him. Bending he sucked one into my mouth, working it with his tongue until I was writhing against him wildly. He released me, but only to go across my chest, sinking his teeth into my other nipple, making the pre-orgasm tightening start between my legs.

Close.

So close.

I just needed to reach into his pants, to free him, to pull my swimsuit to the side, and have him slip inside me. Deep, from the feel of it, overtaking me completely.

God, yes.

I needed that.

I needed it more than I was sure I ever needed any man before.

My nails clawed across his shoulders, holding on as I circled my hips against him.

Now.

I needed him inside me now.

Right that second.

But, no.

No, I added to my brain, hazy and slow with the fog of need swirling around it.

No, I couldn't have him right now.

We had no protection.

And I never took that risk.

If we paused to work out that situation, the moment would be gone. I would think it through. I would realize exactly how stupid it was.

Seeming to sense a shift, Fenway's arm anchored around my waist, turning, shifting, laying me flat on the warm cement, my legs dangling in the water.

"I can't fuck you," he told me, running his tongue between my breasts as he lowered himself into the water. "But I can taste you," he added, arms hooking under my legs, yanking them up.

His hand moved between my thighs, pulling my suit to the side.

Before I could even muster an objection—and, surely, I was going to object, right?—his mouth was on me, sucking for a second before his tongue was working my clit—fast, relentless, never giving my body a chance to lose the orgasm that was building at the base of my spine, a deep fist of tension.

And then just like that, his tongue swiped, and I crashed through my orgasm, crying out loud enough to alert anyone in the house—or in the neighbors' houses—letting them know exactly what was happening out on the patio.

But I didn't care.

I couldn't have cared.

Not with the pleasure exploding through my system, working its tendrils through every inch of my body, overtaking me entirely, leaving me shuddering in the wake.

My swimsuit moved back into place.

Fenway released my legs.

And then he was pulling himself out of the water, his wet body sliding over mine, pressing into me for one glorious moment.

He paused, waiting for my eyelids to flutter open.

And I saw complete and utter triumph staring back at me.

"Good luck trying to convince me—or yourself—that you don't want me now," he told me in that deep, sexy, alpha voice he used far too rarely, considering it was the hottest thing I was sure I'd ever heard. "Darling," he added with a smirk, like he knew exactly what he was doing, how I was trying to separate the two men I had come to know as Fenway Arlington.

Then his lips pressed to mine.

Hard.

Claiming.

Branding.

That was what they did.

They branded me.

But then they pulled away as quickly as they had pressed to me.

He pushed himself upward, away, and walked back into the house, dripping wet, hard as he had been just minutes before.

But victorious.

On a whimper, I reached downward, settling my breasts back into my swimsuit, which was no easy task given tits' tendency to seek separation when you were flat on your back, but I managed.

Lying there, I took a few deep, steadying breaths, my hand pressing to my belly.

"Wasp?" Alvy's voice called a few minutes later as I stayed there like a beached whale. Mostly because I wasn't sure I had complete authority over my own legs yet.

"Yeah?" I asked, taking one more deep breath, then folding upward to face them.

"Fenway said to tell you to be ready in an hour. He has a day planned."

"A day? What does this 'day' include?" I asked, brows furrowing as I reached up to toss my soaked hair over my shoulder.

"Actually," Alvy said, looking puzzled. "I have no idea. He didn't ask me to arrange it. He, ah, he did it himself," Alvy added, the words sounding like a question, like they couldn't quite come to terms with their helpless boss being able to do anything for himself.

"That is a terrifying thought," I told Alvy, getting a smirk from them.

"He's not quite the clueless idiot he can sometimes portray himself to be. I'm sure he has something interesting planned. Interesting," Alvy specified. "Interesting does not necessarily mean good, but if nothing else, you will have a story to tell."

"That's for damn sure." This entire ordeal was one for the books.

"You always have my number if you need an escape route," Alvy reminded me, shrugging, seeming uncertain what to do with themselves when Fenway was somehow taking care of his own affairs for a change.

"You can tag along," I offered, really needing the social buffer. I was reasonably sure that Fenway and I weren't going to jump each other with Alvy nearby.

Only pretty sure, though, mind you.

"I was given the day off," Alvy informed me, shaking their head.

"Oh, *darling*," Fenway's voice called from the second story balcony, making me crane my head to look up, my hand raising to block the sun. "Wear flats," he instructed, grin cocky, still basking in his victory.

Oh, he won the battle, that was for damn sure. I wasn't so prideful that I couldn't admit that. He clearly had the upper hand. He'd taken this one.

But I was going to win the war.

"I don't know if I like that look," Alvy observed, watching me with drawn-together brows.

"Your boss needs to be taken down a few pegs," I informed them.

"You're not getting any objections from me," Alvy said, giving me a smirk. "And I think you might actually be the woman for the job."

"Oh, I am. He's going down," I added, feeling my cheeks heat at that choice of words, wondering if Alvy knew more than they were letting on.

"Just let me know when. I want to be there. With popcorn. And a camera."

"I appreciate the vote of confidence," I told them, standing, making my way on stiff legs toward the door, following Fenway's wet footsteps through the house, up the stairs, across the hall to my room.

Going into my bathroom, I decided I needed to wash off the chlorine.

Making my way to the shower, I reached inside, pausing, hearing Fenway's shower on against the wall of mine, water slicking off his body and slapping against the floor in waves.

But that wasn't all I heard.

Oh, no.

I heard a low, tortured-sounding groaning, making my sex clench in realization.

I am not proud of this next part, I will admit. But it is the truth regardless.

I moved into my shower, pressing my ear against the wall, eavesdropping on a private moment.

Need gripped my system once again as I listened to him jerking off. To the idea of me. My hands. My mouth. Everything else.

My thighs pressed tightly together as there was a slamming noise—his fist hitting the wall—followed by a hiss, then a growling curse.

My sex fluttered in response, a large part of me wishing I was in there with him, coming with him.

"Christ," I hissed to myself, moving out of the shower, reaching in to turn it on.

I needed to get my head back in the game.

I needed to focus.

The sexual chemistry was good.

It was important, even.

It was even better if it was not faked on my part. Because I was pretty sure Fenway would have been able to notice the difference, even when every other man I faked it with didn't have any idea.

Showered, dressed in a simple sundress I had picked up in Qatar, and a pair of flip-flops since I didn't own any other sort of flat shoe, I made my way downstairs.

Chin up, shoulders back, gait confident. Even if my nerves were skittering around, making my heart flutter in my chest, my stomach flip-flop around.

What version of Fenway was going to be taking me on an outing today?

And where the heck were we going?

Maybe the better move would have been to say I was staying home, enjoying the beach and pool.

But what can I say? I wanted to see Indonesia. This was a once-in-a-lifetime opportunity. I wanted to take all I could get from this experience.

"You look ravishing, darling," Fenway greeted, waiting for me in absurd, but somehow charming, pink chino shorts with some sort of tiny blue print on them and a white tee.

"What the hell is on your shorts?" I asked, moving closer.

"Well, you could get on your knees and check it out," he suggested, tone doing that deep, sexy, serious thing again.

The two parts of Fenway I had come to know were starting to blend together more. Which was going to be problematic for me. Because a part of me was starting to like the easy-going and absurd Fenway. The other part was sex-throbbingly obsessed with the idea of screwing the alpha, cocky, serious side of him.

"Oh, sweetheart," I said, adopting an old, trusty persona. The cool, collected sex kitten. My voice purred, my body swayed, sashayed, moving closer, near enough that our bodies almost touched. Almost. My fingertip touched the hem of his shorts, tracing slowly upward, making sure to tease in at the last moment, gliding up his zipper. "I've already gotten all I need from you," I told him, claiming the pool event as my own, taking the power back. "Now," I said, pulling away when I was sure his cock was hard again against his shorts, "Where are you taking me today?"

I could tell by the pained look on his face that I had just won an important battle.

And just like I planned, the playboy Fenway followed after me like a puppy dog.

Considering Alvy had no part in arranging the day, Fenway had set up something pretty memorable.

We started the morning at The Sacred Monkey Sanctuary, seeing families of monkeys, giant stone statues, the breathtaking greenery.

Fenway stopped me frequently, insisting it was the perfect spot for a photo op, then taking pictures all from good angles. And it was right in those moments that I remembered how nice it was to travel with someone else, to share the experiences, to get lost in a new area, a new way of life, to catalog those memories for when you are old and your memory was getting spotty.

"That was great," I admitted as we climbed back in his waiting car. I was even getting used to being driven around which, at first, had felt very awkward and unnecessary.

"How about a trip to the market?" he asked, as if I would turn it down.

"Don't we need to stop somewhere to get money? What kind of money do they use in Indonesia? I don't imagine a place referred to as a 'market' takes credit cards, right?"

"Rupiah is the type of money. It's very colorful," he informed me, reaching into his pocket, pulling out a giant wad of cash held together with a silver manatee clip. "And I keep a stash of it at the house in case of situations just like this. Now, you are not going to deny me the pleasure of buying you some happy, are you?"

"Happiness can't be bought. At least not in a lasting way. But far be it from me to turn down a little temporary happy," I added, enjoying the smile he shot me a little bit too much.

"I'm softening you up, aren't I, darling?"

"Don't be silly, *darling*," I said, patting his thigh. Did I pat him unfairly, torturously high on his thigh? I sure as hell did. And he sure as hell felt it, judging by the indrawn breath that I pretended not to notice. In fact, I pretended not to notice where my hand touched as well, my gaze out the window.

Fenway wasn't quite ready to let me get away with it, though.

His arm landed across my shoulders, pulling me into his side. His lips moved down near my ear, his warm breath sending a shiver over my skin.

"You and I both know you haven't gotten everything you truly want from me, darling," he told me, voice low. "You're not going to be satisfied until I'm buried deep inside you. Until you come around my cock multiple times. Even then, I suspect, it won't be enough. Play your games, pretty girl, but we both know where this ends."

With that, he released me, reaching for his door, pulling it open, making me realize we had somehow gotten to the market and parked without me noticing.

Yes, that was the effect Fenway had on me.

He made the world fall away.

And that was very, very dangerous.

Because I was pretty sure he wasn't wrong.

This wasn't over.

And there was no true way to win.

No matter which way things went, I was pretty sure we were both going to lose.

EIGHT

Wasp

"This is getting ridiculous," I told Fenway as he made a show out of snatching the hat I was trying on off my head and handing it to the shopkeeper with a flourish, telling her we would take it.

It was my third hat.

I also had a bright green and gold Siddhartha mask, a macramé wall hanging, a rainbow woven blanket, a massive white dreamcatcher, an I Love Bali tank top, a pink lizard magnet, beaded bracelets, and two straw purses—one small and round, the other large and rectangular.

Basically, if I touched it, or stopped to look at it for more than five seconds, Fenway decided I needed to have it.

"I love ridiculous things," he declared, handing the proprietor money, telling her to keep the change. From the wide eyes on her face, I imagined it was way over the asking price. "It is also good for the local economy that I am so ridiculous."

It wasn't just ridiculous.

It was generous.

I was starting to see that his way of throwing cash around wasn't exactly for recognition, for envy from others, but simple because he wanted to give; he genuinely liked brightening someone's day.

That was an unexpected and all-too-appealing quality, I had to admit.

"I literally don't have enough space to store all of this. I live on a bus, remember?" I reminded him, stopping myself short of touching wooden wind chimes, liking the idea of them, but knowing the constant clanging while driving Wanda would drive me mad.

"You'll find room," he assured me, dropping an arm across my shoulders, light and amiable, a part of him I was no longer seeing as superficial, but another side to his personality. We were all multifaceted. Judging him on it before had merely been because I'd been seeing him through a cynical lens, not a fair one.

"I think I will have to throw out my hot plate and coffee maker to make room for all of this.

"Food and coffee can be picked up on the road," he assured me, brushing my objections away.

By the time we finally left the market, I had an extra pair of flats, a coffee mug, and a really cute little mama and baby monkey statue.

"To remember our trip today," he told me, snatching it up, handing it to me, then paying for it.

I would never admit this, not even if Raven was giving me her 'out with it, Wasp' eyes, but there was a strange, unfamiliar little tugging sensation in my chest as I held it, as I thought about the sentiment behind it. I even had this insane urge to press the damn thing to my chest like some old long-forgotten childhood toy when finding it tucked in a box in the attic.

Uncomfortable with the sensations coursing through me, I took the statue, tucking it inside the round purse I had put on cross-body. Partly because I didn't want to keep feeling those sensations. But also because I wanted it safe, protected, not lost in the shuffle as we climbed back in the car.

"My feet hurt," I admitted, flexing them as I felt a refreshing blast of cold air from the air vent.

"Well, we certainly can't have that, can we?" Fenway asked, reaching down to snag my legs, ignoring my objection as he settled them over his waist, his hands going for one of my feet, fingers pressing with expert precision into my sore soles.

"You know, if the being a mega billionaire thing doesn't work out for you," I told him, leaning my head back against the window, eyes half closing, "you could really have a career in foot massage," I told him, watching the warm look in his eyes as he gave me a small smile. "Are we going home?" I asked, not knowing what the rest of the plan was because he refused to tell me more than one step at a time.

When I asked why he was being such a pain about it, he'd told me that he wanted it to be a surprise so he could see my reaction when I learned the next destination.

It was an annoyingly adorable thing to say.

I wanted to hate him for it. As I always hated mush, in all of its forms.

But there was no denying that, well, I was starting to feel a little mushy inside when he said things like that.

"Nope."

"Where are we going?"

"It's a surprise. This is my favorite part of the day," he added, smiling. "Don't worry though, darling, I will have time to finish both your feet before we get there."

"Well then, I guess I have no objections," I told him, nudging him with my free foot.

I was liking this too much.

Way too much.

The rational part of me understood this, knew how problematic it could be. The irrational part of me, though, told the other part to fuck off.

"Wasp," Fenway called, a faraway sound in my ear, stirring me from a deep sleep. "Honey," he said, making my belly wobble. "We're here," he added, giving my leg a squeeze.

A low, grumbling noise escaped me as my eyes slitted open, squinting at the afternoon sun.

"I think I have had enough fun," I whined, pouting at him.

"I'm afraid we can't reschedule, darling," he told me, shrugging.

"Why not? We have no plans tomorrow."

"No," he agreed. "But I have already paid the people who run this particular tourist attraction to have exclusive access to this place of the day."

"You... what?" I asked, sitting up, suddenly fully awake. My gaze moved around outside the car, seeing an empty lot save for us and one car with some sort of logo on it that I couldn't read. "You can't pay to rent out a public place."

"Sure you can. People rent out Disney all the time. Churches. Museums..."

"Not entire parks."

"Yes, entire parks," he corrected. "Us being living proof of that."

"But that's not fair to everyone who planned to come here today."

"Sure it is. I paid for them to be able to come here tomorrow with no charge. They were all happy to oblige. Or so I was told."

"But why would we need it to be empty?"

"You'll see," he told me, giving my leg one last squeeze before exiting his door, leaving me to slip back into my shoes and follow.

"What is this?" I asked, looking up and seeing nothing but rolling hills of greenery. Beautiful, lush greenery, but seemingly nothing else. No temples, no statues, just natural beauty.

"So many questions."

"Just one question, actually," I corrected, brow raising.

To that, he rolled his eyes, reaching for my hand, twining his fingers between mine, and pulling me along.

I was supposed to snatch my hand away.

I was making it too easy.

He wasn't going to fall for me if there wasn't some resistance.

I needed to pull away.

But his hand felt good in mine—strong, reassuring, companionable, like we were going on an adventure together.

Which, I guessed, we were.

So I left my hand right there, telling myself that I could find some resistance some other time, that I was just going to enjoy this moment.

From there, we took off on our own, not even stopping to greet the park ranger as we passed, Fenway just giving him a nod that was returned as the man promptly disappeared.

I didn't know how much this had cost Fenway—I didn't want to know—but I had to admit there was something about hiking through this park in complete silence that made the experience almost seem, I don't know, spiritual.

"Fenway?"

"Yes, darling?"

"Um, are we just... taking a hike? Or is there some sort of destination in mind?"

"You haven't figured it out yet?" he asked, raising his brows.

"Figured what out? What is there to figure out?"

To that, he pulled to a stop. "Listen," he demanded.

I was going to tell him I'd been doing nothing but listening when I did, in fact, hear it. I guess I had been listening to my own heavy breathing and internal monologue and not the sounds around us after all.

Because the moment he told me to hear it, I did.

"A waterfall," I declared, smiling.

"Very good," he told me, eyes bright.

"I love waterfalls," I told him. "I have to have at least a thousand pictures of my best friend and me at various waterfalls all across the United States."

"As lovely as all those must have been," he started, pulling me along again, this time with more enthusiasm, which meant I damn near had to jog to keep up. "I think this one will take the cake," he told me, suddenly dragging my body in front of his.

Then there it was.

He wasn't wrong.

It was the best one I'd ever seen.

Not because it was the biggest—it wasn't—but because there was something about its quiet seclusion, about the way it was technically three waterfalls in one, about the way it was surrounded with the greenest trees and moss I had ever seen.

"Wow," I whispered, shaking my head, going ahead and leaning back into Fenway when his arms went around my midsection.

"Right?" he asked, lips down by my ear.

"Wait, I'm not done," I told him when he pulled away, grabbed my hand, started to drag me with him.

"I promise, this will be even better," he told me, dragging me into a tree-lined path, but not one that was well worn like the rest of them. If anything, this didn't seem to be an on-the-map path at all, but merely one a select few people knew about.

And, of course, Fenway was one of those people.

The further we walked, the louder the crash of the waterfall got, until it was all that you could hear.

"This way," Fenway called, nearly yelling, yanking me to the side, then ducking under a squat tree.

Without another choice since he was still holding my hand captive, I followed, hair getting caught on branches as we squat-walked for a minute before we slipped through a hole in a rock formation, where we could finally stand up again, my burning thighs crying in gratitude.

The noise here was nearly deafening.

The spray from the water wet our faces as we got closer and closer to the wide opening to the side of the second waterfall.

"Okay, you're right," I declared, taking a deep breath, wanting to remember this sight, these smells, this one perfect moment.

There were many small, perfect moments in life.

I had pages of memories of them.

But this one felt different, bigger somehow.

Fenway moved in behind me once again, watching the cascading water from over my shoulder as his chin rested there, his arms wrapping me up once again.

Don't ask me why I did it.

I couldn't tell you. Not if I had a lifetime to analyze my motivations.

But my head turned, and my lips pressed to him.

Light.

Sweet.

I'd done a lot of kissing in my life. But it had always had a singular purpose, a lead up to something more.

This, though? This was not that. This was just connection, just intimacy, just taking the sensations that were overflowing out of me and trying to share them with him.

It was the purest, most innocent kiss of my life. I felt it down to my toes, up to the top of my scalp. A tingling that wasn't desire, but something deeper, something stronger, something I wasn't familiar enough with to have a name for.

My heart was beating hard in my chest, a kick-drum to my ribcage, as Fenway's hand rose, gently framing the side of my face, turning me to face him completely.

I didn't bother to fight the urge to wrap my arms around the back of his neck, to press my body tighter to his.

We stayed like that for what seemed like an eternity, lips soft, sweet, undemanding.

Eventually, though, the warmth that was spreading in my core made its way across my belly, over my chest, until every inch of me felt warm, felt the throbbing of desire.

My lips demanded more first, and Fenway's were eager to give me exactly what I wanted, his hand sifting into my hair, tugging a little, making my head arch backward, giving him better access.

My hands moved down his back, gathering the material of his tee, pulling upward.

Our lips broke apart long enough for him to toss it to the side, his hands sinking into my ass, the slinky sundress hardly any barrier at all. I could feel the heat of his palms as surely as I felt the hard length of him pressing into my hip.

When his lips broke from mine again, it was so he could lower down to his knees, his hands bunching up the material of my skirt, pulling it slowly upward, his lips kissing each exposed inch of skin, the sensation of it going not only straight to my core, but higher, seeping into my heart as well, a warm, fuzzy feeling I had no name for, but found both comforting and overwhelmingly terrifying somehow at the same time.

But then his tongue was tracing the outline of my panties, wiping away anything but the desire that was like a stabbing sensation inside, something hot and acutely painful.

His lips didn't move inward, though, but placed kisses across my hip, up my belly, between my breasts, up my throat, then pulling away completely to pull my dress over my head, leaving me in nothing but my barely-there panties, the cool water dampening my skin within seconds, sending a chill through me.

Fenway's hands settled into my hips, turning me, pulling my back against his chest once again, both of us facing the waterfall as his hands covered my breasts, teasing my tightened nipples into harder buds, not relenting until my ass was grinding back against his hardness, desperate for relief from the clawing need inside.

Only then did one of his hands slide up, gently closing around my throat as the other slid down my belly, making a delicious path downward, under the waistband of my panties, then stroking up my cleft, finding my clit, circling it lazily, building the pressure.

Just when I thought I was at the breaking point, his fingers slid downward, slipping inside me, my muscles tightening hard, greedy for the sensation of fullness.

"Feel how much you want me?" he asked, his teeth nipping my earlobe.

And, God, yes, I did.

It was something almost bigger than myself, this need to have him inside me, something urgent, something that refused to be denied.

His fingers started to thrust lazily, hinting at what I needed, but refusing to give it to me, just wanting me whimpering, gasping for breath, fingernails digging crescents into the skin of his forearm.

"Fenway, please," I cried, hips rocking back against him.

A low, growling noise escaped him, his hand leaving my throat as his hips shifted back, his hand freeing himself.

I heard the crinkle of a condom foil, and with my head resting against his shoulder, I could see him raise it up, nip the edge.

Anticipation was a live-wire in my system as he reached between us, protected us, before his hands were on me again, one slipping between my legs, pressing against my clit as my legs parted slightly, my ass arching back and up, begging for an end to the torment.

Luckily, Fenway didn't seem to have much self-control left either, his cock sliding between my thighs, pressing against me for a moment before sliding inside, long and thick as I had expected, filling me completely.

There was one solid moment of nothing, just silent acknowledgment of this singularly perfect moment before the need for release overtook everything else.

Fenway's free hand gathered my hair, wrapping it around his fist, yanking it to the side, exposing my neck, his lips and teeth claiming the sensitive skin as he started to thrust.

Hard.

And deep.

But not fast.

Dragging it out.

The pressure built deep, working outward until it overtook me completely.

His cock buried deep.

His finger swiped.

And I simply shattered.

Shards of me flew in every direction, leaving nothing behind but a strangled cry, a wave of pleasure so acute it was almost painful.

A growl escaped Fenway as my walls squeezed him through the orgasm.

But he wasn't done with me.

He hadn't come with me.

I came back together, gasping for breath, body trembling, only to have Fenway pull out of me, turn me, and press me back against the cave wall, the moss cool and soft against my back as his hand reached downward, hooking my knee, dragging it up high before slamming inside me.

After an orgasm like that, I was sure I was done, that my body wouldn't be able to take anymore.

Apparently, I didn't know myself as well as I thought, because as Fenway started to thrust—harder, faster—I could feel the desire rekindled, the aching need for fulfillment renewed.

He drove me up fast, pushing me to the edge, then tossing me over, but this time, he fell with me, both of us crashing at the same time, bodies sinking into each other as we struggled to find breath, to find strength in our gelatinous limbs.

I wasn't sure how long we stayed like that before we finally broke away, Fenway stooping to retrieve his pants as I tried to talk my body into cooperating with any sort of movement.

"What are you doing?" I asked, watching as he produced a plastic baggy from his back pocket. Where the hell had he even found plastic baggies?

"I hate to be a discourteous guest," he told me, tying off the condom, slipping it into the bag, sealing that, then tucking it back into his shorts.

"Why did you bring baggies?" I asked, shaking my head.

"Well, I knew I would need one for my phone," he told me, finding another baggy, slipping his cell inside it, sealing it, then tucking it into his other back pant pocket.

"Why would you need it for your phone?" I asked as he reached for his shirt, then my dress, my panties.

I thought to hand them to me so we could both dress and head out.

I really should have known better.

"Well, of course I would need one for my phone," he told me, walking over to the cave opening, dangerously close to the edge, in fact. "Otherwise, it would never survive this," he told me balling up our clothes.

I realized his intention a second too late.

As they seemed to hover in the air in slow motion before falling.

"No!" I shrieked, heart dropping. "Why would you do that? I am pretty cool with all of this," I said, gesturing to my naked body, "but not cool enough to walk back through this park and up to the driver of your car stark freaking naked, Fenway."

"Luckily, my darling, that won't be necessary," he assured me, reaching for my hand, pulling me forward toward the opening of the cave, the water slicking my body with spray.

"Fenway, no," I said, trying to plant my heels, but there was no use.

He was determined.

The ground was slippery.

And, quite frankly, I didn't actually want to fight him anyway.

"Oh, darling, yes," he told me, face triumphant. And, God, it was a good look. So good, in fact, that my lips curved up with him, anticipation fluttering through my belly.

"Have you ever done this before?" I asked, leaning forward slightly, trying to see if there were any jutting rocks we needed to be worried about.

"Nope."

"Do you know if it is safe?"

"Nope," he said, smiling wider.

"That is a hell of a risk."

"Oh, come on now, darling, you're not scared of anything."

He was right.

And yet so incredibly, monumentally wrong.

Because I was scared of something.

Terrified, in truth.

And that was of the feeling I had in my chest when he looked at me like that, like I was the only thing in the world, like I was the only person he would ever want to have this adventure with.

Wanting to get away from those feelings, I took a deep breath, my fingers gripping his more tightly.

"On three," I told him, leaning forward slightly. "One..."

"Three," he declared, leaping, taking me with him.

When I looked back on this moment, I would find a sort of poetry in it.

The act of physically falling.

And the fact that, inside, my heart was doing something very similar, something just as frightening, but also as thrilling.

My scream echoed through the empty park right before we broke through the surface at the bottom of the waterfall, last-minute panic gripping me, realizing I had absolutely no idea if this water was deep enough to dive into, if we were going to survive the fall, if I was going to be some Jane Doe in a Bali morgue because no one here actually knew who I was.

But when my body propelled upward again, breaking the surface, allowing me to gasp for air, I decided it had been worth the risk.

I turned, finding Fenway who was reaching up with one hand to swipe his hair back, his grin as triumphant as mine must have been.

Have you ever been skinny-dipping in an Indonesian lake after leaping down a waterfall with a billionaire playboy?

Well, I have.

And let me tell you, it was the best moment of my life.

"You do realize that all of our clothes are sopping wet now," I said, seeing my dress float by us, Fenway's hand reaching out for it.

"I told you that you needed that dress at the market. But did you believe me? Nooo," he teased, eyes dancing.

"Well, had I known that we would end up tossing our clothing into a lake, I might have reconsidered that stance. We are going to be freezing on the ride back to the house."

"Well, then, I guess we will have to warm up in the hot tub together," he suggested, shrugging. "But we can't be too long," he added, reaching for me, pulling me closer, using one arm to keep us afloat.

"Why? Do we have more plans tonight?"

"Not tonight. But we will need time to pack."

Pack?

We were leaving?

And why was my heart sinking at the idea.

"I didn't even get to see the beach yet!" I told him, trying for light and fun when I felt like something was crumbling inside.

"Well, I am taking you to a different beach," he told me, pressing a silly kiss to the tip of my nose. "On the yacht," he added, eyebrows wiggling.

"Well, I can't exactly turn down a trip on a yacht, now, can I?"

"You certainly can not," he affirmed.

I had thought he meant a different beach in Bali.

Really, I should have known better.

This was Fenway, after all.

King of the ridiculous.

Chaser of new adventures.

To Fenway, we had 'done' Bali.

And it was time for a new experience.

And a new country.

Me, I was an eager passenger.

Sometime between the marketplace and the cave, I had somehow completely stopped faking it.

And it wasn't until a week later, my feet cozy in warm sand, when a ding on my phone reminded me of the truth.

That none of this was real.

That this was just a job.

And one that was nearly over.

NINE

Fenway

"Do you think we are going to see one of those giant crab things?" Wasp asked, eyes wide, smile bright.

Most people, when they heard of all the creepy crawlers in Australia, x'd out the entire country as a "nope."

Wasp?

Wasp wanted me to uncover every freaky, ugly, venomous, dangerous creature.

When I'd gotten her on the yacht four days before, after listening to a short lecture about how ostentatious it was before she decided we needed to break in the hot tub, she had pulled out her phone, finding some articles about all the weird and wondrous creatures that inhabited the Land Down Under.

"There are one-hundred-and-seventy snakes native to Australia. Want to know how many are venomous?"

I didn't actually, but her enthusiasm was infections. My hand moved out, tucking the hair behind her ear that had fallen in her face. "How many?"

"One-hundred! Oh my God. They have snakes that can eat crocodiles. Look at this kangaroo. He looks like he is 'roided up and ready to fight," she told me, turning her phone.

I'd brought hundreds of people to thousands of places in my life. Not one, not a single one, was half as excited about things as Wasp was.

She'd cooed over monkeys. She'd stopped at every single stand at the market, admiring goods. She'd stood for every photo op, claiming she needed the memories for when she got old and boring.

As if a woman who would jump naked down a waterfall after having sex in a cave could ever be considered boring.

"Not likely, darling, they are more likely to be seen in the Cook Islands. We can head there next," I offered, not nearly done with her yet.

In fact, there was this niggling little voice in the back of my mind that got louder in quiet moments before bed, like after Wasp had passed out like a starfish only to curl up on my chest, saying crazy things.

Like maybe I would never be done with her.

That I wanted her to stay.

"We aren't going anywhere," she told me, rolling her eyes. "You promised we could find a Megabat. I need to get a picture of one to terrify my nephew with."

"What a sweet aunt you are," I declared, dropping an arm across her shoulders.

"It is the job of the cool aunt to mess with the littles. And also to buy them wildly inappropriate gifts that will drive their parents crazy."

"If you ever need pointers on ridiculous gifts, I am the man to consult with."

"What is the craziest thing you've given someone?"

"I accidentally gave a friend a barnyard pig instead of the mini pig she had wanted for years."

"That's a pretty big oops."

"She still adores it. I am on swine-sitting duty for life should she ever want to go on vacation."

"Sounds reasonable," she told me, pulling me down onto the beach behind the resort we were staying in. "These are absurd," she declared as we came up to one of the many round beds with a shade top. "And absolutely amazing," she added, climbing up onto it, giving me a great view of her nearly-bare ass as she did so. I needed to get a picture of it, I decided, reaching for my phone before it was too late.

"Seriously?" she asked, dropping down after she heard the shutter, rolling her eyes at me. "What could you possibly need a picture of my ass for?"

"I am going to have it printed on a pillow and sleep on it at night," I declared, only half joking as I moved to lay down beside her.

"Okay, Fenway Arlington," she said, voice serious. "Tell me something serious," she demanded.

It was her new favorite game, wanting a peek below the curtain. It was my own fault. I'd let her see other parts of myself on more than one occasion.

Somehow, though, I didn't mind her having access to something only two or three other people in my life ever had. I didn't know what that meant. I didn't want to find out.

"What do you want to know?"

"Tell me about your childhood," she decided, having already asked me about random things. Losing my virginity, political opinions, my personal feelings on climate change given my 'blatant disregard for carbon emissions while traveling.' It was only a matter of time before she got to the dirty stuff. The stuff I didn't talk about to anyone, save for that one time when I was assed-out drunk, and made some choice comments to Alvy about it after having gotten a phone call from back home.

"It wasn't happy," I told her, being honest, not entirely sure why I didn't brush her off, why I didn't make light of it like I usually would, quip about how my silver spoon was thrown away and replaced after every meal, and move on with the conversation.

"Why not?"

"I came from three generations of men who took themselves, their lives, their wives, and their children very seriously."

"There is nothing serious about a child."

"Therein lies a lot of the unhappiness. Children in my circle, they aren't told to go out and play in the backyard while the grown-ups talked. We were expected to be at every dinner party, every charity function, every tennis match and golf course and hunt. We had to dress and act the part, be adults without any of the maturity or self-control that comes with age."

"That sounds very un-fun," Wasp decided, giving my thigh a pat.

"It wasn't just me in that. It was all of us. So there was some comfort in that. But my father's expectations were harsher. He was Type A and anal about every small detail of his life. My clothes had to be arranged a certain way, my bed made with military corners, my floors swept, my surfaces dusted. And the servants were forbidden to help. They were an earned privilege. The older I got, the more I chafed at the restraints."

"What did he do?"

"Tried to beat it out of me at first," I admitted. "Do you have any idea how humiliating it is at fourteen-years-old to be beaten so badly that you piss yourself?" I asked, looking over at her, seeing the pain slice across her bright eyes.

"No, I don't," she told me, leaning her head on my shoulder. "I'm sorry he was such a dickwipe."

He was that.

"When the beatings no longer satisfied him, he shipped me off to Avon Mills."

"I'm almost afraid to ask what Avon Mills is."

"A school for 'troubled' kids from a certain tax bracket. A sort of hyper-militant survivalist institution where they strip everything you have away from you, strip you yourself down to the rafters. We were denied every sort of pleasure. No TV. No music. Only unseasoned food. We were forced to do military-style workouts for eight, ten hours a day. In the sweltering heat. In the snow. You cried, you puked, it didn't matter, you had to keep going. You slept on the floor or outside when they thought you misbehaved. They couldn't actually beat us, but they did everything in their power to make us suffer."

"How the hell did they get away with that?"

"Well, firstly, it wasn't in the US. Secondly, you'd be surprised how many places just like that actually do exist in the states."

"How long were you there?"

"Five years."

"Five *years*?" Wasp shrieked, pulling away, looking down at me, her brows pinched. "Nonstop? Like that was home?"

"That was home," I agreed, nodding. "I didn't leave for summers or for holidays like many of the others. Which always made it worse on me. A lot more one-on-one attention."

"So you, what? You aged out?"

"Just shy of my eighteenth birthday, my grandfather died, giving my grandmother control of most of the family assets. She gave my father an ultimatum. Get me out, or be written out of the will."

"Thank God for your grandma," Wasp grumbled, sadness gone, replaced with rage.

I jumped back and forth between those two emotions as well when I thought back on all those long, cold, lonely, years without a single amusement, without anything fun or light, without a break from the never-ending work, the back-breaking torture.

"Yeah," I agreed, nodding. "She is what you might think of when you think of a matriarch of an old money family. Strong, stern, often disapproving, but with a soft spot for her loved ones, even if her way of showing it at times is not affectionate.

"What happened after you got out?"

"I went to stay with my grandmother for a few months, trying to adjust to a life outside of that world that had been all I'd known for so long. And then she released my trust to me on my eighteenth birthday. It was supposed to be on my twenty-first, but she had it changed. Out of guilt, I would imagine, for not having found a way to step in sooner. But in many ways, she was as helpless as I was much of the time, stuck under my grandfather's thumb for her whole adult life."

"And when you got all that money..." Wasp started, lips curving up, knowing where this was going.

"I sought every form of entertainment I could find. I made a life out of fun and light and easy, all the things I had never known for myself. Sprinkle in a strong desire to find any way I could to embarrass my father, and you have an idea of the life I have lived since getting free of that toxic life."

"Is your father still alive?" she asked.

"No."

"Good. I know, that's cruel, but good. The bastard."

He was a bastard.

I had swallowed my pride to go to him on his deathbed, to try to make some sort of amends, get closure, whatever the hell it was that the shrinks told me was important.

He spent an hour telling me all the ways I had been a bitter disappointment to him, how I was an embarrassment to the family, that my ancestors were rolling around in their graves knowing that I would carry on the family legacy, that he wished he'd never even had a son.

I walked out, learning later he died an ugly death, gasping for air, unable to catch his breath until he eventually died after sixteen torturous hours.

I was going to hell for thinking it, but all I could think when I'd heard the news was: Good. Good. That was the end he deserved.

Then I went right back to my old ways.

"So that is why you have this light outer persona but that darker part that shows its face every now and again," Wasp mused. "For the record, the dark part is kinda sexy," she told me, eyes going molten.

"Yeah?" I asked, lunging forward to grab her at the hips, dragging her up on my lap, smiling at the squeal she let out, then the shuddering breath when she felt my cock press against her eager pussy. "What about the light side?" I asked, reaching up to trace the line of her bathing suit between her breasts.

"The light side is lots of fun. It's the best of both worlds," she declared, happy open.

But then something crossed her face, something that made her brows draw together, that made her eyes go guarded.

"What's wrong? Wait," I said, trying to grab her as she climbed off of me. But she dodged away, rushed off before I could stop her.

She'd had more than a handful of moments just like that one since the cave.

There seemed to be a cycle with her. She gave and gave and gave, and just when you got used to it, she ripped it away, leaving you wondering what the fuck you did wrong, what you said to piss her off.

It didn't escape me, either, that while she badgered me for intimate details about my life, she hardly ever gave me any of hers. I knew she had grown up with both parents. But they were dead. I knew she had siblings, but not their names, not their locations. I knew she had a best friend who was wealthy and had kids. I didn't know what kind of childhood she'd had, what she did for a living. If she did something for a living. If she did, why was she able to leave it behind to traipse around the world with me?

And what kind of job could she do from a converted school bus home?

Burning questions, all, but she'd proven stealthy at changing the subject when I tried to press a topic.

She often used her body to do this.

And being a man who very much appreciated every curve of that body, I wasn't exactly mad about her dirty fighting methods.

"You're not going after her?" Alvy asked, dropping down at the foot of the bed, handing me a drink.

"She's only going to distract me from finding out what is wrong by using my body."

"Oh, you poor thing, you," Alvy quipped, laughing.

"I know, right? How dare she. I am more than my penis," I shot back, taking a drink. "I can't figure her out."

"That's the appeal, though, isn't it?" Alvy asked, watching me. "That's why you're not bored of her yet."

"I'm not bored of her yet because she is interesting even without all the details."

"Maybe she's not giving you the details because she thinks the mystery is the only reason you are interested in her, "Alvy suggested.

"Alvy, you might be a genius," I declared, but then thought better of it. "You know what, no. I don't think so. She's too much of her own woman to give a fuck if I am interested."

"Possibly."

"You sound suspicious of her."

"I wasn't at first," Alvy said, draining the rest of their drink. "But the longer this goes on, the less sure I am about her."

"What do you think, that she's after me for my money?" I asked. "Even if she were, which I don't think she is, how does that make her any different from every other woman in every other corner of the world who I've shared some time with?"

"Because this one is getting under your skin," Alvy said. "You might not want to admit it. Hell, you might not even realize it yet. But she's in there. And that makes her a threat that all the other gold diggers weren't."

"I may be a great many foolish things, Alvy, but I think we can both agree that I have done well enough with the family money."

There was no argument to that. I spent money like water. But I made it just as easily. It may have even been a final 'fuck you' to my father, increasing the family fortune more in a decade than he did his entire life.

"I wouldn't worry so much if I knew you knew more about her."

"You're not wrong," I agreed. "I will figure more out. Especially if she sticks around for a while."

"I just think it is in your best interest," Alvy said, shrugging. "I know it's not my place. I just wanted to make sure you were thinking with your big head," they said, giving me a smirk as they walked off down the beach.

I will admit, I had been enjoying our little adventures enough not to let myself sweat the details. In fact, I was simply not someone who sweated details in general. But Alvy was right. If she was going to be more lasting than others in the past, I needed to know who I was getting into bed with.

Now if only she would stop being so damn good in bed, I might actually get somewhere.

I drained my drink, heading back to the hotel, ready to coerce some answers out of Wasp by any means necessary.

Even if that meant withholding orgasms until she gave me some small detail about her life.

In fact, I really liked that idea.

And she got so desperate for release that she would probably give me what I was after too.

If nothing else, I would enjoy the hell out of it.

"Oh, darling!" I called, opening the door to our suite, finding her lounging on the couch, still wearing her bathing suit, legs draped over the arm, one hand up, twirling her hair like I found she did when she was thinking about something.

"I want to be alone."

"I have a game I want to play."

"I don't like games."

"Says the queen of them," I shot back, watching as she turned her head on the cushion to glare at me. "Are you going to try to deny it?" I asked, stalking closer to her, dropping down on the ottoman at her side. All I got to that was another glare. "You only like the games you can win."

"Sweetheart," she said, slowly unfolding, a cat ready to strike. "When are you going to learn?" she went on, moving to straddle me, running a finger down my jaw. "I always win. In fact," she said, wiggling around on my lap, feeling my cock already pressing against her, "I believe I already have." With that, she hopped over, turning, attempting to walk away.

My hand shot out as I got to my feet, grabbing her wrist, jerking her around, slamming her back against the floor-to-ceiling windows at our side.

"Want to bet, *darling*?" I asked, yanking her suit down, sealing my lips over her nipple, feeling the tremble course through her body.

For a woman who loved to be in control of situations, she melted into a puddle of need when you took charge in bed.

I was going to win this.

And, sure, she was going to be a sore loser afterward.

But that was a problem for later.

The only problem now was figuring out which way I was going to torture answers out of her. My fingers. My tongue. My cock. She was a sucker for all of the above.

I guess we could employ all the weapons in this battle.

My fingers slid her suit aside, thumb moving up to stroke her clit, two fingers thrusting inside her, working her exactly how she liked it until I felt her walls start to tighten around me, threatening oblivion.

"Fenway, please," she cried, fingers digging into the flesh of my neck.

"You can come," I assured her, doing one careful tap to her clit. "Once you tell me when you lost your virginity and to who."

"What? Why are you—oh," she whimpered as my finger did another tap. "I was fifteen," she told me.

"Was he your first love?" I asked, doing a swipe.

"No. I don't do love. He was my next-door-neighbor. He was thirty," she admitted. "You promised," she reminded me, hips squirming when I paused, surprised by her admission, at the laissez-faire way she described what most states would consider statutory rape.

"I did. I promised," I agreed, working her clit, sending her crashing through an orgasm.

She barely managed to catch her breath before I was moving down to my knees, running my tongue up her.

Thankfully for me and this plan of mine, Wasp was multi-orgasmic, something I was using to my advantage, driving her up once again. "What do you do for a living?"

"Fenway, this is-oh. Fuck," she hissed, her hand slapping down on the top of my head when I sucked hard on her clit. "Fuck, please..."

"Just tell me your job title, and you can come."

"I'm... I'm a... fuck. I'm a... dog trainer," she declared, sucking in a deep breath as my lips sucked again, sending another orgasm coursing through her body.

"A dog trainer," I repeated as she came back to her senses, breathless, flushed.

"Yes. I train dogs. Really badly behaved dogs." There was something in her voice, a tone, an insinuation I didn't understand, an inside joke I wasn't privy to, perhaps? I didn't know. I wasn't going to press. I was happy to get an answer at all from her. Taking a deep breath, she reached up to run a hand through her hair, making it settle more to one side as she looked down at me, eyes small, smile wicked. "I didn't think you could play that dirty."

"Oh, darling, I am full of surprises," I told her, shooting upward, shoulder going to her center, tossing her over my shoulder, her ass high in the air, just begging to be slapped.

"Ow!" she hissed, body jolting when my hand landed there with a satisfying smack.

I carried her through the suite, tossing her onto the bed, watching as she bounced, standing there at the foot of the bed, stripping out of my clothes, watching as she tried to keep unaffected eye contact, then failed, hungry eyes trailing.

"Take off your suit," I demanded, watching her eyes flare, knowing she loved being bossed around even if she would never admit it.

Moving to the nightstand, I got a condom, put it on, watching as she made a show of undoing her straps, pulling the suit down to her waist, then slowly lowering down onto the bed, planting her feet, bridging upward

"I need help," she told me, giving me that ball-stabbingly hot sexy pout of hers.

My cock twitched as I moved back to the foot of the bed, fingers teasing the outside of her ankle before both hands grabbed both ankles, yanking, pulling them out from under her, then twisting, forcing her onto her stomach. My hands moved into her hips, pulling her ass up high toward me, then yanking the material down to expose her perfect ass.

My hand landed with a slap, harder than before, leaving a pink mark on her cheek, dragging a ragged whimper out of her as I slammed inside her without preamble, taking every inch.

"Fuck," she hissed, fingers fisting the sheets, ass angling out further, begging for more.

My hands went back to her hips, using them to slam her body back against me as I thrust forward. Hard. Merciless. Completely lacking any self-control, something Wasp ate up, her whimpers becoming moans that became hushed curses as I drove her up to the edge.

"Why did you agree to come with me to Bali?" I demanded, pulling nearly all the way out of her.

"No. Damnit. Don't stop," she growled, trying to wiggle against me. "Fenway..."

"Answer me," I demanded, landing another slap to her ass.

"Fuck. Fine. I thought it would be fun to play with you," she admitted, and everything about it rang true.

I slammed back inside her, deep, feeling her walls pulsate around me wildly, milking my orgasm out of me as well, sapping all my strength, making me crash forward over her on the bed, gasping for a deep breath.

"You're an asshole," Wasp declared when she got her breath back, throwing her body weight, tossing me off of her onto the mattress as she sat up, glaring down at me.

"I am," I agreed, putting an arm behind my neck, happy with my victory. And the methods by which I secured it.

"You know you just upped the stakes, right?" she asked, chin lifting, challenge making her eyes even brighter than usual.

"Oh, I am looking forward to the next battle.

"It is going to get ugly," she promised me.

"You know what? You're lucky you're so pretty," I told her, watching her brows furrow.

"Why is that?" she asked, a sliver of ice slipping into her voice.

"I—"

"Describe me," she demanded, cutting me off.

"What?"

"Say someone asked about me. How would you describe me?" she asked, body getting tense.

"Well, you're beautiful," I started, knowing the second it was out of my mouth that it was exactly the wrong thing to say, that I had somehow made a point she had in her head as she went up on her knees, leaning over me.

"What a *lousy* way to describe me," she snapped, poking me hard enough in the center of my chest to hurt. "I am *brilliant*. I am *resourceful*. I am *enigmatic*. I am fucking *interesting*. Don't you dare reduce me to just 'beautiful' again, Fenway," she hissed, hopping off the bed, grabbing her robe off the chair in the corner, and storming into the bathroom, slamming the door hard enough to make me wince.

Well.

Alright then.

That was probably the first time I'd ever been scolded for complimenting a woman.

It was pretty impressive how things had gone from epically good to a complete shitstorm in a matter of two minutes.

I couldn't pretend to understand why being beautiful—which she was, and she had to have known she was, and that everyone noticed that first because that was what they were looking at when they met her—was so bad, but she wasn't wrong.

She wasn't *just* beautiful.

There were plenty of *just* beautiful girls in the world, ones who built their entire personas around what was on the outside, the ones who chased fading beauty with Botox and filler and lipo and implants and lifts and nose jobs, knowing down to their core that all they had was what was on the outside because they hadn't taken the time to cultivate a personality along the way.

But Wasp was right.

She wasn't just pretty.

She was brilliant and resourceful and enigmatic and, yes, above all else, interesting.

Dare I say it? She was the most interesting woman I'd had the pleasure of meeting. And I only knew a small chip out of the iceberg.

There was so much more to uncover, so much more to become enthralled with.

I would have told her that, given the chance. But she'd cut me off before I could tell her just how amazing I thought she was, how I hadn't met anyone like her before, how my life felt a lot brighter with her in it, that I was enjoying seeing the world through her eyes.

I would tell her all of that.

Once she cooled down.

Once she realized she hadn't given me a chance to answer the question before she passed judgment.

"Wasp," I said, tapping my knuckles on the bathroom door.

"Fuck off, Fenway," she growled.

Alright then.

She wasn't ready to talk.

"I am going to go down to the pool."

"I don't care," she shot back, making my lips curl up.

I hadn't ever been a man who enjoyed angry women. I could see the theory about hot make-up sex. But I had dealt with enough anger in my life. I didn't want to romanticize it for the sake of a good lay.

So I pulled on my swim shorts and made my way downstairs, figuring she would be calmer after she got some time alone.

And she was.

But the tightening in my gut said that her calm as I came back into the suite wasn't a good calm.

No.

It was much like a calm before a storm.

Like that perfect stillness right before a tornado ripped through the town and destroyed everything you had come to care about.

I had no idea how right I would be about that.

I just enjoyed the amiable dinner, the easy conversation, even if my gut twisted recognizing something wrong in her posture, something tight in her voice, something that hinted at trouble, but I couldn't figure out what it was.

Hell, I was pretty sure even if I had years to analyze all the possible ways this whole situation could go belly-up—and why—I couldn't have come anywhere near to the truth.

I just basked in her smile.

I laughed at her jokes.

I told her I had a lead on her giant bats.

We talked about New Zealand and China, about Japan and India, all these places we were near enough to visit next, about all the possible tourist attractions there, about the food to be eaten, about the experiences to be shared.

I had no idea that she had absolutely no intention of going to New Zealand, China, Japan or India with me.

I had no clue, in fact, that she didn't even plan on finishing out the week with me in Australia.

TEN

Wasp

What the hell was wrong with me?

The sound of the door slamming set my teeth on edge as I lean back against the marble wall, hands pressing over my face.

Had he fucked me hard enough to knock my brain loose? Really, that seemed like the only possible explanation for what was going on here.

I was having an affair with a client.

I was having sex with a client.

I might not have been morally against it, but I damn sure wasn't exactly all for it either.

It made a situation stupid and messy when it should have been smart, carefully calculated, and neat.

For Christ's sake, I didn't do weekenders, let alone drawn-out multi-continental affairs with men. Not normal men. Not men I'd met in a bar and liked enough to go home with.

Let alone clients.

Clients who clearly were only interested in me because I was pretty. Because I had a good ass. Because I was all-too-willing to spread my legs and play by their rules.

Oh.

Good.

God.

Had I fallen into Fenway's dicksand? Was that what this was?

The signs were certainly all there, weren't they?

Letting him whisk me away into his world, overwhelm me with his likes and desires, forgetting about my own plans, my own goals, my own desires?

And getting screwed so well that I lost some brain cells in the process.

Ew.

I was *that* woman.

I vowed never to be that woman.

And it was even worse that I was *that* woman to *this* man. This man who was clearly terrible enough at some point in his life, had hurt some woman badly enough in his past, to have her seek me out, pay me an exorbitant fee, and hurt him deeply on an emotional level.

Fenway was not my Roman.

He wasn't a good man.

He was fun, sure. He was entertaining, yes. He was even more layered than most people would know. And, of course, he was probably the best lay of my life.

But he wasn't good.

He was just another dog off his leash that I was hired to train, to bring to heel, to modify their behavior.

No one hired me for the little jobs, the guys who forgot Valentine's Day or shushed you when the game was on.

They hired me for the hopeless cases, the ones everyone had already tried to train.

I was for the lost causes.

I was a last resort.

I had gone and fallen into the dicksand of a man so bad that someone was willing to pay me a hundred grand to make him suffer.

What the hell did that say about him?

About me?

"God damnit," I growled, taking myself into the glass enclosure, turning the water to cold, hissing through a frigid shower.

This was over, I decided as I dried off.

I was giving it a couple more days without the sex, without the snuggling, without falling into the trap of his infectious enthusiasm.

I was close.

I knew it.

So close.

If I withheld sex, if I had him slobbering after me, I could get those words.

Once I got those words, I was done.

I was on a plane and I was fucking *done*.

I didn't know what that would mean for my mental health, if I was going to have some issue coming to grips with not only sleeping with a client, but losing my professional edge.

But that would be a problem for when I was back in the US, back in my skoolie, back on the road, back to freaking normal.

This had been a fantasy world.

I was playing Adventure Barbie and Yacht Barbie and What-The-Fuck-Were-You-Thinking Barbie.

This was not me.

Even as I went through the rest of my day trying to believe that, a niggling little voice at the back of my head was whispering things I didn't want to hear.

That if this wasn't me, then why had I felt more at ease with myself over the past couple of weeks than I had in the previous few years?

That if this wasn't me, why did my shoulders suddenly feel lighter, my heart warmer, my life brighter?

"Oh, Jesus," I hissed, hand flying to my heart when I went to open the bedroom door, only to find Alvy standing there.

Standing there like they were waiting for me, like they had something important to say.

"Let's talk," Alvy said, in a tone I hadn't expected from them, in one that was firm, cold, maybe even, I don't know, suspicious?

I could handle firm and cold.

Suspicious, though, that was cause for concern, wasn't it?

"We could talk about how your boss is a superficial dog who thinks women are only good for their looks," I suggested, breezing past them, making my way into the kitchen area, deciding breezy and a tad bitter was the truest reaction I could muster at the moment.

"Fenway is a lot of things. Superficial is one of them," Alvy agreed. "But I think you are smart enough to know that he wouldn't be dragging you all around the world just because you're pretty."

"Why not? Men do it all the time," I told them, reaching for the bottle of pink champagne, not caring that it was too early in the day for drinking.

"Sure. But, for the most part, Fenway doesn't."

"For the most part is not 'never,' Alvy."

"True. There have been brief infatuations in the past. But I have been here for longer than anyone else. I know this isn't that."

"I really don't think this conversation is appropriate," I said, leaning into the boss-employee mindset, hoping it would throw Alvy off enough to walk away.

"I have been in charge of buying Fenway condoms and lube for years, Wasp, I think we have crossed the line of appropriateness a long time ago. Besides, I'm not overly concerned with Fenway's behavior."

"So you're concerned with mine."

"He doesn't know your real name."

"He doesn't need to know my real name."

"He does if—"

"Oh," I said, scoffing. "Oh, well, that's real nice, Alvy," I said, shaking my head. "You are worried I am after him for his money."

"Well, you are staying in his suite. You did go to his yacht. You do have bags and bags of souvenirs."

"I think you must know as well as anyone else that Fenway enjoys spending his money. Have you ever tried to take out your wallet when he was around? He never lets you use it. And he will throw more and more money around to get servers and people in shops to take *his* side. I have never asked him to spend a penny on me. If you must, you are free to ask him that yourself. I can guarantee his words will line up with mine. And furthermore, I am insulted that you would even insinuate that. I am not some gold digger. I make my own way in life."

"As a dog trainer. A traveling dog trainer."

"It is not any of your business, but yes."

"I don't believe you."

"I don't believe I give a shit," I shot back, my anger being of the short fuse variety. "I'm not asking you to trust me, Alvy. Quite frankly, it is not your place. What Fenway thinks is what matters. And I have a feeling I know what Fenway would think about you coming in behind his back and trying to grill me over something that doesn't involve you."

"Are you threatening me?"

"I am telling you that I don't appreciate you coming to me with baseless accusations about wanting him for his money," I corrected, putting down my glass, making my way toward the door. "You know what, Alvy? I liked you," I told them in the doorway to the hall. "Really, I did. You were a good ally there for a minute, offering me escape routes should I ever get overwhelmed. That was a much better look than this one. Don't worry, though. I will keep this between us. And don't worry. I don't want his money. My most recent job set me up for quite a while."

With that, I slammed the door.

"Shit," I hissed, stabbing my finger in the elevator call button. "Shit shit shit," I mumbled over and over to myself as I rode down, the door sliding open, bringing in a woman who shot me small eyes. "Like you've never heard a curse word before. Please," I grumbled, my mood too sour to care about being a good human right then.

I wasn't sure if Alvy had gotten to Fenway yet, if that was their next step.But if that happened, it had the potential to ruin everything.

If there was one thing wealthy men hated, it was being told that a woman only liked them for their bank balance. It fucked with their ego. It made them feel small. And when men were made to feel small, they got mean.

I couldn't exactly picture Fenway being mean, but I also didn't imagine he would be fond of the idea that I was after him for the shopping sprees and the private jets and the yachts.

It would ruin everything if he started to wonder—even if just an infinitesimally small part of him started to wonder—if I was disingenuous.

Frustrated, needing an outlet for it so I could think straight, I took myself down to the pool, doing laps until my arms screamed, until my shoulders burned, until I felt a bone-deep sort of exhaustion settle over me.

I took myself back to the room, changing into shorts and a tee, falling into the bed, curling up under the covers, trying to figure out how to get Fenway in love with me, then secure enough to admit it, before the week was out.

This had to end.

Soon.

Because I was getting invested.

Because I was losing sight of the job.

Because Alvy was suspicious of me.

Because, despite my outburst, I actually didn't hate that Fenway thought I was beautiful.

I should have.

I always did.

From birth, that was all anyone had to say about me.

It didn't matter if I was a straight-A student, that I made high honor roll. I even distinctly remembered my seventh grade male English teacher pulling me aside after class when I asked to do an extra book report, and telling me that he was afraid I was taking on too much, that he'd hate to see pretty girls like me getting stressed out over grades.

Because all pretty girls were good for was marrying and pushing out pretty babies, right Mr. Radleigh?

Because I couldn't possibly have dreams or ambitions.

Every man—and many of the women—I encountered in my life believed my worth started and ended with the way my cells had happened to come together. My accomplishments, my intellect, my wit, the things I had a hand in creating, meant nothing.

I lost my virginity at fifteen to a perv neighbor because he called me clever. Not pretty. Not hot. Clever.

It took a long time for me to be able to work the hand life dealt me, to get what I wanted from men by taking advantage of the fact that no one thought someone like me actually had a head on their shoulders.

I was known for walking away from men at bars who complimented me. It was a running joke in my family.

When pretty became my job—the bait I used to lure in those men who needed to be punished in one way or another—I had learned to detach myself from everything superficial. It helped you feel less slimy when men talked about your eyes, your mouth—(and what they'd like to do to it)—, about your tits, about your ass, about your feet, for the foot fetish guys.

But it didn't feel slimy when Fenway said those things.

No.

It felt good.

And that was not good.

He couldn't have that power.

I had to get the hell out of here before it was too late.

"Darling," Fenway greeted me when I emerged from a self-pitying nap, finding him changed into one of his tan suits, this time with a light blue shirt on underneath. "Whatever did you say to poor Alvy?" he wondered, buttoning his center button, head tilted to the side, watching me.

"Why do you think I said something?"

"Because they tore out of the hotel, telling me to keep an eye on you, and claimed they were going to spend the rest of the week in a different hotel."

"We had a disagreement," I admitted, shrugging.

"Might I ask what over?"

"You may ask," I told him, nodding, "but I told Alvy I would keep it between us."

"Did they say something about not trusting you?"

"Fenway, I gave them my word."

His gaze slid away, looking out at the ocean. "I've never known Alvy to get involved with my personal affairs."

"Are you saying you don't trust me either?" I asked, letting my voice whine, making sure my lips parted, my eyes went rounder.

Fenway's shoulders slumped, his arms moving outward, hands beckoning.

As I slid my feet across the floor to him, letting his arms wrap me up, pressing my face against his chest, I should have been feeling triumph. But that sinking, swirling sensation in my chest and belly seemed a hell of a lot more like guilt than victory.

"Alvy works too hard. And is very loyal," Fenway said, rubbing his hand down my spine. "They probably just need a few days away. I'm sure you two will work it out."

I was just as sure that I wouldn't be around to do so.

There was a deep, stabbing sensation in my belly at that, something I chose—in that moment—to blame on hunger.

So we ate.

We talked about our plans.

We didn't talk about the argument earlier.

I gave him a few more pieces to my puzzle, but only things that would never lead back to me: silly little stories from when I was a kid, some of the crazy things that had happened on the road with Raven, mishaps in building my skoolie.

He needed the details, the little pieces that he could attach himself to, the intimacy that was bred by shared disclosure.

That was what he had to have to get him where he needed to be, to get him to the point of no return.

To get the look.

To get the words.

And then I was gone.

Back to my life.

But back to what, *exactly?* That annoying, persistent voice demanded. *Loneliness and the same old roads, the same old sights, the same old everything?*

Maybe my life had gotten stagnant, predictable, unfulfilling.

But it was mine.

This?

This wasn't mine. This was a job. And when I got back to the States, I would collect on it, hop in Wanda, and get lost somewhere, get my head back together, make a plan to shake things up.

"You've been distracted today," Fenway observed two and a half days later as we walked down the beach, his pockets full of mermaid toenails, his hand pressed to the small of my back as I absentmindedly kicked the waves as they teased my feet.

"Have I been?" I asked, leaning into his shoulder, letting myself have that little bit of closeness, of intimacy.

It was a bad idea.

I'd been careful not to touch him because I knew my body was too attune to his, was too attracted to his, and I really needed not to fall back into bed with him again.

Because I needed to keep him chomping at the bit. Not because I was worried what it might begin to mean to me if we kept doing so. I mean, of course it wasn't that.

To his credit, when I'd pulled away in bed that first night, he'd just snuggled in behind me, pressing a kiss to my head, and falling asleep. And hadn't made a move since. He probably thought I was on my period. And that worked well enough since I clearly had some self-control issues around Fenway. At least this gave me some space I desperately needed.

That said, if he couldn't have sex, he still needed intimacy.

A part of me needed it as well, but we weren't going to talk about that part. I was doing my best to keep that part bound and gagged until I could finish this job, get home, have some space to pick apart this whole situation, come to terms with whatever I found.

"What have you been thinking about?" he asked, wrapping an arm around my back. "Aside from my devilish good looks, of course," he teased.

"Well, whatever could I possibly think of beside your good looks?" I quipped, getting a chuckle out of him. "Everything. Nothing. I don't know. What are you thinking about?"

"How excited you would get to see all the vending machines in China," he admitted, throwing me off.

"What? Why?" I asked, stopping walking, turning my head up on his shoulder to look at his face.

Looking down, his gaze went soft, his free hand raising to tuck my hair behind my ear. "Because I like seeing the world through your eyes," he told me.

The swirling feeling in my stomach told me that I had him.

It wasn't those three words, but it was just as good.

And the sinking sensation in my chest said that he had me too.

I had to go.

I had to go before I fucked it all up.

Oh, who was I kidding? I already fucked it up. But at least things were still salvageable.

Even if I had some asinine idea to stay, to admit the whole truth to him, there was no way this ended with us in China, and him looking at me like he was looking at me right then.

Because he would know it was all a fraud.

He wouldn't be able to trust that anything from me was genuine.

There would be no way to tell the truths from the lies in the past, or in the future.

He wouldn't be able to live with that uncertainty.

And I couldn't stomach the idea of seeing the betrayal on his face when I told him the truth.

No.

There could be none of that.

No truth.

No explanations.

Just absence.

I waited until he was asleep, creeping through the suite, slipping into shorts and a tee, grabbing my luggage. Most of my souvenirs were still on the yacht. Wherever that was. But I had brought the little round purse with me to Australia, and had tucked the monkey statue inside it. Along with a rock I had taken from the waterfall.

It was overly sentimental for someone like me, but as I made my way through the suite for the last time, I found myself clinging to the rock, the sharp edges poking into my palm.

Physical pain could dull emotional pain.

I wasn't one for self-mutilation, but just this once, I understood the need for that kind of relief, that kind of distraction from the swirling void inside.

I didn't leave a note.

I didn't leave anything.

Except, of course, a part of me I had given to him, a part of me I hadn't known I could give to a man.

But he had it.

And I would have to figure out how to go on without it.

ELEVEN

Fenway

"What do you mean, she's gone?" Alvy asked, having taken one step into the suite I had been pacing for almost an hour waiting on them to get there.

"I mean she took all of her luggage and left," I told them, raking a hand through my hair, barely able to think through the breakneck pace of my head, jumping from one conclusion to another.

"Did she take anything?" Alvy asked.

"I just told you she took her luggage," I reminded them, frustrated, needing them to be on their game when I was clearly spiraling.

"I meant anything of yours, Fenway," Alvy clarified. "Did she take your wallet? Cards? Those diamond cufflinks?"

"So that was it," I said, voice going low, cutting, foreign enough to Alvy that they straightened.

"What is?" they asked.

"The argument you and Wasp had. She said she told you she wouldn't talk about it, so she wouldn't give me any details. That's what it was about. You insinuated that she wanted me for my money."

"It is a valid question for someone with your income, Fenway," Alvy reasoned.

The thing was, they weren't exactly wrong. That was the ugly part about all of this. You did have to be on your toes. You did have to suspect ulterior motives when someone got close to you fast.

Clichés were a cliché for a reason.

Rich men attracted trust fund chasers.

It was just part of the gig.

That said, it never felt great to think that was all someone saw when they looked at you.

The idea of Wasp seeing dollar signs when she was with me made bile rise up in my throat.

"That wasn't your place, Alvy," I told them, watching as their chin lifted a bit, refusing to back down.

"You wouldn't do it for yourself."

"No," I agreed. "And maybe I never would have. But that would have been my decision. If I ended up led by the throat to an altar without a prenup, that would be my business."

"You couldn't have been seriously thinking about marrying that woman," Alvy said, shaking their head. "You don't even know her real name."

"And now, it seems, I never will."

"It wasn't my fault, Fenway," Alvy insisted. "If she was going to leave about our disagreement, she would have left immediately. Not three days later."

They weren't wrong about that. The timing did seem off. As did the fact that she didn't say anything. Wasp liked having the last say. She liked letting people know she was coming out on top. She was competitive by nature—something I'd learned after making the mistake of playing cards with her one night on the yacht, getting my ass kicked mercilessly as she gloated.

If she was leaving to make some sort of point, she would have woken me up, made her declaration, then sauntered her sweet ass out of the suite in those skyscraper heels she loved so much, leaving me salivating after her.

She would have loved that.

It was just her style.

Sneaking out while I was sleeping?

That was a coward's move.

Wasp would hate to be called a coward.

She would despise that being her legacy.

So why would she do it?

"Are you sure she didn't take anything?" Alvy pressed.

"I'm sure," I insisted, not having actually checked, not needing to. She didn't take anything. Except, I was starting to worry, a piece of me.

"Then why leave? Without saying anything?"

"That's what I am trying to figure out."

"Do you know how long she's been gone?"

"I have no idea. We went to bed around midnight. I got up at six. Anytime in that window."

So she could have been well and gone.

On a plane heading who-the-hell-knew-where.

Likely never to be seen again.

"You look like someone kicked your puppy," Alvy observed, eyes piercing.

"I believe the impossible has happened, Alvy," I declared, going over toward the line of liquor bottles on a sideboard, twisting the top off a bottle of Scotch, filling a glass. "I think I might have fallen for her," I admitted, saluting them with my drink before throwing it back.

"Shit," Alvy hissed, reaching up to rub the back of their neck.

"Yeah," I agreed, nodding. "That about covers it," I agreed, going back for seconds.

"You're sure you haven't fallen for her like you did that movie star? Like the mafia guy's wife? Like the hotel heiress?"

"Little infatuations," I told them, throwing an arm out, nearly sloshing my drink all over the floor. "This? This was different. She was different."

"Alright. So, what kind of different was she?" Alvy asked.

"I'm not sure what you mean by that," I admitted, feeling a delightful warmness bloom across my chest. The Scotch kicking in. Thank God. Because the feeling it was replacing—a sharp, undeniable stabbing sensation—was proving hard to think past.

"Well, is she just a story you want to have in your back pocket? The woman with the funny name who traipsed across the world with you only to sneak out on you without another word? Or is she someone you want to see again?"

"I need to see her again." If for nothing else than to get an explanation.

"Okay. So, we'll figure it out."

"And how do you propose to do that?"

"It's a long shot, but I have her number. If she is trying to cut ties, I doubt she will answer. She probably already blocked me," they added, reaching for their phone, scrolling, then putting it on speaker as they dialed.

"Disconnected," Alvy hissed when the automatic message started playing. "She's on top of things, I'll give her that."

She would be.

If she was going to pull a power move like a genuine ghosting, she would do it in a way that made it impossible for you to get any kind of closure.

Sting once.

And keep on stinging.

That was how she operated.

That was the legacy she wanted to be known for.

"Fuck," I snapped.

"Well, you know what this is."

"What?" I asked, mind racing.

"Another international incident, don't you think?" they asked, eyes bright, smile wry.

"You know what, Alvy, I think you might be right!" I declared, feeling some of the weight lift from my shoulders.

It was never hopeless.

There were always people to pay to fix problems.

In fact, I had an entire team I used to fix all of mine.

"Besides, it has been so long," I added, warming to the idea. "They surely miss me by now. I want to—"

"I am already getting the yacht lined up to take us back to the jet," Alvy told me, already clicking away on their phone.

The yacht lined up to take us back to the jet.

I never would have thought twice about that phrase before Wasp, before her eye rolls to the ostentatiousness that had been a normal part of my life.

"No," I said, shaking my head.

"No?" Alvy asked, brows knitting, looking up at me.

"I don't want to waste the time. Book us flights back commercial."

"Commercial"?" Alvy repeated as though the words made no sense, like I'd begun speaking a foreign language.

"First Class. Let's not get too carried away," I told them, smirking.

"I, ah, alright then," Alvy agreed. "How soon do you want to leave?"

"How soon can we get things here wrapped up?"

"If you want, I can hang back here and handle all of this. We have to get the jet back to the States anyway."

"Of course," I agreed, realizing just how little I actually thought the practical things through. If it weren't for Alvy, that jet would have stayed where it was until I realized I needed it again, and it was nowhere to be found. "That will work. As soon as you can get me out of here then. It's a long flight, if I recall."

"And you're going to have to endure it in a seat brushing up against strangers," Alvy teased.

"A horror I fear I must endure to learn the truth. And quickly."

With that, Alvy burst into action, getting me a small bag of luggage packed, arranging the flight, getting a car to drive me to the airport.

Then I was off, heading back to Navesink Bank.

Back to Quinton Baird & Associates.

If anyone could find Wasp, it was them.

The team of professional fixers who had gotten me out of every sticky situation I'd ever been in.

They'd never steered me wrong before.

TWELVE

Wasp

"Okay," Raven said, dropping down on the bed beside my body. "You've been curled up in bed for three days. Three. Days," she repeated, reaching downward, pressing a wrist to my forehead in a move that was so motherly that it was almost funny. Almost. Unfortunately, I found myself short on things like humor. Or smiles. Or anything but this free-fall sensation inside.

"I'm not sick," I told her, yanking the blanket back up under my chin.

"No?" she asked, her perfectly shaped brow raising. "Because you're acting exactly like one of the kids when they don't want to go to school. Lazing about in bed, curled under the covers, overcome with nondescript ailments that don't add up to anything."

"I'm not faking being sick either," I told her, flipping onto my other side. "I just don't want to get up yet."

"Yes, well, it's after one in the afternoon. And you didn't want to get up yesterday either. Or the day before."

"I'm an adult. We can dramatically take to bed without all the judgment. It's one of the perks of not having anyone in control of our lives anymore," I told her, wishing she and Roman had a smaller guest room. With a twin-sized bed. Because this queen was begging me to notice how empty the other side was.

I wiggled into the dead center, not feeling any better about taking up the whole thing, but finding myself too unmotivated to move back.

Unmotivated.

That was one of the best ways to describe how I had been since I landed back in New Jersey.

I wasn't motivated to get back in Wanda and hit the road. Or to unpack my things. Or eat. Or get out of bed. I think it went without saying that showers and me, we weren't on speaking terms either, despite having a beautiful one all to myself just a few feet away.

"I'm worried about you," Raven told me, voice tight, airless.

I knew she was.

She'd done everything she could to try to lure me out of bed. When that failed, she sent her little gremlins in to try to annoy me out of bed.

You knew you were a whole new level of pathetic when young children decided you were a lost cause, got up, went to the door, turned off the light, and left you alone in your misery.

"I don't need you to worry about me, Raves," I told her, turning to stare up at the ceiling.

"And yet, here I am. Worried. What is going on with you? What the hell happened in Paris?"

"Paris. Qatar. Bali. Australia. The yacht."

"Okay. We will get back to the world tour, Wasp. But what *happened*?" she asked. "What were you doing?"

"A job," I admitted.

"You were on a job in Paris. And Qatar. And Bali. And Australia. And on a yacht."

"Oh, and the jet. The jet too."

"The jet," Raven repeated, brows scrunching together. "Okay. We will get back to that. And the fact that I wasn't in on any of that. Which is a problem. But I want to get to the most important thing first."

"My bad tan lines," I quipped, but there was no levity in my voice.

"Wasp, look at me," Raven demanded, voice sad, hollow, drawing my gaze to her face, finding her blue eyes wide, panicked. "I am going to need a straight answer from you right now, okay?"

"I can try," I admitted, not wanting to promise her anything I wasn't sure I could give her. Because I was too confused about this whole situation—and my reaction to it—to give her any kind of rational explanation about it.

"Did something happen?" she asked, words heavy, hanging in the air like summer humidity, thick, hard to ignore, making breathing difficult. "Did the job go south? Do you need me to come with you to the police station?"

"The police station?"

"Did he hurt you?" she asked, point-blank, making guilt kick me in the stomach.

Of course her mind would go there. Mine likely would have too if a once lively, carefree friend suddenly took to the bed, barely eating, unable to bring themselves to do basic daily necessities.

"No. No," I added more firmly, sitting up against the headboard.

"You can tell me if it happened. Or not tell me, but let me take you somewhere to tell someone."

"It's not that, Raven. But I appreciate that."

"If it's not that, what is it? I really don't understand. I want to understand. This is not like you. I don't recognize this person. And I know you inside and out. What happened?"

I took a deep breath, swiping my knotty hair out of my face, shrugging my shoulders.

"I think the con was so good that I fell for it myself."

"I don't understand," Raven said, shaking her head. "What was the con? Who was the mark? What went wrong?"

"It was a sweetheart scam."

"You make them fall in love with you."

"Exactly."

"To what end? For money? For access to information? What did the client want?"

"They wanted me to break his heart."

"Oh," Raven said, head jerking back. "That's not a common one."

"No," I agreed, nodding.

"He must have really hurt someone to make them want that kind of revenge."

"I wasn't provided a lot of detail. Just a bottom line. And it was too good to refuse."

"Who was the mark?"

I should have kept it to myself.

But this was Raven. I never kept anything from her for long.

"Fenway Arlington."

"Fenway Arlington. Fenway... that sounds familiar."

"He's very rich. And very generous. And known for being a bit of a playboy."

"I think I've heard Roman mention him. You know how men in business like that are," she said, shrugging. "They all know each other. If by nothing else but a common friend or something like that. So you followed this Fenway guy to Paris."

"Yeah. And he brought me to Bali and Australia. He's a bit... impulsive."

"Gee, that sounds like someone else I know," Raven teased.

Impulsive.

Yeah.

That was part of the problem, wasn't it? I hadn't given a single step of this job nearly enough thought.

"So what happened between Paris, Bali, Australia, and you showing up on our doorstep?"

"At some point," I started, feeling the truth like a boulder in my chest that needed to be chipped away at, made into smaller, more manageable pieces. "At some point, I stopped acting," I admitted, wincing. "It was fun," I admitted. "It was fun and we had a good time at the monkey sanctuary and the marketplace. And in the cave. God, the cave," I groaned, closing my eyes, trying to force the images away, trying to focus, not let myself go back there.

"What happened in the cave, Wasp?" Raven asked, knowing me too well, knowing there was a story there. "Wasp?" she pressed when I sat there with my eyes closed, finding the words harder than they should have been to admit.

This was my best friend.

We talked about sex all the time.

But this was different.

Because, I guess, in the past, sex had always been a power move on my part.

Sex with Fenway was perhaps the only time I'd been with a man and given even a small bit of my power away.

"I slept with the client," I admitted, finding that the separation, the choice not to use his name made it easier to admit.

"Okay," Raven said, trying to process this information. "You slept with the client because it was good for the job, or because you genuinely wanted to do it?"

"I wanted it," I admitted. "And then I continued to want it. Day and night. For about a week," I told her, shaking my head at myself.

"I think we both know that sex is sex. It doesn't have to be more than that unless we want it to. So my question is this. Was it just sex? Or did it mean something to you?"

"You know the answer to that."

"I want to hear it."

"It meant something to me. And it was more than sex. It was everything. We fucked in that cave, and then suddenly, I wasn't a conwoman and he wasn't a mark. I was just a person. Who was kind of into this other person."

"Into," Raven repeated as though the word didn't make sense. And, to be fair, it didn't make sense. Not as it related to me and the opposite sex.

"Yes, into. Like a normal woman is into a normal man."

"Wow. Okay."

"That's it?" I asked, feeling my lips curve upward slightly. "That's all you have to say to this revelation?"

"I'm processing," she told me, taking a deep breath. "If someone asked what phrase I would be more shocked at coming out of your mouth—that you were going to shave your head, forsake all material things, and dedicate your life to meditation in a hut in the woods all alone, or that you might have feelings for a guy, I'd consider the former the much more plausible option. And you'd have to be barefoot to do that, and we both know how much you like your heels."

"I know it's crazy. It took me a long time to see it too." I was still processing it, if I was being honest.

"So what was it about him that was so different?"

"I honestly don't know," I admitted. "He was utterly ridiculous. He was not someone I should have been into."

"Utterly ridiculous sounds interesting. You've always had a thing for interesting."

"That's true."

"How was he ridiculous?"

"He is just over-the-top in every way. He decides at the drop of a hat to hop onto his private jet or his massive yacht and just take off to some other part of the world. He does things like rents out an entire tourist attraction so that he can show it to you when it is empty. He buys everything you look at for too long at a market. It was just... it was all crazy."

"Maybe that's your type."

I guess I wouldn't know. I'd never wanted a man for more than a night, so I didn't stop to consider what about them I would be into. Aside from being able to hold a halfway decent conversation in the bar before heading back to a room somewhere.

I always knew that if a conversation started with something along the lines of, 'Hey did you hear about this new conspiracy theory blowing up Facebook?" or "So, the Illuminati," I knew I was out.

I liked lighter hair and swimmer's builds instead of tall, dark, and handsome or insanely jacked.

Outside of those sorts of things, I didn't have a 'type' because I never spent that much time with those men.

It was entirely possible that I liked ridiculous men.

"I thought opposites were supposed to attract," I told her, knowing that I was generally the craziest person in any given room, someone willing to run off at any given moment to do something fun or interesting, someone who ran cons for a living. Sweetheart cons, nonetheless.

"You're a nut," Raven told me, though I sensed a 'but' coming. "That said, you are very rational and grounded. Sometimes people don't see that right away. Being a conwoman who lives in a skoolie and wears ankle-breaking heels to concerts makes you seem a lot more irrational than you are. But you are a good businesswoman. You have more street smarts than anyone I know. And I am including more than those biker brothers of yours. You might be crazy, but you balance it out. Does this Fenway guy balance himself out?"

See, the thing was, he did, didn't he? No one saw that. I wasn't even sure those closest to him saw that because he was really convincing at being flip and outlandish. But he had a serious side. He was someone who had worked to increase his family's wealth—despite how much of it he blew with his ostentatious lifestyle. He had endured a hard life that had given him discipline. Though he typically chose not to use it, it was there should he want to.

"He does," I told Raven. "I think his crazy side is the dominant one, but he does have another side as well."

"You know what I like about that?" she asked, looking wistful, a little dreamy, having moon eyes for the idea of me with a happily ever after like she had.

"What?"

"That there is no *completing* the other person. Neither of you are lacking. You have it all. But you have personalities that commingle nicely. I like that."

"Well, it doesn't matter now," I said, reaching for my blanket again, pulling it up to my chin like a little kid.

"It does matter," Raven countered, shaking her head. "And I am going to need some more details."

"Like what?"

"Like how it ended. Like what has been going on in your head since you got back here."

"I finally felt confident that he had strong feelings for me," I told her, unable to use *that* word. You know the one. The one that would hurt too much to admit. "Then I packed and left while he slept."

"No note?"

"No note. The mystery is what hurts the most when you get ghosted," I reminded her. We'd been over it many times in the past, but she was retired, rusty.

"Do you feel guilty?"

"We don't do guilt in our business."

"Wasp," she said, shaking her head. "Come on. We're not talking about the countless other assholes. We're talking about this particular asshole. Do you feel guilty for knowingly hurting him?"

"Yes," I admitted, the taste of that word bitter on my tongue.

"Okay and now for the important one," Raven said, raising a brow at me. "Did you love him? I know you said feelings. And feelings can be a lot of things. But did you love him?"

"I think I was starting to," I admitted, feeling a sting at the backs of my eye, blinking it away. I didn't cry. That wasn't my thing.

"Shit," Raven said, shaking her head.

"Shit?" I repeated, feeling my lips curving up—my first genuine smile in days. Raven had never been one to use swear words even before children. Now it was an even more strict rule for her.

"Yeah, that about covers it, don't you think? Shit. Or 'What an utter clusterfuck" works too," she added. "Well, what now?"

"What do you mean what now? There is no what now. I drag myself out of this bed when I get to that point. And then I get back on the road. I get back to my life."

"Running more cons."

"Yes, seeing as that is what I do for a living. What you used to do for a living," I added, actually sensing judgment in her face, despite all the years she had done the exact same thing.

"Look, I don't think what we did was wrong, per se. I just have some distance from it all now, and I can't figure out why the hell it felt like such a passion of ours for all those years."

"We did it for all womankind. For all of our fellow women who got screwed over by shitty men. They deserved a chance to get some closure. We provided that. Or we helped them prove their spouses were cheating so they could get the proper alimony. No, wait," I said, holding up a hand when she went to speak. "Let me throw a hypothetical at you, okay?"

"Okay," she agreed, nodding.

"Imagine a year from now, you start to suspect Roman is screwing around behind your back. I know, I know. He's perfect. But they *all* are, aren't they? Until they're not. So suspend your disbelief. Imagine sitting up in bed at night while he sleeps like a baby as you wrestle with the knowledge that those hands he puts on you are the same ones he had on another woman just hours before. Sit with that a minute. Feel how that might feel."

"Wasp—"

"Now imagine you finally got the nerve to tell him you were done, that you want out, that he could have his other women, but not you at the same time. And you take the kids and you go. And you find out that he canceled your cards. And he removed your access from accounts. And you are forced to get several low-paying jobs just to keep your kids in a shitty motel room because you can't afford anything else, and all you have left goes to a lawyer to try to get him to pay the alimony he owes you since he invalidated the prenup for cheating on you."

"I get your point, Wasp.

"And imagine he hires a shark, someone who wants to bite you and your children to shreds, to leave you with nothing. So, your piece of shit cheating husband can go on with his life like nothing happened, like he was through with all his responsibilities. You know this happens. We've heard almost this identical story dozens of times over the years. They have no recourse. Or they *had* no recourse. Until we showed up. We helped them get what was rightfully theirs by proving their spouse was a cheater. Pictures and all. Is it a morally gray area? Yes, absolutely, but that doesn't mean it isn't a needed service. Shitty men should have to pay."

"But not all men are shitty men, Wasp. That is the point I am trying to make, I guess. What if Fenway isn't a shitty man? What if some woman just blew something out of proportion? For as many shitty men we have come in contact with, we have seen truly disgusting, mean-spirited women too, ones who were just vindictive and ugly-hearted, ones who just wanted to screw with someone's life because there was a misunderstanding or something like that."

"Yeah, but we could smell that from a mile away."

"True. In person. Like all our other meetings have always been. But you never said anything about meeting this woman."

That was true.

But it was also true that I had slowed down on in-person meetings a while back because I no longer had Raven around to do a meeting when I was on a job or vice versa. The workload had made me automate some things that had once always been handled manually, with face-to-face meetings and carefully outlined plans.

"It was a lot of money, Rave. Don't tell me you would have told me to turn it down. Back when we were still on the road. Back when money was tighter for both of us."

"No, you're right," she agreed, looking out the window of a house that everyone would collectively call a mini-mansion. "And we both know that if he was an asshole at some point, he likely has more than enough money to try to make sure that never got out to ruin his public persona, or blowback on his family. But I have a hard time believing he was a dickhead if you were falling for him."

"Why not? Great women fall for shittacular men all the time."

"Well, that is the damn truth," she agreed, snorting.

We'd seen it far too many times in our lives. These amazing, intelligent, successful women for some reason ending up with men who sat around and watched sports all day, who had no ambition, who left them to handle all the housework along with the breadwinning.

Why?

That was a good question.

We'd never been able to come to a satisfying explanation for the phenomenon.

"Because I know you. He would have to be a skyscraper of a man to make you take a second look, let alone catch feelings. Maybe somewhere along the way, he pissed off the wrong woman by doing nothing other than being himself. And maybe that self was not right for *that* woman, but it doesn't mean it isn't right for you."

"Yeah, well, even if that were true, there is no chance, Rave. I took money to con him. He believed me. And that means he would never be able to believe me in the future because he knows how good an actress I am. It's a nonstarter."

I expected some empty platitudes that we both knew I would see right through. I didn't get those, though.

"I think you're right. And that sucks. And I hate this for you. But I'm here, okay? And you are welcome to stay in this bed and mope for as long as you need to. So long as once a week, you get your ass out of that bed so I can wash the sheets."

"That sounds reasonable," I said, giving her a weak smile. "Thank you, Rave," I told her.

The aching feeling in my chest was hard enough. I couldn't imagine having to deal with it all alone in Wanda, just traveling with no direction, the loneliness seeping in through the cracks in the windows, curling its long fingers around my throat until I couldn't breathe through it anymore.

At least here, even if all I was doing was wallowing in my room, I wouldn't ever be alone. I could hear Raven moving up and down the halls, the kids squealing and laughing, Roman coming home. I wasn't part of it, but it was all around me. It was a comfort of sorts.

Eventually, I had to have faith, this would fade. Then I could get back on the road, get back to my life, let Raven and her family get back to their normal without the creepy aunt in the attic bedroom, haunting the halls with her misery.

"Can I perhaps interest you in a shower?" Raven suggested, making a snort escape me.

"Is that a hint?"

"You're starting to smell, babe," she told me, wrinkling her nose.

"Well, we can't have that, can we?" I asked, throwing off my blanket, making my way off the bed.

"I will clean the bedding while you're gone."

Alone, I let the water rush over me. And because no one was around to see them, and because I had plausible deniability of their existence as they merged with the water running down my face, I finally let the tears come.

I didn't remember the last time I'd cried. When my father died, most likely. A lifetime ago.

I slid down the slate wall of the shower, squatting under the stream of too-hot water, heels of my palms pressed into my eyes as I cried with the reckless abandon of a child, until my body was shaking with the sobs, until I was starting to worry they might never stop.

Until, eventually, they did, leaving me hollowed out inside, like someone had reached inside and scooped something out of me, discarding what they found.

I moved through the rest of the shower in a blur, drying and dressing in oversized sweats, making my way back into the bedroom on numb legs, finding the bedding fresh, the room aired out, drinks and snacks on the nightstand in case I needed them.

I didn't want food.

I wanted sleep.

I wanted oblivion.

I wanted the thoughts of him to stop.

Except I found my dreams plagued with memories and impossible possibilities, things that we could never have, never do, never be.

Days tripped into one another, a blur of a zombie-like fog that only got broken up on Raven's chosen bedding wash day.

Then back into that bed—and that misery—I fell.

There were no signs of it letting up, no light at the end of the tunnel.

I was just about ready to accept this patheticness as my reality.

When, suddenly, there was a knock at my door.

And I realized Raven hadn't given up on me.

She'd called in reinforcements.

My brothers were at the door.

THIRTEEN

Fenway

"Nia!" I greeted, leaning in her office doorway, watching as she lifted her unamused brown eyes, inspecting me for a moment before leaning back in her seat, flicking her black braids over her shoulder.

"What do you want, Fenway? I'm not on your case."

"No, you're not," I agreed, nodding. "But I believe you should be, you Mistress of the Keys, you."

"Mistress of the Keys," she repeated, a rare smile pulling at her lips. "I like that. Alright, fine. I'll bite. What do you want from me?"

"I know your boss is running his usual investigation angles. And he hasn't steered me wrong in the past, but I think I need you to look around."

"Why is that?"

"Because I think you would be able to find someone who goes by the name of Wasp somewhere online. She made a comment once about arms dealing in her family. That's an angle I think you could work too."

"What would make me want to abandon my current work to deal with your little issue?"

My little issue.

I'd been involved in international scandals, in corporate takeovers, in every sort of ugly, backstabbing situation you could think of.

None of them felt quite in the same league as this *little issue* of mine.

Maybe because all that other shit, it was background noise, it was something pesky to have dealt with, so that I could go back to my normal life.

This?

I was attached to this.

And I wasn't sure anything would go back to normal again.

But I could maybe find a new normal if I found answers, if I found her, if I got closure.

Even as I thought it, I wasn't sure that was true. But I was choosing to let myself believe it. At least in part.

"What do you want? Triple your usual fee? A summer home in Tuscany? Name the price, Nia," I demanded, moving to sit in one of the chairs on the other side of her desk, leaning back, tired down to my bones.

"Name my price," she repeated, steepling her fingers, observing me over the tops of them, trying to figure out if I was being honest or not. "What if I wanted your jet? Your yacht?"

"If that's your price..."

To that, her brows knitted, her lips pursed. "Okay. What is going on here?" she asked, waving a hand at me. "I'm newer here than a lot of the others, but I've seen enough of you to know that this rumpled suit, no shave, dark eye circle look is not you. When's the last time you got some sleep? Because, frankly, Fenway, you look like shit."

I had just enough humor left to snort at that. Even if I knew she was being honest. Painfully so. As was her nature. She was one of the few women in a male-dominated field. She had to be tough to get by.

"The last time I slept was the night she walked out of our room in Australia," I told her truthfully.

"How long ago was that?"

"I don't know. Two weeks, give or take." It had taken three days to get into see my team of fixers since, for once, my problem wasn't of the "someone is going to kill me if you don't step in" variety.

From there, it seemed like they'd just hit dead-end after dead-end.

"She really got under your skin, huh?" she asked, leaning forward, grabbing a notepad and pen off her desk. "Alright. I'll bite. What do you know?"

"She goes by Wasp. She has a best friend. I think she called her Raven. And then the two brothers who are in the arms trade somehow. She converted a skoolie."

"A skoolie."

"A school bus. Into an RV, of sorts. She told me she is a dog trainer."

"Alright. What else? The more details, the better.

The problem was, I didn't have anything really solid to go on. I had little details, general preferences, but no names or events or even a home state to drop a pin in.

"All details are good details," Nia told me, shrugging. "People share everything on social media. You never know what might be an important part of the search."

"She likes classic movies. She has a strong aversion to gross feet and bad grammar. She's traveled a lot. But it sounds like just across the continental US. She mentioned a lot of different tourist traps and restaurants."

"Alright," Nia said, nodding. "This is a good start. Oh, Jesus. Stomp your feet or something," she snapped, making me turn to see who she was looking at only to find a tall, massive man with tanned skin and a short crop of hair standing in her office, looking for something on a shelf. "No worries, man. You're not interrupting or anything," she added to the man who ignored her completely. "Yep, I wanted your hands all over all my shit. We don't do boundaries at this office or anything," she went on as the man continued to ignore her.

"It's nice to—" I started, trying to introduce myself to someone who was clearly a new member of the team. He would likely be on one of my cases more than once. It was always good to get on their good side early.

"Don't bother," Nia told me, rolling her eyes at the man's back. "He has no people skills to speak of. Or manners. Or respect for someone else's property," she added as the man tucked something under his arm and made his way out of the room.

"Who was that?" I asked, jolting when he slammed the door.

"Holden," Nia said, shaking her head."He's new."

"What is his job title?" I asked, knowing that each of them had a particular specialty, and that their names reflected that. The owner, Quin, was The Fixer. The man who helped people in sticky situations was The Ghost. There was a Messenger, a Negotiator, a Cleaner, a Babysitter. More recently, a friend of mine became a member of the team under the title of The Executioner. Nia, appropriately with her impressive computer skills, was The Hacker.

"The Inquisitor," she said, snorting. "I know. It's ridiculous, right? So pretentious. Like he is going to come riding into your town, round up your wild women who were accused of witchcraft, and put them on the rack until they admit to it. When all he really does is go into our communal fridge and steal other people's meals. Meals they put a lot of time into preparing."

"Why, Nia, if I didn't know any better, I would say you have a crush."

"Oh, ew," she said, cringing. "God, no. He's not my type."

"I've heard that before. Doth you protest too much?"

"Doth?" she repeated. "And no. Not at all. The stoic, silent type with bad tempers aren't my type. I like men with some levity."

"Oh, Nia, dear thing, you can just come out and say it. You're hopelessly in love with me. You've been carrying a torch all this time."

"Yeah," she agreed, smirking. "That must be it. I'm in love with your pain in the ass self. Cleaning up grown-ass men's problems gets my panties wet," she drawled.

"I am afraid to inform you, but I find myself in love with someone else."

Those words sounded clumsy on my tongue, unpracticed, my lips struggling to form the right sounds.

But there was no denying the truth in them.

I didn't even know the woman's real name, but I had fallen for her.

I had to figure out where she went, why, what would possess her to cut ties completely. When things had seemed to be going so well, when we had all sorts of plans to keep exploring the world together.

"Wow. You love her," Nia repeated. "I wasn't sure you were capable of loving anyone other than yourself."

"Neither was I, honey, neither was I. Alas, it seems I am not only capable, but very much afflicted with this love shit."

"This love shit," she laughed, but her smile fell fast, reading something on my face that she didn't like. "It sucks, right? Love. It's a real mother fucker."

"That it is," I agreed.

I hadn't been able to think of much else since I woke up alone. Business calls and emails went unanswered. Or, more likely, redirected to Alvy to delegate for me. I didn't go out. I didn't even think about it.

I just lay in a hotel room waiting until it was an appropriate hour to drink, then doing so until I passed out. Only to have dreams plagued with images of her.

I needed this case figured out.

I needed answers.

I need to track her down and talk this out.

Confrontation was not in my nature. It was why I had people in each of my companies to handle the reprimanding and firing and all that other unsavory shit. It wasn't for me. I'd gotten too much of it in my life already. I didn't want to invite more when it wasn't necessary.

Just this once, though, it seemed necessary. "Figure this out for me, Nia," I demanded, hearing an edge to my voice that had never been there before. Desperation, perhaps? Or something as equally unsavory.

I knew she liked a challenge. She thrived on them. The impossible cases, the information no one else could track down. Once she had a case, she worked on it day and night, barely catching snippets of sleep until she finally found what she was looking for.

"Okay," she agreed, nodding. "But I am going to hold off on naming my price."

"You have an IOU without an expiration date, honey. Anything you want."

"Wow," she said, shaking her head. "You really are lovesick for her, huh?" she asked as I climbed out of the chair, buttoning my center jacket button.

"Sounds about right," I agreed, heading out of her office.

Love, yes.

That explained the borderline obsessive thoughts of her, memories of her.

But sick, yes, as well.

It explained the aching in my chest, the pit in my stomach, the lack of motivation, the siren's call of my bed.

I had to get some answers.

Even if they weren't what I wanted to hear.

It was better to know.

That was new to me. I'd always been perfectly content accepting a half-truth or a full lie if it made life easier, if it let the party go on, if I got to keep the status quo of light and easy and carefree.

I never needed to know someone's deep dark secrets, their motivations, their reasons for their decisions.

But I had to know Wasp's reasons for blowing into my life and out again, pulling some vital part of me along with her, refusing to give it back.

I had to know.

Then things could go back to normal.

I could go back to normal.

At least that was what I was trying to tell myself.

It wasn't a long wait, in the grand scheme of things. Nia's obsessive need for answers produced more in two days than the rest of the team had managed in two weeks.

"Nia," I greeted her as I opened my hotel room door, finding her looking puffy-eyed and paler than usual, exhaustion taking its toll.

"You are not going to believe this shit," she told me, brushing past, charging into the dining room area, waving at the empty seat.

"You found something?" I asked, hope a skipping sensation in my chest.

"Something," she scoffed, dropping a file on the desk. "Try everything."

"What did you find?" I asked, my chest feeling tight, my stomach sloshing around ominously, and I hadn't even gotten to the drinking part of the evening yet.

"Your girl, Wasp—you're not going to believe where she's from."

"Where?"

"Right fucking here," she said, eyes huge, waving an arm toward the floor-to-ceiling windows.

"She's from Navesink Bank?" I asked, not ready to accept that kind of coincidence.

"Her daddy was a biker. The local Henchmen kind of biker. But a long time ago. He was killed, leaving behind a wife, two sons, and a little girl," she told me, waiting for me to put the pieces together.

"Her brothers," I started, remembering her comments about them being arms dealers. Like the local outlaw biker club did for a living. "They're Henchmen."

"They sure are. Meet Reeve and Cyrus," Nia said, flipping open the file, grabbing a picture of two men with light hair and eyes, one with longer hair, the other with a distant, tortured look to him. "And this is Raven. Her best friend. She is married to a man named Roman who also lives here," she told me, producing a picture of a beautiful black-haired woman and a man who looked vaguely familiar, like someone I'd brushed shoulders with in the past, but hadn't made any sort of connection with.

"How did you figure all of this out?"

"I got the pictures you gave to the rest of the team. And I ran them into a search."

"You found her on social media?"

"No, actually. Your girl is a complete ghost. Not even any old defunct pages from her teen years. Nothing."

"Then how did you find her?"

"Raven, whose real name is Rebecca, had a big, fancy-ass wedding. Fancy enough to make the local paper in Navesink Bank. And her maid of honor was right there next to her. Took fucking forever, but that was how I found her."

"What's her real name?"

"Yeah, see, that's the thing. I have no idea. And you know how much I hate saying that. But I have looked really hard. I can't find it. She was named in the paper as Wasp. And once I made the connection to Rebecca/Raven, I found her social media. Where she had posted a throwback to when they were teens. Her,

Wasp, and the two brothers. But I couldn't get any records from Wasp's birth or anything. And her brothers don't really do much social media either. You know how outlaws are about that shit."

I didn't. But I could imagine that when your career and life involved something as illegal as arms dealing, the rules about what you posted online were strict.

"What about the local high school? She must have gone to class with Raven."

"I know," Nia agreed, dropping down on the chair across from me, what was left of her energy seeming to seep slowly out of her limbs. "The old yearbooks aren't scanned in. I have to wait until Monday to go to the school to look. Normally, I'd wait until I had all of that to give you. But with how wrecked you looked in my office, I figured the sooner the better with whatever information I have. You have the brother lead and the best friend lead. If you want to follow through with those. Or have the rest of the guys on the team handle it."

I didn't have time to wait for my team of fixers to find some diplomatic way of figuring this out, approaching the brothers or the friend.

I had to handle this myself.

Which would be pretty new for me.

Handling my own damn business.

"Nia, you are every bit as good as you think you are," I told her, getting a smile. She never pretended to be humble about her skills. I always appreciated that about her. "Better, even," I added. "Thank you for this."

"We have to pull out all the stops for our most notorious client," she told me, and the price she was paying was clear.

"Go on. Go get some sleep, Nia," I told her, reaching for my wallet, grabbing some cash. "And have a nice dinner on me."

"A nice dinner," she said, taking the cash, looking up at me. "This is nice dinner for a month."

"Then have nice dinners for a month. You earned it. And you have my IOU for when you need it," I told her, leading her to the door.

"I know you're going to try to go get your girl," she said, stepping into the hall, turning to face me. "Can I offer you some advice?"

"I'm sure I could use it," I admitted.

"Let her talk," she said, shrugging. "You come at her too hard, you're only going to lose her again before you even get any answers. Then you're never going to be able to get some sleep."

With that, she was gone.

I went back to the table, flipping through the file, checking out the faces, wondering which would be the straightest route to her.

The best friend, I decided, looking over the wedding pictures. In my experience, when a woman found a man she looked at like Raven looked at Roman, she wanted that kind of thing for her best friend too.

There was also the added perk of Raven not likely wanting to kick my ass like her brothers might.

Decision made, I showered, changed, threw back some coffee, and made my way across town to the development of mini mansions that Nia had provided me the address for.

"I got it!" A woman's voice called from inside when I'd hit the bell. "It's probably the Chine...oh," she said, pulling the door open.

She was every bit as pretty as her wedding pictures, but wearing a silk tank top that had some sort of purple smudge on the stomach, her hair wrapped up in a bun on the top of her head in a frazzled mom look everyone recognized.

Her bright blue gaze slid over me, settling on my face, lips curved up ever-so-slightly.

"All that money," she started, shaking her head, "And it took you this long to track her down?"

"I had the best team on the job," I admitted, feeling relief wash over me. I'd picked the right person. She was happy to see me. She wanted me to be able to talk to Wasp. "Is she here?" I asked. It was a rhetorical question. Wanda was parked way in the backyard.

"She's staying here temporarily," Raven told me, nodding.

"May I see her?"

"Well, there's a problem."

"What kind of problem?"

"I waited for you to show up. When you didn't, I had to call in reinforcements."

"You called her brothers," I mused.

"Yes. And they convinced her to get up, get pretty, go out tonight. Made her an offer she couldn't refuse. An underground casino."

"Those poor bastards she's playing," I said, snorting, getting a big smile out of Raven.

"I know, right? I've never won a single game against her."

"This underground casino..."

"It's invitation only."

"Oh," I said, feeling my hope deflate.

"Oh my God. Look at those sad eyes," She said, grin getting huge. Like she was pleased I was miserable. "I will give you this," she said, producing a black and gold casino chip. "But you have to promise to hear her out."

"That's the second time I've heard that tonight."

"Yes, because men aren't exactly known for their listening skills," Raven said, shaking her head.

"That's fair. I want to hear her out. That's why I spent the past few weeks trying to track her down."

"Alright," Raven said, nodding. "Here you go," she said, tossing the chip, making me grab for it.

"Thank you, Raven. I really appreciate this."

"Yep. Go have your chat. Oh, and Fenway?" she called making me turn back.

"Yeah?"

"If you hurt my girl, I will hire someone to toss you off that fancy yacht of yours. And make it look like an accident."

"Should it come to that," I said, giving her a smile, "Might I suggest you turn to Quinton Baird & Associates for your crisis management?" I said, then turned and walked away. "They've never steered me wrong."

I might as well get them some new business.

I was pretty sure I was retiring from the international scandals over the fairer sex.

I'd have my hands full with just this one.

FOURTEEN

Wasp

"I'm going to kill Raven," I grumbled, looking at the pity in my brothers' eyes. "I'm fine. Go back to your clubhouse with all those yummy biker brothers of yours. Leave me alone."

"How long have you been moping in here?" Cyrus asked, moving to the side of the bed, dropping down next to my body.

"I'm not moping. I'm... recovering from some pretty epic jet lag."

"Jet lag," Reeve repeated, arching a brow as he moved in the room, but didn't come too close. When it came to respecting boundaries, Cyrus didn't exactly understand the concept, while Reeve very carefully gave you the space he thought you wanted. "Last I checked, jet lag doesn't make you puffy-eyed. Like crying does."

"I never cry," I insisted, not wanting to admit to them that was no longer true.

"Wasp," Reeve said, tone much like our father used to use, impatient, yet indulgent.

"I was on a job. It got a little crazy. I am getting a little R&R. It's no big deal."

"You've never needed R&R before," Cyrus insisted.

"Yes, well, I am getting old, asshole," I told him, getting a small smirk out of him.

"Come on," Reeve tried, moving to the foot of the bed, putting his hands on the footboard. "We all know that Raven wouldn't be calling us unless you were in bad shape. That's your girl. She has been able to handle you for your whole life. If she needs reinforcements, this isn't that you're tired from a job. You can tell us to fuck off, but don't lie to us."

That was fair. We weren't always the closest of siblings, what with my traveling all the time, but we didn't bullshit each other either.

"I caught feelings for a mark. There. Are you happy?" I grumbled, wishing I could throw the covers over my head, hide my heated cheeks.

"Hey," Cyrus said, patting my leg over the covers. "You don't need to be embarrassed with us. Shit happens."

Shit happens.

That was such a Cy thing to say.

He was the proverbial duck with everything sliding off his back.

Reeve was much more serious, more introspective, someone who thought things through deeply.

"Yes, well, *this* shit doesn't happen. I don't fall for marks. Marks are assholes. That's why they're marks."

"So, asshole is your type," Cyrus concluded, shrugging. "I'm not exactly surprised. Who else would want to put up with you?" he teased, nudging me.

"I'm not so much worried that you caught feelings for a mark, Wasp," Reeve said, dragging my attention in his direction. "I'm worried why we've been told that you've been in bed for weeks. You. Who could never sit still for more than five minutes."

"I mean, I got a call from your heels today," Cyrus said, looking grave. "They said they're worried about you too. They haven't seen you in ages."

"Look. It's not a big deal. I'm just in a mood. It will pass."

"It will pass," Reeve repeated, raising a brow.

"Yes."

"Moods don't just pass, Wasp. You know that. You deal with them and move on. Or you fall into a hole because of them."

Reeve would know. He lived in a hole for far too long.

"I'm fine," I insisted, but the words fell flat even on my own ears.

"If you were fine, you'd have blown out of this town a week ago," Reeve said, and we all knew he wasn't wrong. "You're putting down roots because you want your people close. Because you feel like shit. Well, we're here. Tell us what's going on. Let us help you stop feeling like shit."

A big part of me didn't want to tell them, didn't want to admit to my little failures once again. But when Cy put an arm around me, the words just burst out, each of them tumbling over one another to try to get out first.

"So, now you see why I am in a bed, dealing with my mood. Because there is nothing I can do about this. I screwed up. I can't fix it. So I just have to deal with the aftermath."

"Is it written somewhere that you have to deal with it in bed?" Cyrus asked.

"I want to be here."

"Yeah, well, give the mattress some time to miss you," Cyrus said, reaching into his pocket, producing a small black and gold gambling chip.

"What's this?" I asked, seeing an address on it.

"It's an invitation. And I damn near had to promise my next child to get it. So you are going to take it, you are going to get dolled up, and you are going to go use it. Get your ass out of bed for a while. You're not going to feel any better if you lie around endlessly."

He wasn't wrong.

I had to admit, the more I stayed in bed, the more I wanted to, the further away motivation got.

I thought I just needed to rest, to sort through my feelings, to come to terms with what had happened.

I guess that was the tricky thing with sadness. It let you think you could outsmart it. Then it kept pulling you deeper and deeper. Until there was no motivation left to pull yourself back out of it.

I'd seen Reeve go through it.

And the only thing that got him out was us, being there for him, demanding he try, forcing his hand at times when he couldn't find the will to do it himself.

Slowly, surely, he got there; he started to rebuild his life.

If he could do it, with a much more horrific situation than mine, then I could do it too.

"I like gambling," I said, running my finger over the chip, trying not to remember Fenway's loud assertions that I was cheating when I kept beating him.

"I imagine it is even more fun when it is underground and illegal," Cyrus observed, clearly never having been there himself, despite being part of a big criminal empire in Navesink Bank.

"I'm happy to stay here in bed."

"Yeah, well, too fucking bad, kid," Reeve said, shaking his head.

Reeve never pulled the big brother card, so the fact that he was doing it now was telling. All the times I'd screwed up, all the times I did things he didn't approve of, he'd always kept his mouth shut.

He wasn't going to let me stay in this bed.

And maybe he was right. It was toxic. Sure, it felt like there was something gouged out of me with a hot poker. But it had been weeks. Staying in bed wasn't helping. It was time to try something else.

"Okay," I agreed, nodding. "I'll go gamble. Are you both coming?"

"Neither of us are coming," Cyrus told me. "It was hard enough to get one chip. We're connected, but, apparently, you need to be a whole other kind of connected in this town to be invited to Eamon Awan's casino. That address on the chip will bring you to a street somewhere where one of Awan's men will be. You and whoever else is there will be blindfolded and loaded into a stretch. They'll drive you around, then lead you down into some basement somewhere. Then you get to take off the mask. And have a good old time. They will deliver you back to that spot later, or to your house. Or, in this case, Raven's house."

"How the hell did you guys find out about this?"

"Gotta love our incestuous little town," Cyrus said. "I heard it from someone who heard about it from someone who has been there. But I have heard from reliable sources that it was safe and they had a lot of fun. We wouldn't send you if we thought it was seedy. But we figure it is just crazy enough to pique your interest. Shaking it up might be good, y'know? I hate seeing you like this," Cyrus said, nudging me with his shoulder.

"This isn't you," Reeve agreed. "I get that shit went down and you are feeling it, but don't let it change who you are—"

"Because you're fucking perfect," Cyrus finished for him.

"Oh look at you two. Being all sappy," I told them, forcing a smile because their efforts deserved it.

I had a feeling it was going to take a lot of forcing to get myself out of bed, showered, dressed, and out of the house. But, let's face it, I was the queen of faking things. I could fake entire identities, actual relationships, and no one was ever the wiser.

I could fake the old Wasp for the evening.

Maybe if I did it well enough, I could even convince myself it was true.

"Thank you guys. For coming. I'm usually the one doing the ass-kicking in this family, but I'm happy to know you guys are willing to do it too when I need it."

They left half an hour later, and Raven plied me with cups of coffee as I went through the process of getting myself together.

Something about the ritual of general self-care helped break up some of the dark clouds that had been hanging overhead, letting little slices of light shine through.

It wasn't happy.

It wasn't even status quo.

But it was better than sobbing in the shower.

It was better than barely being able to force myself out of bed.

I guess there was a reason for that old 'fake it 'till you make it' phrase.

"I'm sorry, who are you?" Raven asked when I made my way down the stairs after slipping into the highest pair of heels I owned. They were what I called "sit down shoes," but I figured that I would be spending most of my night at a poker table, so they would work. "The only guest we have staying here has giant mats in her hair and a permanent pillow indent on her cheek."

"Do you think it's too much?" I asked, waving down at the skin-colored silk bow-tied open back dress. The hemline was of the mini variety, and the bodice dipped low, leaving very little to the imagination. It was the sexiest dress I owned. I figured if I was going to do it, I was going to do it right.

"I think it is just enough," Raven shot back. "But hold on. You need something," she told me, getting up, rushing upstairs, coming back down with a simple gold necklace with a small golden bee pendant. "I had this picked out for your next birthday, but I think it completes the look," she told me, going behind me to slip it on. "There. That's perfect. I know you still feel like garbage, but sometimes getting your warpaint on can help. I hope you have a lot of fun."

"Did you see my car pull up?"

"Yeah, they're waiting. Get super wasted and take them for all that they've got. And given the kind of people I hear frequent those types of places, that is a lot. Like a vacation house a lot," she told me, wiggling her brows. By the time the car was dropping me off at the location on the chip, I could feel anticipation starting to bubble up inside.

It was smart of my brothers to pick an illegal casino over something tame like going out to dinner or the movies. The thrill of it was possibly the only thing that could penetrate the thick wall of regret I'd been building inside.

"Oh, now, look at this one," a tall, svelte blonde woman with ice-blue eyes said as I walked in their direction. She was in a pair of champagne-colored slacks and a blue silk top, giving her an air of casual sophistication —not to mention money, judging by the diamonds at her ears.

"If she is coming with us tonight, she's not looking to work for you, Faye," a tall, attractive bald black man in a gray suit told the woman, then turned to give me a smile.

"Aero," he said, extending his hand. "And this is Faye. You are?"

"Wasp," I told them, inclining my chin toward the man walking up behind them.

"Oh, and this is Richard Balefire," Aero introduced.

"You're bringing your girls now, Faye?" Richard Balefire said, inclining his head at me.

"I'm not entirely sure if that is a compliment or insult," I told Richard, getting a smirk from him.

"Faye is a madam," he explained.

"So you think I'm a prostitute," I mused, feeling my lips twitch.

"A very, very expensive call girl," Faye corrected.

"Well then, I guess that's a pretty good compliment."

"You're new here," Richard Balefire concluded.

"I'm not from around here," I told them. "Anymore," I added. "I am just in town for a few weeks. I needed a fun night out."

"What's your game, Wasp?" Aero asked.

"Oh, honey," I cooed, giving him a once over the way the old Wasp would, always running a con even when I wasn't working. "It doesn't matter. I always win," I told him, watching as his smile went a little devilish.

"I bet you do, babe. I bet you do."

"Really, are you sure you don't want a job? A side gig?" Faye asked. "I'm pretty sure you just made Aero come with that look," she added, smirking.

"If you're done trying to recruit, Faye," Richard said, but sounded amused, like he had a soft spot for her, "our ride is here."

"Wasp, I hope you don't mind a blindfold," Aero said, taking one from one of the men who had emerged from the limo, handing out a pile of blindfolds.

"With a sight like you here, I'm sure she is thankful for it," Faye teased, getting a chuckle from Aero.

With that, we all climbed into the limo, putting on our blindfolds, and riding in silence as we seemed to be driven around aimlessly.

I'd grown up in this area. I knew the back roads as well as any local kid who'd ridden their bike around every afternoon after school. As such, while we drove for about half an hour, I was pretty sure I knew the general vicinity of this private location.

We all were helped out, led down a set of stairs.

The next thing I knew, hands were at the back of my head, undoing my blindfold.

And there I was.

In Navesink Bank's invitation-only underground casino.

It didn't have the same cheesy glitz of a casino in Vegas or Atlantic City —all neon lights and harsh colors.

Whoever Eamon Awan was, he clearly had taste.

Everything was in shades of black—some shiny, some matte—with the occasional splash of red. Understated. Upscale. The kind of place millionaires dropped salaries of the average middle-class families in a matter of hours.

"Wow," I said, and just for a single second, that was all that was on my mind.

Only a second though, mind you, because, inevitably, my mind wandered back to Fenway, thinking about how much fun this would have been to enjoy with him. I would sit there winning endlessly. He would keep losing with a smile on his face as I scolded him about wasting so much money.

It would be an amazing experience with him.

But, I reminded myself, I would have to find a way to enjoy it without him. As I would with all future adventures in my life.

"What do you say, Wasp?" Aero asked, offering me his arm. "How about you whip my ass in poker?"

"That is an offer I can't refuse," I told him, being led over to the table exchanging cash for coins as everyone else did.

Our dealer was a silent man in his later mid-life in a pitch-black suit and salt and pepper hair.

"So, Wasp," Richard said a few moments later. "What brings you to Navesink Bank?"

"Oh, I'm visiting with a friend," I told him, arranging my cards.

"And how did you manage to snag an invitation?" Richard asked.

The only spot open was beside Faye who was across from me. I couldn't help but wonder if it would only be the four of us, if this place was that exclusive, or if others would make their way in later, in a different limo.

"A treat from my brothers."

"And they are?" Richard asked. They were probing, and I couldn't' quite figure out if they were just a tight-knit group, or if they were somehow suspicious of me.

"Local outlaw bikers. Henchmen," I supplied, figuring that if they were the kind of people who would be regulars at this casino, that they were also the type who could figure out exactly who I was.

"Oh, that's a yummy group," Faye said, tossing a couple chips in the pot. "They're not clients," she told me, looking at me from under her lashes, "in case you wanted to know."

"I sincerely hope they didn't find themselves so lacking in game that they had to pay for it," I said, smiling.

"You'd be surprised how many men prefer not having to chase. Despite the stereotype. Alright. Who's trust fund am I stealing tonight?" she asked, shooting me a wicked smirk.

Between the two of us, we'd won three rounds before Aero declared he needed a drink before the next hand.

"Can I get you a drink, Wasp? What's your poison?" he asked.

"I—"

"Pink champagne," a voice said behind me. *That* voice. The one that made an ache slice through my chest, the voice I still heard in my ear in quiet moments.

But no.

No way.

He couldn't be there.

He was in freaking Australia.

Even if he did come back to the States, what were the chances that he would be here, in this town, in this underground casino?

Slim to none.

Yet, there was no denying it was him.

I knew that voice as well as I knew my own.

My body was already warming, thawing, at the sound of it.

"Unless that was a lie too, *darling*," he said, making my stomach plummet.

Across the table from me, one of Faye's well-shaped brows lifted, intrigued.

"I have a feeling it's a tequila night, Aero," I told him as Fenway moved out toward my side, going around the table. "Thank you," I added, my gaze following Fenway as he took the empty seat beside Faye.

"That's a nice dress, Wasp," he added, his cool gaze on me.

Cool.

That was the right word.

Cool.

This wasn't fun, easy-going Fenway.

This was the darker, sexier one.

And if I wasn't mistaken, he was pissed.

Did he know?

Surely not.

I was very careful about my reputation.

"And who might you be?" Faye asked him, giving him an assessing glance.

"You mean he hasn't been one of your clients?" Richard asked, smirking. "With his reputation with women? This is Fenway Arlington," he said.

"Richard. It's been a while."

"Still Scotch?" Richard asked, rising, buttoning his suit jacket.

"Always," Fenway said, gaze barely leaving me.

"So how do you two know each other?" Faye asked, clearly picking up on the tension, and seemingly enjoying it.

"We met in Paris," Fenway supplied since my tongue felt paralyzed in my mouth. "Toured the world together," he added as I numbly accepted my drink from Aero as he returned, taking his seat, oblivious to the dark mood around the table.

"Did you do anything fun?" Aero asked, shuffling his chips around.

"Would you like to tell them about the cave in Bali, darling, or should I?"

"Scotch," Richard cut in, saving me from having to answer. "Fenway, are you still a terrible player?" he asked as the dealer started handing out cards.

"Apparently," Fenway agreed, and I was pretty sure everyone but Faye and I missed his double meaning.

"So, Wasp," Aero said a moment later, shifting in his seat, sensing the tension, but not able to pinpoint it, just wanting to mitigate it. "What is it you do for a living? And no need to pretend here. We are all open about our... more unsavory dealings. Nothing leaves this table."

"I'm a dog trainer," I claimed, my go-to, and also what I needed to say with Fenway's gaze boring into me like it was.

"Really?" another voice asked from behind me, making me tense up as I felt the owner of it moving close. So close, in fact, that he rested a hand at the back of my chair, knuckles touching my bare back as his other hand moved around me. Expensive, spicy cologne teased my nose as his fingers traced down the length of my cold chain, toying with the bee pendant. "That's not the way I hear it, Wasp," he said in a delicious accent—English or maybe even East African—making me tense again. "The word on the street is our new guest here is a conwoman," the stranger claimed, making bile rise up in my throat as Fenway's eyes widened. Surprised? Hurt? Both? I didn't know. But this man refused to leave it at that. "Known for sweetheart cons, if I'm not mistaken," he added, finally releasing my pendant, moving out from behind me, going around the table, giving me my first sight of him.

Eamon Awan, I decided.

The man looked like a model with his Middle Eastern coloring, his inky black hair, his pristine shape-up, and his short beard. He wore all black, giving him an intimidating look that was right there in his surprising light green eyes.

"See!" Faye declared as my gaze followed our host, wondering why he was outing me, what he stood to gain from that, keeping my focus there because I couldn't stomach the look of disgust I was sure was on Fenway's face right about then. "I knew I liked you," Faye added, smiling. "This is Eamon, by the way," she said. "The owner of this lovely establishment."

"You'll learn to forgive me," Eamon declared, keeping unnerving eye contact with me as he moved behind Faye, clamping a hand on Fenway's shoulder.

"I'm not so sure I will," I told him, voice tight.

"You can live a lie all you like outside of these walls," he told me. "But in here, we air our dirty laundry. It keeps everyone from being able to use anything against the other guests."

From a business perspective, I could respect that. If I was a true guest here, a regular like the others seemed to be, I would be appreciative of that sort of measure.

But as a woman sitting across from a man who had been her most recent mark, who was in love with him despite not believing I was capable, I was furious.

"Yes, well, I think I am no longer going to be a guest of your *fine* establishment," I snapped, rising, turning, making my way toward the door.

"Hey, you can't—" a guard warned me, hand curling around my arm.

I wasn't anyone's martial arts Barbie.

But I'd taken a couple self-defense classes with Raven as a sort of business move, always wanting to make sure we could take care of ourselves and each other should a job go south.

I'd only ever needed to use my memorized moves once in the past. A part of me was convinced that the only reason I'd been successful was because the man had been tanked.

And my advantage here seemed to be that this man didn't think I would turn on him.

Because he didn't even try to defend himself when I planted my hands on his shoulders, using his body as leverage to ram my knee up between his legs.

I didn't pause as he collapsed, just dashed up the stairs, threw the door open at the top, rushing past the guards there, men who likely never expected anyone to disobey the rules, to rush out, to ruin their secret location.

I didn't give a damn about their location.

I never planned on returning.

I just had to get the hell out of there.

I had to get away from him.

I couldn't face him now that he knew the truth.

The only reason my job worked in the first place was because no one ever saw me again.

And having to face the one mark I'd screwed up and gotten unprofessional with? Yeah, I couldn't do this.

I didn't get far.

It was naive of me to think I would.

A hand closed around my arm, pulling me to a stop.

"While I admire your willingness to try to run in those heels, Wasp, you're going to break something," Fenway's voice said, barely winded. "Do you really think you can run away from this?" he asked, hand loosening enough to allow him to move in front of me, looking down at me. "Look at me," he demanded, voice firm, brooking no argument.

Sucking in a deep breath, I forced my chin to lift, my gaze to move to his face, knowing this confrontation was going to need to play out. Whether I liked it or not. No matter how much it would hurt.

"How did you find me?"

"I keep a fixer firm on the payroll."

"Why does that not surprise me?"

"When you left without a word, I came back here to them. I wanted to find you, so I could figure out what possessed you to up and leave in such a way."

"How did you know I was here?" I pressed. "At the casino," I clarified.

To that, his lips curved up ever so slightly as he reached into his pocket with his free hand, producing a chip.

"Your best friend thought I might need this," he said.

"Raven gave me up?" I asked, the words not making any sense. She would never do that. She always had my back.

"You can't be mad at her."

"Actually, I can. She had no right."

"What about me, darling? What rights did I have in all of this?" he asked, chin lifting, daring me to try to lie to him again.

"I don't want to do this, Fenway," I told him, hearing the crack in my voice, not trusting the floodgates to stay strong. Not with him standing there looking at me with accusation and—much more devastating—pain in his eyes.

"I'm sorry, darling, but that's just too fucking bad," he told me, tone cutting.

"Wasp, Fenway," Eamon's voice joined us, making me turn to find him approaching, arms raised. "I see you two have a thing going on right now. But I feel I need to warn you that you are standing on gang territory with a ten-thousand-dollar Rolex and a two grand gold necklace on," he said, making me glance around, seeing the group of young guys on the next corner over. "You might have some moves, babe," he went on, looking at me, "but I don't think you can knee them all in the cock at once. Why don't you take my car back to, well, anywhere else but here," he added, brow lifting, making it clear we didn't have a choice.

"He can take the car. I will get a ride."

"Oh, but I would enjoy it much more if you two had to endure each other on the ride back to the pick-up location," Eamon told us, snapping, making his guards move toward us.

The bigger guard moved over toward Fenway first, grabbing his arm.

Fenway stared daggers at me as he was led away. The other guard grabbed my arm, starting to pull me in the direction of the limo as well.

"You're a real asshole, you know that, right?" I asked Eamon as I moved past him.

"I do, babe, I do know that," he told me, lips curving up like he enjoyed my anger. "Don't bother trying to plot your vengeance, sweetheart," he told me in that annoyingly delicious accent of his. "I don't do love."

With that and nothing else, I was shoved none too ceremoniously into the back of the limo, making me half-topple over Fenway who made no move to help me get back up as I tried to get as far away from him as possible.

The car lurched to life as the silence in the back became nearly unbearable. I kept my gaze out the side window, willing my stomach to tolerate riding sideways because it gave me an excuse not to look in his direction.

"Don't," I demanded, catching his lips starting to part.

"I'm afraid you're not in control anymore, Wasp," he told me, voice low, lethal. And, damnit, a little too sexy given the situation. "We're going to do this. And you're going to give me answers. I deserve that, at least."

It was hard to argue with that.

Still, I felt like I had to.

I had to gain some ground. I was stumbling on the small plot I was standing on.

"Look, everyone who gets conned is embarrassed and angry. It's natural. I get it. But that's just how it is. You'll come to grips with it."

Being snippy—even if I was faking it—was the wrong move with Fenway's apparently volatile mood.

One second, he was in his seat.

The next, he was shooting across the space, dropping down next to me, fingers snagging my chin, forcing me to face him.

"Tell me, Wasp, do you fuck all your marks?" he asked, voice tight, barely holding onto his anger.

The revulsion in his face was a hot knife to the stomach.

I didn't recognize my voice when it came out, small, weak, choked.

"No."

"I don't know if I should believe you," he said, jaw so tight a muscle ticked there.

"I know you're angry, Fenway," I told him, wincing, "But you're hurting me," I told him, trying to pull my chin away.

His hand yanked backward like I'd burned him, face jolting back as though I'd struck him.

He wasn't a violent man.

He didn't hurt people. At least not on purpose. Which only served to prove just how badly I'd affected him.

"Why?" he asked, voice small, pained, another stab wound in my chest. "Why me? What did I ever do? What did you want from me? And don't," he cut me off when I started to speak. "Don't try to tell me it doesn't matter. It matters. You fucked with my life, Wasp. That matters. I deserve to know why."

I swallowed back the plea for him to forgive me that bubbled up and threatened to burst out, steeling my voice.

"I was hired for the job."

"Hired by whom?"

"I don't know who. I got an email through my website. They didn't give me much information other than your name, whereabouts, and the fee they were going to pay me to do the job."

"And what was the job?" he asked, eyes accusing. I deserved it, but it still hurt to see in those eyes that had only ever looked at me with kindness and wonder and humor and affection.

"To make you fall in love with me. And then break your heart," I told him, feeling the sting of tears, blinking them back. It wasn't the time or place. I just had to hold it together for a little while longer. We weren't that far from the pick-up location.

"Why?"

"I can't answer that, Fenway. I didn't ask. But, usually, this kind of thing is because you hurt someone else," I told him, eyes begging him to understand, to see this through a lens other than his pain. Maybe then he could see mine. That was selfish, but I couldn't help it.

He had a right to his pain.

But he wasn't the only one hurting.

I felt like my heart was getting crushed to dust inside my chest.

"I haven't been a saint," he admitted, eyes cold. "But I have never been cruel enough to make someone love me, then fuck them over for the hell of it. Oh, forgive me. Not for the hell of it. For something much worse. For money."

I couldn't... I just couldn't do this anymore.

"Hey," I called, seeing us drive right past the pick-up location. "Hey," I called to the driver again, turning to look at him. "You're supposed to let me out there. Hey!" I yelled when he ignored me, just pushing the button so the privacy window slid into place. "Let me out!" I shrieked, flying at the window, fists pounding on it. "Let me out, damnit. I have to get out of here," I added, hysteria rising up and bubbling over.

I never understood people who lost their ever-loving shit. Until that moment. When I was yelling and slamming my hands against a window, tears flooding my eyes.

"Let me out!" I tried again, voice catching.

"Hey, hey," Fenway's voice called, hands grabbing my wrists, pulling them away from the window. "Calm down," he demanded.

"I need to get out of this car. I can't breathe in here," I added, yanking against his hold. "I can't breathe," I hissed, my throat tight, invisible hands closing around it, cutting off my air, making my pulse pound, my face feel tingly.

It was just a panic attack, I tried to reason with myself. It wasn't a big deal. I was going to be fine. But I sure as hell didn't *feel* fine. I felt like my heart was going to break through my ribcage, like it was going to pound out of my chest.

"You need to take a breath," Fenway reasoned, voice calm, frustratingly kind.

I couldn't take him being nice.

Not after what I'd done.

"Don't," I demanded, trying to pull away. "You don't have to be nice to me," I told him, yanking out of his hold, throwing myself across the car to the other seat, hand closing around my throat.

"Wasp..."

"I get it, alright? I fucking get it," I snapped, breathing coming out in strange strobes. "I'm a bitch, okay? I'm an asshole. I hurt people for a living. You hate me. I get it, okay? I get it," I added, voice cracking as the floodgates finally failed, tears overflowing, spilling down my cheeks in fast, hot waves, blurring my vision.

I've had a lot of low moments in my life.

Havig a panic attack and hysterical breakdown at the same time in front of the only man I'd ever cared for? This was the lowest of the lows.

"I don't hate you," Fenway's voice said a moment later, low, almost hard to hear over my frantic breathing, the sniffling as I tried to pull myself back together.

"Bullshit," I shot back, swiping at the tears that refused to stop cascading down my cheeks.

"I wish I did," he said as though I hadn't spoken. "It would be a lot easier if I hated you."

"Of course you hate me," I said, placing my elbows on my thighs, pressing my head in my hands. "*I* hate me."

That admission, something I had been trying to tamp down for weeks, this realization that was too ugly to admit even to myself, seemed to create a crack right down the center of me, making my voice catch on a God-awful shrieking, dying animal noise.

"Alright," Fenway said, voice soft, making me realize he had moved across to my side. "Okay," he hushed, arms reaching for me, holding on even when I tried to jerk away, pulling me until my legs draped over his, until my face was tucked against his chest.

I had no right to take comfort from him right then. A small part of me—the sliver that was still capable of rational thinking—knew that. The other part was too busy crumbling to care that my fingers were curling into his suit jacket, that my tears were soaking through his shirt. "Wasp, it's alright," he told me, voice a little louder, trying to break through.

"No, it's not," I managed to choke out before the sobs became the loud and utterly humiliating sort. Even knowing that, even feeling that, I couldn't seem to stop them, they overtook me completely.

Fenway said nothing after that, just held me tighter, like maybe he thought if he squeezed me hard enough, he could keep me from falling apart.

It was too late for that.

I was dust.

Nothing could put me back together again in the exact same form. I had no idea what I was going to look like after all of this, but I had a feeling it wasn't going to be pretty. Just a vague facsimile of the person I had been before.

"I'm sorry," I whispered into his neck what felt like forever later, when my insides felt dry as sandpaper, when my face felt raw from the tears.

"I know you are," he told me, fingers sifting into my hair. I had no right to enjoy that either. But I did. God, I did.

"I've never slept with a mark," I told him, truth spilling out. What was the use trying to protect myself anymore? There wasn't much left of me to protect. "That's not how it works. I don't get involved. I don't get attached," I added, struggling to get that last word out.

"Attached," he repeated.

"Yes, attached. I don't do that. Ever. Not on a job. Not in my personal life. I don't do it. It's not me."

"But?" he prompted, sensing it hanging there in the air.

Squeezing my eyes tight like the admission would somehow be easier if I did so, I let the truth slip out. "But I felt more like myself with you than I think I ever have."

"That's why you had to leave? Because it wasn't just a job?"

"It was a job."

"But not just a job. You weren't just a conwoman. And I wasn't just a mark."

"You were supposed to be."

"But I wasn't," he pressed, hands sinking into my shoulders, forcing me backward.

"No," I admitted, gaze lowered, unable to give him the truth with those eyes boring into me.

"When did it stop being a con?"

"I don't know," I admitted.

"Before the cave?" he pressed, refusing to let up. And after what I had done, I had no right to deny him the truth.

"Yes. I think sometime between arriving in Bali and the pool. And then more after the pool and during the day that followed. It was more me than it wasn't me, if that makes sense," I said, gaze on his throat.

"When wasn't it you?" he asked, hands settling on my hips.

"When I was pushing you away," I admitted. "When I was picking fights. That's what you're supposed to do. Reel them in. Then push them away, keep them coming back."

"Keep me coming back," he corrected.

"Yes, you too."

"Why?"

"Why what?"

"Why do you do it?"

"I get paid for it. I am good at it."

"Why, Wasp?" he pressed, one hand going to my chin, gently forcing it up.

"Because some men get away with things they shouldn't be allowed to. Because I can help some women get even."

"And because you get to use your pretty against them," he mused, daring me to object. "It didn't escape me how you flipped whenever I called you beautiful. And now I am thinking that is because you were born pretty, right? Came out that way. Got prettier every year. Pretty enough that no one gave a shit if you had anything else to offer."

'They still don't," I said, shrugging, trying not to be bitter about it.

"I do," he corrected. "Yeah, you're gorgeous. I notice that. It's a factor. You like how I look too, darling."

"That's fair," I agreed.

"But that isn't it. I didn't keep you around because you were pretty. Pretty is a dime a dozen. I'd have gotten bored of pretty before we left Paris. The night we met, I was surrounded by pretty," he reminded me. "I walked away from them for you. And kept coming back for more."

"Yeah, because that's how it works, Fenway. Catch and release. It's a trick."

"It wasn't that I couldn't have you."

"That is all it could have been."

"No. There was something about you. I could feel it the moment you walked in. Before I even saw you. The air changed when you walked in that bar. Maybe you think all men see is the pretty, but there is something else too. The way you carry yourself. That look in your eyes. Everyone projects a vibe. It's why women can spot a creep from a room away. And maybe I saw all that pretty, Wasp. It's hard to ignore. But that vibe was what pulled me away from my table. I knew there was something there. I wanted to get closer to it."

"And then," I prompted, needing more.

"And then you stopped with the bullshit long enough for me to get to know you a little. And the more I knew, the more I liked. This," he said, running a fingertip down my jaw. "This is all wrapping paper. It's pretty. It draws your eye. But what you really want is underneath all that. Christmas would be pretty boring if all you had were piles of pretty wrapping paper."

"I like that analogy," I decided, lips curving up slightly.

"Tell me it was more real than it was fake," he demanded, vulnerability a breathtaking thing on his face.

"It was a lot more real than it was fake. It was almost all real. I had to leave because it was getting too real," I told him. "I knew that if I stayed any longer, I was going to tell you. And that even if I did, there was no chance for us. Because you would never be able to trust me again."

"Trust is a funny thing," he mused. "Sometimes you think it's been broken, when it's just been tested."

"How could you call this tested? I lied to you. I took money to lie to you. I met you and I had every intention from day one of hurting you. That's not a test."

"No, but maybe this is," he suggested. "Getting it all out there."

"There's no way you could go on and believe me in the future."

"No? I think that's my place to decide, darling, not yours."

"You couldn't possibly want me now, knowing what I did."

To that, a humorless smile pulled at his lips as he reached into his pocket for a handkerchief, gently swiping at my face. "You have a good hand with the makeup, but it's not waterproof. You look like you haven't slept since you walked away from me," he told me, touching the smudges I knew were under my eyes. "I think you've probably beat yourself up enough about what happened. You don't need me to pile on."

"It's not about what I need. You have a right to pile on. I did something awful to you."

"Did you, though?" he asked, tucking the makeup-smeared handkerchief away. "Falling for you wasn't so bad," he teased, lips quirking up. "One might be even able to argue that I quite enjoyed it."

"Quite," I scoffed, shaking my head.

"I do need to know one thing, though."

"What's that?"

"What's your real name?" he asked.

"Oh, anything but that," I groaned, knocking my forehead into his shoulder.

"I'm afraid it's a deal-breaker, darling. How bad could it be? Do you have some old lady's name or something?"

To that, I snorted, taking a deep breath, sitting back. "It's Bella."

"Bella. Meaning 'beautiful,'" he said, eyes shining, understanding why I hated it.

"In both Italian *and* Latin," I agreed, rolling my eyes. "My parents really had to add insult to injury on that one."

"It's a beautiful name. Even if I think Wasp suits you a little bit better. Maybe I will only call you Bella when I want to piss you off."

"You're planning on doing that often?"

"Just about every chance I get," he promised, eyes bright. "You're kind of sexy when you're pissed off," he told me, smile devilish.

"So you plan on seeing me in the future," I said, needing confirmation, too scared to let myself hope without hearing the words.

"Seeing you? Yeah," he said, hand slipping up my side, over my ribs, a place he knew I was sensitive. "And doing a lot more than just seeing you," he told me, fingers moving up, teasing the low bodice of my dress, not even touching my skin, but managing to send goosebumps washing over my skin in anticipation.

"Fenway, be serious for one minute," I demanded.

"Oh, darling, if there is one thing I am serious about," he started, eyes going molten, "it's about making you do... yeah that," he said when his hand slipped under my bodice, closing over my breast, his thumb moving over my hardened nipple, making me moan. "Now, isn't that better than talking?" he asked, using his thumb and forefinger to roll my nipple, making need bloom in my core.

"We need to talk," I insisted even as my hips did a little shimmy, moving higher on his lap, feeling his cock pressing against me, making me let out an airy sigh.

"We can talk," he said, one hand sinking into my ass, grinding me against him. "About how wet you are for me," he told me, jerking his hips upward, making his cock hit me right where I needed him, dragging a ragged moan out of me. His other hand went behind my neck, dragging me closer. "We can talk about how we are going to keep you quiet when I fuck you, so the driver doesn't hear," he told me, hand moving from my ass to slip between my thighs, sliding under my panties.

"Fenway, please," I whimpered, rocking against him. "It's been too long," I added, instantly regretting those days when I'd held him at arms' length.

Luckily, Fenway was just as out of control, not wasting any time slipping on protection, ripping my barely-there panties, and guiding me up so I could slide down onto his length.

"Fuck," I whimpered, taking a deep breath.

"Yeah, you never faked that," he told me, smirking as he jerked his hips upward into me as I started working in slow circles.

It wasn't long before all control snapped, leaving me riding him hard, fast, his hand crushed over my mouth to muffle my cries as I got closer, as I flew over the edge, crashing down into my orgasm.

Fenway followed on the tail-end of my orgasm, hissing out my name—my real name. And maybe I didn't hate the sound of it on his lips.

"You realize Eamon Awan probably has a camera in here, and just watched us get it on," I told him, pulling backward after I caught my breath.

"Yes, well, the poor ugly bastard probably can't get any himself.

"Ugly—" I started.

"Work with me here, darling. I have some pride," he told me, grinning.

"Oh, right. Yeah. He's just... hideous. If there was a race of aliens that were about to go extinct and needed a man's sperm, and the women came down, and Eamon was all the world had to offer, they'd probably decide they'd rather let their race die out."

"I know, right? The poor man. I clearly could not imagine being so unfortunate-looking," he said, grinning.

"Seriously, though. He probably has cameras in here. Why the hell else are we driving around Navesink Bank in circles?" I asked, looking over his shoulder at a building we'd already passed. "Unless he plans on killing us," I concluded. "You know... for figuring out his super secret location."

"Hm," Fenway mused as I climbed off of his lap, tucking my panties into his pocket. "Maybe he'd be more forgiving if we went back, and I dropped a small country's GDP at one of his tables," he suggested, zipping up, then sliding to the side, knocking calmly on the glass. "I have a hundred grand burning a hole in my pocket," he told the driver when the window slid down.

"I'll see what he says," the driver told us, closing the partition again.

Fifteen minutes later, we were back at a table, Fenway making easy business conversation with Richard Balefire as I tried to pretend to ignore Faye's knowing look.

"It's clever, you know," she told me as she shifted her cards around.

"What is?" I asked.

"A dog trainer," she told me, smirking.

"Yes, well, you know how they behave when they are let off their leashes," I told her, getting a humorless laugh.

"Chasing after every bitch in heat," she suggested.

"Well, yes. But not if they're scared of having their balls chopped off," I added, shooting Fenway a saccharine smile as I rearranged my hand, knowing I'd won again.

"Oh, I'm not a cheater," he said, eyes narrowing as I laid down my cards for him to see. "Unlike *some* people," he added, raising his brows at me. "There's no way you have that hand."

"Oh, hush, and hand over the twenty grand, *darling*," I added, getting a big smile out of him. Eye crinkles and all.

I could get used to that look directed at me.

Maybe, if I was lucky, I could.

After I was done taking all his money, that is.

Priorities.

FIFTEEN

Fenway

I imagine other men might have run for their lives when her truth came out. Perhaps that was even the most prudent of choices.

But, really, when had anyone ever accused me of being careful?

Besides, many jobs were steeped in suffering of some sort. Everything from food production to finance to fast fashion. There was harm done whether it was human or animal or environmental. It would be hypocritical to judge her for causing harm if I didn't go out of my way to blame others for their negative impact on the world.

And on top of all of that, there was the simple fact that I believed her. Women could fake things. And fake them well. That panic attack and breakdown in the limo? That was real. She couldn't have faked that. The Wasp I knew would have been too mortified even to try. Her mask was the cool, calm, and collected sort.

She cared about me.

If it wasn't love yet, it was heading in that direction.

She left because she was moments away from telling me the truth. And she was terrified that by doing so, she would not only ruin any future since she thought I couldn't trust her, but also lose out on the money. It was the definition of a damned-if-you-do, damned-if-you-don't situation.

I didn't blame her for taking stock and running.

Lesser men would have wanted groveling, would have wanted her begging for forgiveness, tearfully swearing she would never lie to me ever again. My forgiveness didn't need to be earned on the back of her pride. If your ego required someone else to make themselves small to be able to welcome them back into your life, maybe it was time to reevaluate your relationship dynamic.

After she took me—and Aero—for all we were worth, we went back to my room at the hotel, falling into bed and each other for hours before her phone started—and refused to stop—ringing.

"It's probably Raven," Wasp told me, grumbling as she rolled off my chest, walking bare-ass naked out into the living space to grab her phone out of her purse. I went ahead and enjoyed the view before climbing out of bed and following, going for my own phone, texting Alvy, telling them to send Raven flowers and set up a meeting with Richard Balefire, half paying attention to Wasp's conversation that started with her trying to sound firm while telling her friend she was in big trouble, then slipping into excited whispers as she recounted the evening.

"She wants to officially meet you," Wasp told me after hanging up. "Expect very harsh judgment. And some veiled threats."

"Hate to break it to you, darling, but your best friend is more of the direct threat sort of woman."

"She already did it? And I missed it? Damn. Did she threaten to jam something up your urethra? Because that's my threat."

"It involved a boating accident that would never be traced back to her."

"She's perfectly capable of that," Wasp declared, moving over toward me, dropping down on my lap, reaching for the scotch I had discarded before the casino.

"I don't need Raven's threats. You scare me enough," I told her, tugging her hair.

"As I should," she agreed, giving me the glass to finish as she leaned her head on my shoulder. "So, aren't you at least a little bit curious?" she asked.

"About what?"

"Who hired me," she said, shaking her head a little. "That was a lot of money. I don't think your little trust fund chasers would have been able to bankroll the job.

"You don't have a check?"

"We did it crypto. Normally, they'd pay cash or Paypal me. But because it was so much, I wanted it in crypto. It's a bit more complicated to turn it back into USD, but it saved me from having to worry as much about the IRS. I have enough of an issue explaining my profession to them every year."

"You actually pay your taxes?" I asked, snorting. "What criminal pays taxes?"

"The kind who don't want to get Capone'd."

"Capone'd?"

"You know, they technically got away with all their crimes, but they threw tax evasion charges at them."

"So do you actually tell them you're a dog trainer?" I asked, teasing.

"I do, actually," she said, smiling up at me. "I am a very expensive dog trainer. But, of course, I am worth every penny."

"What was your plan for when you were done with dog training?"

"I have been carefully investing. I was hoping to maybe partially retire, find some side gig that I found fun and interesting. But, apparently, I could have a very successful future as a high-end call-girl," she mused, pursing her lips. "Perhaps I should be giving Faye a call..."

"I don't think so, darling. No one is going to get to put their hands on you but me from now on," I told her. I'd never been a possessive person in the past. But I'd also never had a woman as a steady fixture in my life, a woman I could picture a future with.

"Well, clearly, if this becomes a thing, a future with contracts kind of thing," she said, pussyfooting around the word 'marriage,' "I would have to find something to bring in money. Since you are on a one-man-mission to lose your entire fortune."

"Oh, but what a fun way to go into destitution," I declared, getting a chuckle out of her. "This plan for semi-retirement," I started, knowing this was a tricky area. "When was that supposed to start?"

"I didn't have an exact date. I figured there would come a day when I just knew I was done. By then, I should have saved up enough to take a year or two off to figure out my future plans."

"So you have a year or two?"

"Well, thanks to your job, absolutely."

"Good. Because you're officially retired," I told her, watching as she arched a brow at me. She knew she was too, but this was not a woman who liked being told what to do. "Come on. We have to check out all those vending machines. You said you would come with me."

"I believe I said it would be fun to go with you, not that I would."

"Come on. You know you want to." She did, too. Her eyes were already bright with excitement

"We can't just jet off to China."

"Sure we can. Alvy brought the jet back to the States for me."

"That's not what I meant," she said, rolling her eyes, but she was smiling. "You have to meet Raven and Roman. And if my brothers catch wind of your presence, they will want to size you up as well. We will have to stay in the States for a little bit."

"Well, if we are going to stay for a while, maybe we can plan a trip for you to meet someone too."

"Your grandma?" she asked, looking touched.

"Yes. She's up in Connecticut. We can fly up after we spend some time with your family. We can even fly... commercial," I said, pretending to gulp hard.

"I have a much better idea."

As it turned out, her better idea was to take Wanda.

I learned something new about Wasp on the road trip up to my grandmother's estate.

She drove like a church lady on her way to a potluck with a giant pot of soup—without a lid—on the floor of the passenger set.

"There is a gas pedal, you know, darling," I told her, getting a withering glance. "Here I was thinking you'd be the sort to say fuck it to speed limits since you know you can charm yourself out of a ticket. But here you are, hands at ten and two."

"Have you ever driven a school bus?"

"I have not."

"Then shush," she demanded, taking a turn at about three miles an hour.

Her skoolie—aka Wanda—was nothing like I thought it would be. Namely, not cold and oppressive, tight-feeling.

She'd clearly done the work to make sure it was airy and open feeling, so that despite it's minuscule size, I didn't feel like the walls were closing in on me. I could see how she and Raven had comfortably lived here for years.

Even if I much preferred flying and using the yacht, to be perfectly honest. If for no other reason than that we would actually make it there in good time rather than a day later than planned. Not that my grandmother would mind, of course. She was used to me being late.

"This neighborhood is silently judging Wanda. She can feel it," Wasp declared a couple hours later after we finally turned into my grandmother's gated community, getting a raised brow from the guard.

"They probably just think you're casing the joint. Driving four miles an hour and everything," I teased, getting a smirk from her. "This is the one," I told her, pointing to the maple tree-lined property.

The house was set far back from the street as they all were, a towering French country style home with pristine white bound and batten siding and black shutters. My grandmother was particularly fond of her vibrant hydrangea bushes in white, pink, purple, and light green. Apparently, their whole marriage, my grandfather had claimed snowball bushes were 'lowbrow,' and he refused to have any on a single one of the family properties.

I admired the ultimate fuck-you move of her ordering her bushes the week after his burial.

They were thriving now, lush, in full bloom, bees buzzing around them happily.

She would have fresh cuts of them scattered around the house, in practically every single room, sitting on tabletops or windowsills.

"You know, for being so massive, it is still somehow homey-looking," Wasp decided, slipping into her heels. She'd already ducked into the bathroom to slip into a simple white sundress with oversize black buttons down the front. It was demure by any standards—especially hers—but, to me, it was maybe the sexiest thing I'd ever seen her in. "You're sure I shouldn't pull my hair up?" she asked, tossing some of the wild mass over her shoulder. "I know I have decidedly *un*refined hair."

"I like it that way," I assured her, taking her hand, pulling her onto her feet, pressing a kiss to her temple. "You look beautiful. And you have no reason to be nervous."

"No? The matriarch of one of our country's old money families is going to be scrutinizing every inch of me from the childbearing potential of my hips to my tacky nail polish color. I think I have a reason to worry."

She'd been fretting about the nail polish in a bright red color that she'd wanted to pull over and wipe off.

"My grandmother is partial to red nail polish. It was another thing my grandfather hated. Red nail polish, apparently, was for street walkers."

"Well, I have a very attractive street-walker position waiting for me should I need it," she teased, taking a deep breath, then taking my hand as I led her up the paver driveway. "Also, can I repeat that I love your grandmother's style. Doing absolutely everything her overbearing husband told her not to while they were married. She's a badass."

"That she is," I agreed. I'd never been able to see it while my grandfather was around, when she was under his thumb, when she bowed to his wishes. But when he was gone, she really became her own woman. And she was a fearsome woman to behold.

"Mary-Ellen," I greeted the middle-aged woman who had been my grandmother's housekeeper for over a decade. "I like the red," I told her, meaning her hair. It had been dishwater brown since I'd met her. The red made her blue-green eyes pop.

"I never thought I'd see the day when you brought a girl home," Mary-Ellen said, shaking her head, giving Wasp a warm smile. "Can I get you something to drink?" she asked as we moved into the entryway.

"An entire bottle of vodka with some crushed Ambien around the rim?" Wasp quipped, making Mary-Ellen chuckle.

"Don't worry, honey. Charlotte is a fair woman. She is waiting for you in the solarium."

With that, she was gone, leaving me to lead Wasp through the house.

"Hey, you can't bring me to a certifiable mansion and not let me gawk a little," she demanded when my hand pressed into her lower back, pulling her along with me.

What can I say?

I was eager to get the introductions started.

My grandmother had been the only family member I ever felt like gave a damn about me. Even after she freed me from Avon Mills, she'd never batted an eye to my increasingly outlandish antics. She never faulted me for going wild after being kept so contained my whole life. I guess because she understood that feeling all too well.

I had plenty of extended family, but my grandmother was my only close relation. I found I was anxious to let her meet the woman I was starting to see a future with. Not to get her approval, per se, but to share something exciting with her, something and someone who was becoming important to me.

"I promise you can gawk all you want later. But let's go say hello first," I told Wasp, giving her ass a tiny pat before putting my hand back to the small of her back as we stepped into the opening of the conservatory, a sprawling space of gleaming windows, a myriad of houseplants, and all white furniture.

My grandmother was seated on one of the chairs, a teacup perched on her knee.

A woman of eighty-four, she could have easily passed for twenty years younger. She'd always been tall and lean, dressing in casual cream slacks and solid silk blouses. Today, she had on a dove gray which went well with her perfectly style shoulder-length gray hair. Her face was etched with some years, but she'd aged gracefully, and there was a keen, intelligent look to her bright green eyes.

"Fenway, handsome as ever," she greeted, arm out, ushering me forward to press a kiss to each of her cheeks. "And the woman who could finally slow you down," she added, smiling at Wasp. "Bella, it was, correct?"

"Yes," Wasp agreed, shifting her feet. "It's nice to meet you. Fenway has told me a bunch of amazing stories about you. I have to say, I am a big fan of your spite-garden," she said, smiling.

The big smile that spread across my grandmother's face was all I needed to see to know she already approved.

"Spite-garden, I like that. Please, have a seat. Would you like some tea?" she asked as we sat down on the couch. "Mine has a little brandy in it," she added in a low voice. "But don't tell Mary-Ellen, she doesn't approve. It can be our little secr—and *that* is why I do not approve of day drinking, children," she cut off abruptly, waggling her finger at us, her eyes dancing, making Wasp and I turn to see Mary-Ellen making her way in with a tea set.

Wasp had to press her lips together to keep from laughing as Mary-Ellen turned and my grandmother produced a flask, slipping a little more into her cup, then quickly tucking it away.

"I made some of those bergamot madeleines you are so fond of, if you'd like some," Mary-Ellen offered. Never having had a mother to do the mothering type things like cooking and baking for me, I appreciated that Mary-Ellen had always treated me like one of her many children when I was around.

"I hope you made more than last time," I told her, shaking my head.

"Yes, how could I have been so stingy? Only making you three dozen," Mary-Ellen shot back, smiling. "I will bring some in."

With her departure, Wasp settled her teacup and saucer on her thigh, looking as prim as a lady at a garden party.

"So," my grandmother started, making our gazes shoot in her direction. "Wasp," she said, making Wasp stiffen, and I could practically hear her thoughts. *We didn't tell her my nickname.* "Tell me, when, exactly, did it stop being a job, and turn into something real?"

Wasp's eyes were round, her lips parted.

"Grandmother, what are—" I started, getting cut off.

"The plan truly was just to teach him a lesson, my dear. But I must admit, I'm not all-together put off by this outcome either."

And right then, a moment later than Wasp realized what was going on, I did as well.

My grandmother.

That had been Wasp's client.

That was who bankrolled her trip to Paris, who had sicced her on unsuspecting me.

"Oh my God," Wasp hissed, putting her teacup back down on the tray. "Oh my *God*," she said again.

"You hired Wasp?" I asked, recovering before Wasp, who was staring at my grandmother like she'd grown another head and it was cursing her out in a different language.

"I did, my dear, I did. I'm afraid I have been too lenient with you," she said, looking at me. "Yes, you were practically a grown man when I got you out of that hellhole, but it was my place to impart some wisdom in you. While I may have accomplished in some ways, I failed you terribly in others. Namely, when it came to relationships. I stood by and let you believe the disposable way you treated women was acceptable. It is not. It never was. When this lovely young woman's name was tossed around at a charity event I had gone to earlier this year, it got me thinking. I had an opportunity to teach you a lesson."

"You wanted her to break my heart," I clarified. Sure, my grandmother could be old school at times, believing a swift kick in the ass did more in a moment than thinking and talking could in a decade, but she'd never been someone who went behind your back to accomplish something. She'd always been more in-your-face about things she was passionate about.

"I did," she agreed, nodding. "I could talk until I was blue in the face about how to treat women, about how to approach relationships. But I know you, my dear, it would have gone in one ear and out the other. I figured I had to get inventive with my methods. And, luckily, this young lady provides a much needed service to society."

"Provided," I clarified. "She's retiring."

"I have an offer to be a high-priced call-girl," Wasp volunteered, getting a smile from my grandmother.

"Yes, well, it is always smart to have a back-up career, should you need it. I never imagined this pairing, but the more time I have to think about it, the more I like it," she concluded, looking between us. "I have a feeling this woman isn't going to let you get away with anything."

"She thinks I am careless with my money."

"A toddler would know you are careless with your money," Wasp said, rolling her eyes. "He rented out an entire park in Bali when we were there."

"As ostentatious as that might have been, I have to admit, I am not disappointed that you seem prone to grand romantic gestures, my dear," she said, giving me a soft smile. "Every woman deserves a man who will spoil her."

"Speaking of men who could spoil you," Wasp piped in, jerking her chin out the back window. "Please tell me you're banging the pool boy."

"Martin? He is hardly thirty-five years old. And I'm—"

"Older, not a monk," Wasp cut her off. "I bet he has a lady of the manor fantasy."

"Wasp, could you not try to hook my grandmother up? At least in front of me," I conceded when she raised a brow at me.

The rest of the afternoon went much the same way, the two of them bonding, Wasp pulling out a young, girlish side of my grandmother I had never known before, my grandmother slowly introducing Wasp to the very different kind of lifestyle we lived.

Far too soon, it was time for us to get back on the road again, my grandmother following us out onto the front stoop.

"It was so nice meeting you. You have my number. I am going to need you to call me as soon as you climb out of bed with your pool boy," Wasp demanded, giving my grandmother a smile before making her way to Wanda, giving me and my grandmother a moment alone.

"I like her for you."

"You should. You chose her," I reminded her, smiling.

"I have always had impeccable taste," she said, one of her hands going over the other, sliding off the ring on her left ring finger. "It's too soon, I know," she said, holding the ring up to inspect it. "But I want you to have it for when the moment is right."

"I can't take your engagement ring, Grandmother."

"You can. You will. Listen, this was never a symbol of great love for me. I think you were always mature enough to understand that. To know mine had never been a great love story. So I want this ring to have a second chance to be a part of a real love story, to be able to represent something that beautiful," she told me, reaching to slip it into my breast pocket. "Treat that woman how she deserves to be treated," she told me, pressing her hand to my cheek.

"I will," I told her, giving her a firm nod.

"You better."

I gave her a kiss on the cheek and made my way back to Wanda, finding Wasp already slipping out of her heels, flexing her feet.

"These shoes might have to retire. I'm pretty sure the only less strenuous job for heels other than sit-down-heels is casket-heels. And I'm not ready to go just yet," she told me, undoing her top dress button, not used to being so covered up. "I love her," she added, beaming at me. "I've never had a grandma. So even if things don't work out with us, I'm claiming her."

"I think I will be willing to share her. Even if she did betray me," I said, dropping down on the couch that acted as her passenger seat, making me ride sideways. But that was alright because I got to watch her the whole way without looking like a creep.

"Did she betray you, or did she give you the best thing that has ever happened to you?" she declared, pressing a hand drastically to her chest.

"I guess you have a point there," I agreed, feeling the weight of the ring in my pocket, the responsibility attached to it. Suddenly, there was no doubt in my mind that I would use it, that I would give it to her, that we would give it the legacy it deserved.

This was the woman for me.

With her crazy hair and chipped nails and her absolute inability to be a gracious winner in card games.

She was the one.

I hadn't even been looking for her, but I'd known it the moment I saw her. And each day after had only reinforced that initial thought that there was something special about her.

I couldn't have known at the time, of course, that she would come to mean as much as she had.

But there was no denying it.

This was the woman who was going to wear my ring, carry my name, tour the world with me, build a future with me.

"Okay. Where are we headed?" she asked, grabbing the wheel. "I am ready for a new adventure."

"We can have all the adventures you want, darling, but not in this thing."

"How dare you insult Wanda!" Wasp hissed, giving me small eyes.

"Actually, Wanda is fine. The problem, I'm afraid, is you. I fear we will both grow old, die, and turn to ash before we get to our next destination."

"I don't drive that slowly," she insisted.

"Do you want me to call Raven for confirmation? I asked, reaching for my phone.

"No," she grumbled, knowing I was right. "Okay. Fine. I will drive her back to Navesink Bank. I can probably convince my brother to store her for a while. But we are going to take her out again."

Not if I could help it.

We were going private or first class all the way.

I would happily use naked persuasion should I need to.

It would be a real hardship, let me tell you.
But I would do it for my woman.

EPILOGUE

Fenway - 2 weeks

"In what way is this the 'most reasonable' of all the houses your real estate agent sent you?" Wasp asked, holding up a binder with a picture of the estate on the front.

"Possibly because one of the first ones she showed me cost eighteen million."

"You can't be serious."

"There is a lot of money in this town," I told her, shrugging. "Rock stars live along the Navesink River."

"I'd like to go on the record and say that it is absurd for them to have eighteen-million-dollar homes as well."

"This one isn't eighteen-million, darling," I reminded her, always getting a kick out of how shocked and outraged she was over the cost of some things I had long since stopped noticing.

"Oh, right. Only eight million. Only," she scoffed. "It has eight bedrooms. Even if you slept in a different one every night of the week, you'd still have one to spare."

"We," I corrected.

"What?"

"If *we* slept in a different room every night of the week, *we* would still have one to spare," I told her, watching the way her smile went almost shy.

Yes, shy.

And, yes, Wasp.

They were two words that shouldn't have gone together, but any time I mentioned a future that involved the two of us in it, she got that same smile. Sometimes, her cheeks even went the smallest bit pink.

"Besides," I went on. "We will need guest rooms."

"Not if we are going to be in Navesink Bank. All our friends have homes here already."

"Alvy would like their own room."

"Okay. That is one extra bedroom. So three would be the bare minimum. Master, Alvy, and guest. Plenty of space. Oh, my God. Is this a spa? A spa? In a private home?" she asked, flipping through the laminated pages.

"You like a good soaking tub."

"There is a massage table. And a water feature. And a meditation room."

"If it makes you feel better, we can use the spare bedrooms as space for foreign exchange students or something like that."

"Oh, please. Like I would ever expose a poor, innocent child to your debauchery," she teased, smiling.

"What about kids?" I asked, worrying it was too soon to ask, but also seemingly unable to stop the question while we were sort-of on the topic.

"What about them?"

"Do you want any?" I asked. "You seem fond of all your nieces and nephew."

"Well, a large part of my enjoyment of them is teaching them dirty innuendos and buying them obnoxious toys. You know, the things that I would hate if I had to deal with said child on a daily basis. Honestly, I haven't really given it any thought. It was never part of my and Raven's plan to grow into stylish old spinsters in New York City and have boy toy boyfriends half our age catering to our every need. But I guess, if the impossible happened and I got pregnant, I would, I don't know, see it as a different kind of adventure. Can you imagine how badass a kid I would raise?" she asked.

I could imagine. Which was why I was asking. Like her, I had never really given it thought either. I guess, in an abstract way, I saw myself in a family way some day. A steadier lifestyle, a constant woman, a kid to be happy to see me when I came home. It was a nice idea. But it had always been a far-off thing.

Now, though, it didn't seem quite so off in the distance.

"Okay. This binder needs to go back to the agent," Wasp decided, closing it with a snap. "There was a gift wrapping room."

"We would need somewhere to wrap the gifts."

"On the dining room table or the living room floor like normal people."

"What about this one?" I asked, grabbing the next binder.

See, Wasp wasn't the only one capable of running a little con. I had showed her two obnoxiously ostentatious homes first. Then I saved the one I really wanted for third when her expectations had been shifted. It was an old marketing trick. You offer someone something at a high value price point and when they refused, you offered them something at a lesser price point. The trick was, you never intended to sell the first thing, and people really hated saying no to people. So when you offered them the thing you really wanted to sell them and they had already needed to be the 'bad guy' by saying no, you increased your chances of them biting by ten-fold.

This was our future house in my hands.

I knew it because I knew her.

She didn't object to oversize houses. She just wanted them to be somewhat practical. She was attracted to beauty, but not necessarily something showy.

This was the house.

It was a Second Empire house built in eighteen-eighty. Two and a half floors with a Mansard roof—hipped with two pitches, dormers, black shingles, deep-set eaves and decorative brackets. The siding was cream. There was an abundance of windows in a two-over-two, one-over-two style, in both rectangles and rounded topped, all of them framed with black shutters. There was a wrap-around porch on two sides, original hardwood flooring throughout all the levels, and even stained glass in the master bathroom.

It was a big house with five bedrooms, four baths, a living room, a family room, a den, and a study. There was an extra room up in the attic that could act as a bedroom, office, workout room, *gift wrapping room*, or, let's face it, a place to store all the souvenirs we would collect over the years.

The price was set around three million thanks to a four-acre property that was uncommon in the area and the fact that it had been painstakingly restored by a previous owner, so everything was new, even if it looked historical.

"Oh look at all these trees," she said, taking the binder from me. "I love Weeping Willows. They are perfect for picnicking under."

I had her right then and there.

While she was cooing over the interior, I was texting the real estate agent, telling her we were going to need a walkthrough.

It was all for show, though.

I knew it right then and there that we'd found our home.

Now I just needed to convince her to marry me.

One step at a time, though.

Wasp - 4 months

"Fenway," I called, looking at the package on the front porch.

The one with breathing holes in it.

And movement within.

"Yes, darling?" he called in a singsong voice because we were in a tiff about one of his naked lady paintings that he wanted to hang in the entryway.

I was no prude. I thought all those paintings from plague times with women lounging around on couches with their tits out were lovely.

I did not, however, think his monstrosity that had a naked woman made up of fifteen different women on a canvas the size of a kitchen island was lovely. In fact, it looked like some kind of veiled threat from a serial killer who liked to dismember his victims. I'd told him as such, too. Because, yeah, no, that damn thing was not going in the entryway. If I had my way, it was going to one of the other houses in his portfolio. Or, you know, straight into the garbage bin.

"There is a package here for you?"

"I didn't order anything," he told me, footsteps making their way in my direction.

"I think this is from someone named Karma," I informed him, pressing my lips together as I listened to the creature inside smack around at the sides of the box.

"Karma?" he asked, moving to stand next to me, staring down at the box.

"Also known as Payback For Buying Your Friend A Farm Pig, Industries."

"Oh, yes," Fenway concluded, nodding his head. "I guess I did have this coming. Well, let's see what it is, shall we?" he asked, picking up the box, careful not to get his fingers near the holes in case whatever was inside bit.

He carried it into our beautiful kitchen with its Viking stove I was starting to think I should learn how to use, butcher block countertops, and white cabinetry, dropping it down on the island to grab a scissor and carefully cut it open.

"Alright. Let's see it," I told him, watching as his eyes went worried as he reached his hand inside.

"Fuck," he hissed, ripping his hand back out, cradling it to his chest.

"Fuck fuck fuck fuck," another voice chorused, making my mouth fall open.

"Darling," I said, trying to hold in a laugh. "Did your old friend send you a foul-mouthed, ornery parrot as payback?"

"There's a note," he told me, nodding his chin toward the box, clearly not willing to risk his fingers again. And since I was pretty fond of those fingers—and the things he could do with them—I peered over the box, finding the note pinned to the side, pulling it out.

The bird inside was somewhat small in size, a gray and white parrot with a black beak and a bright red tail.

"Hi, my name is Leonard. I like almonds. I hate men. My favorite phrase is 'Fuck you, asshole,' followed closely by 'Shut the fuck up.' I will say these things loudly, confidently, and at the most inopportune times. Be advised, I will live for another fifty years, so you have the whole rest of your life to love me.

Signed, Leonard.
Also, your old friend Miller says: Gotcha, Fenway."

"Well, if it isn't my own bad decisions coming back to bite me in the ass," Fenway declared, running his finger under the tap. "I will need to call Alvy to have them figure out what an African Gray parrot needs to be happy and healthy."

"You're keeping it?" I asked, surprised, as the parrot pinned me with a freaky yellow-eyed glare, his pupils dilating in and out.

"Of course we are keeping it. Pick him up, darling. He must want to get out of that box."

"Why do I have to pick it up?"

"His note clearly states that he prefers the fairer sex."

"It says he hates men. It says nothing about liking women," I told him, put slowly lowered my hand inside. "Oh, I think he likes me," I declared when Leonard dipped his head down, seeming to ask for scratches. Which I happily gave him.

"Of course he does. It is impossible not to like you," Fenway said, moving in at my side. At the sound of his voice, Leonard whipped his head up, staring down Fenway, whispering 'Asshole' under his breath.

"Hey, look at that, he knows you so well already!" I declared, getting a slap on my ass from Fenway. "Have you ever had a pet?" I asked, offering Leonard my hand, feeling the surprising weight of him as he stepped up on my finger, letting me pull him out of the box.

"I have not," Fenway told me, trying to lean closer to look at Leonard, but making the bird lunge at him, trying to grab his nose in his sharp beak.

"Me either," I told him, feeling Leonard press his beak to my cheek, making a little kissing noise.

"Well, maybe he will be a good trial run."

"For what?"

"Children. I mean, of course, it is utterly different. This curses and bites and uses everything as a personal bathroom."

"Fenway, have you ever met a child? Because they like to curse, bite, and use everything as a bathroom as well."

"Well, if it has eyes like yours, I guess I could forgive it anything," he told me, reaching over to tug my hair, but getting chased away by the angry little guard bird. "You are enjoying this far too much," he accused when I got another kiss from Leonard.

"I can't help it if all the men fall in love with me," I told him, eyes dancing.

"Yeah, I guess I can't blame you, Leonard. But I fell for her first, so I get dibs."

I would never get used to hearing that.

And Fenway said it often.

Maybe because he sensed a part of me was still struggling to accept it, to believe it. Not through any fault of his own. Like everything else, Fenway did love with everything he had. But I guess I was always waiting for that other shoe to drop, for him to tell me he was bored of me, that he was done with me, that I had to pack everything back in Wanda and hit the road.

This insecurity might have been the big reason I'd insisted on keeping Wanda even though we had been traveling by plane and yacht for months now. I wanted to be sure she was there for me should Fenway change his mind like he was known to do.

It was proving hard to accept that the infamous playboy billionaire fuck-up had hung up his party hat in favor of nights on the couch watching classic movies with me.

He'd used naked persuasion more than a time or two to get me to admit that I wasn't sure if he could go from globe-trotting and all-night-partying to hanging out with me without feeling like he was giving up a lot.

He'd reached for me, got his sexy-serious voice on, and told me that he'd spent so much of his life hopping from place to place because if he stayed too long, he would realize that something was missing from his life.

"And that something was you," he'd told me, giving me a squeeze. And I swear my heart squeezed as well.

"What did Alvy say?" I asked when Fenway's phone dinged, making him reach for it.

"'LOL.'"

"I think that means we are on our own with this one," I concluded.

Since I'd become more of a permanent fixture in Fenway's life, Alvy had taken a step back, letting me handle keeping Fenway somewhat grounded, and to make sure his suitcases got packed and his driver was given enough notice when we needed him.

Alvy and I had made amends, both of us agreeing they had always had Fenway's best interest at heart, and that I was nobody's gold digger.

With all that free time, Alvy had finally purchased a home to house that ten-thousand-dollar living room set in.

Last we'd seen them, Alvy and their partner were settling in nicely.

It looked like Fenway wasn't the only one who found some stability.

And me?

I found the one man who didn't need to be taught a lesson.

The one man who saw beneath the surface of me.

But I was going to hold onto Wanda just a little while longer.

Fenway - 1 year

She hadn't been ready.

That was the reason I still had my grandmother's engagement ring in a pouch in my pocket a full year later.

It was easy to believe that all women had been raised on Disney movies with their happily-ever-afters, and that they were all living their lives in search of that supposed ideal, that once they had it, they dove headfirst into it.

That was not Wasp.

She wasn't built that way.

She had made her life and her living on the backs of failed happily-ever-afters of other women. It had made her overly cautious and jaded. It made it so that she didn't even trust herself and her own feelings. She'd met with far too many women who'd fallen blindly into love, had devoted their lives to men, only to have them spit on everything they had built.

"Treat her the way you would a dog that's been kicked one time too many," Raven had suggested one night while Wasp ran off to show her nieces and nephew her old favorite show as a kid—without telling Raven, of course, that her favorite show as a kid was *Unsolved Mysteries*, and that the kids would likely have nightmares for a week. "She needs time and consistency and trust. I promise you, she is not as cold and hard as she can seem on the outside. She had a huge heart. She's just afraid someone is going to crush it."

Luckily, Leonard had taught me a thing or two about healing and patience. Clearly, one of the previous owners had been a loving woman and an abusive man, making him distrust me. But after weeks and then months, we were finally able to be in the same vicinity of each other without there being any bloodshed.

I learned not to take offense when Wasp insisted on keeping Wanda parked in the back of our property. Or that she didn't take her website down, just slapped a notice on there saying she wasn't taking any clients at this time.

Life had taught her that men couldn't be relied upon.

I had to show her that I could.

Which meant I had to take my time, wait it out, not rush her into anything.

Which was why I was still hanging onto the ring.

But my fingers reached into that pocket, opened the pouch, grabbed the ring.

It was finally time.

We had flown out to Italy the week before, Leonard riding in a carry-on under Wasp's seat since she insisted we didn't need to take the private jet each time we traveled, that flying commercial would keep me humble and in-touch with the common man.

We had no plan in mind. We never did when we traveled. Someone would throw out a name of a destination, and then we would pack, we would head out, we would hit the streets, see what there was to explore.

I'd been everywhere five times over, but everything was still new for Wasp. And I never got sick of seeing the world through her eyes.

So far, we'd spent a lot of our time seeing monuments and museums and eating every single classic dish known to mankind.

But I'd finally managed to get her to agree to take the yacht away from Florence where we'd been spending most of our time.

We were on our way to one of the most romantic destinations in the world.

Cinque Terre.

It was a collection of villages in a place where cars were banned and the seafood was some of the best in the world. Along with the pesto. Which we'd eaten a giant pile of for dinner before hiking through the towns, hitting a few of the shops.

Wasp had long since stopped fighting me when I insisted on buying her souvenirs. All our mantles at home, our bookcases, our shelves, were riddled with little trinkets we'd picked up from around the world.

Colorful Maasai beads from Kenya.

Castañuelas—finger clackers—from Spain.

Nesting dolls from Russia.

Niren Zhang painted figurines from China.

So far, we'd only managed to get to seven countries. Which was not many by my traveling standards, but a lot for Wasp. She'd traveled extensively in our homeland, but claimed it was different, that while there were always smaller cultures to explore, it was nothing like visiting a different country. She liked to take longer, less frequent trips, to be able to sink her feet in, to tour the place like a local.

Besides, we had a home to take care of now, friends that liked to see us on a more regular basis. It was surprisingly nice to have roots.

Wasp had chosen Italy as our next destination.

I had been the one to get the yacht to come out, to meet us in Cinque Terre. Because I knew it was the perfect place.

And I knew it was the perfect time.

I knew she was ready.

Because when we'd mistakenly walked into a little wedding dress shop, since my Italian wasn't nearly as good as my French or Spanish, and the woman had mistaken her for a customer, had draped her head in a gauzy lace veil, and led her over to the mirror to look at herself, her eyes had gone dreamy.

Yes, Wasp's eyes.

Dreamy.

Another set of words that didn't seem like they went together.

Yet, there it was.

A dream in her eyes.

And that dream was to wear that veil and walk down an aisle toward me, one of her arms-dealing brothers at each of her sides.

It was a dream I'd held for a year now.

She'd eventually seen the look in her reflection, had whipped off the veil, and rushed out of the shop. I'd stayed behind, paying for the veil, asking the proprietor to have it wrapped in something plain and then shipped to our hotel.

It didn't matter that the dreamy look was short-lived.

It had been there.

And that meant it was time.

Finally.

I'd never been considered a patient man. I was pretty sure Alvy was wondering if aliens had come down, taken the real me, and replaced me with a clone, knowing how long I had been willing to wait to ask her to marry me.

After dinner, I'd had the captain take the yacht for a tour around the ocean while Wasp crashed on the bed below deck with *It Happened One Night* playing on the TV, then when it was just starting to get dark, I'd had him bring us back to Cinque Terre, but only in the marina just outside of an cove.

Cinque Terre had this one lovely little marina where the houses raised up off the cliffs in bright, happy colors. Pinks, yellows, oranges, light blues. And as it got dark, the lanterns around the towns set the area in a romantic glow.

It was straight out of a movie.

As much as she would scratch and hiss if you so much as implied it, Wasp was a sucker for a romantic movie. But only of the classic variety.

She liked the grand romantic gestures.

This was the best I could do on such short notice.

"Oh, *darling*!" I called down the steps that led back into the master bedroom.

"I ate too much. I can't move," she called back.

"I need to show you something," I told her, hearing a grumble as she rolled out of bed.

"It better be good, or I am throwing you off the yacht," she called, making her way up the stairs, her blonde hair a charming mess.

"If I didn't know you loved me, I would be concerned with the number of times you threaten my life on any given week," I told her, smiling, as I pressed a hand into the small of her back, leading her around the boat, needing to get the placement right.

"Well, maybe if you stopped being so throw-off-a-yacht-able, I wouldn't have to threaten you with that possibility," she teased, giving me a warm smile. "Okay, what am I supposed to look a... oh," she said, her air rushing out of her body as she looked at the image in front of her.

While she was distracted, I took out the ring, lowered down.

Behind me, I could hear one of the staff moving in, someone who I'd learned over the years was handy with a camera, someone who was going to make sure we had this image captured.

We had a lot of artwork on our walls.

Many of them led to mild bickering over their merit as art.

But I had a feeling Wasp was going to have no problems with this particular image hanging on our walls.

"You are uncharacteristically silent," Wasp mused, still oblivious to the way things were about to change for her. For us. For the future. "Did you..." she started, turning, taking a second to realize I was down on my knee.

I'd gotten good at reading her over the past year, this woman who had trained her whole life to hide her real emotions to be able to effectively do her job. She wasn't, I found, as good an actress as she thought.

It was all right there in her eyes.

It always was.

And right now?

There was shock and awe and caution and anticipation.

And most of all, hope.

For a future she never would have envisioned for herself. For the happily-ever-after she so long believed didn't exist in real life.

"Fenway..."

"Marry me," I said, cutting her off, knowing I needed to get this out before she started listing silly reasons this might be a bad idea. "I know it terrifies you. I know you are never going to be fully ready. But I'm asking you to take a chance. Say yes. Go on a new kind of adventure with me."

There was a telltale glistening to her eyes then.

It didn't chase away everything else still reflected there.

But this was Wasp. My Wasp. She had no fear. She was always ready for a new adventure.

Her shaky hand lifted, stretched out toward me, allowing me to slip the ring on her finger.

I could hear the camera shutter going off wildly behind us as I pressed a kiss to the ring, then looked up at her, finding a tear sliding down her cheek.

Standing, I pulled her close, kissed her until my lips went tingly.

She was the one to break away first, taking a deep breath.

"Okay, let's have the ugly talk."

"The ugly talk?" I repeated, brows furrowing.

"Yes, the ugly talk. The prenup talk. It will come eventually. Better to get it over with now."

"There is nothing romantic about discussing prenups."

"Yes, well, I think we have long established that you are the romantic one here. I'm the pragmatist. Which is a scary thought seeing as I am the one who is not allowed to have her nieces spend the night anymore."

"A belly button ring really isn't that big a deal," I reasoned.

"Right? It's her body. But yeah. Since you are the flip one, I have to be the reasonable one. And the reasonable thing is to discuss the prenup now."

"Okay," I agreed, leading her over toward the couch. "Let's talk about the prenup. I don't want one."

"Well, then you're an idiot," she declared, eyes rolling. "What if I was running an ultra-long con on you?"

"An ultra-long con, huh?" I mused. "Involving that time we both got food poisoning and both slept on the bathroom floor of the hotel, taking turns vomiting? If that was part of the con, darling, you have earned the money," I told her, smiling. "That damn lobster—"

"We agreed you would never say that word ever again," Wasp accused, skin going gray at the memory. And, to be fair, that had been a rough long weekend. But how did you know you truly loved someone if you hadn't lived through mutual food poisoning together, and still wanted to be with them?

"I think a small part of you is still worried I don't trust you because of our... unconventional courtship. I think this should wipe away any of those residual concerns. I trust you. You can marry me tomorrow and run away with half my fortune the day after that. That is how much I trust you."

"That is very foolish," she told me, scooting closer, throwing her legs over mine. "But thank you," she added, resting her head on my chest. "What did you have in mind for the wedding?"

"Something ostentatious," I declared, making her chuckle.

"I wouldn't expect anything less from you."

"And I want it soon."

"Of course you do."

"And I want to invite everyone from the casino," I added. We'd been regulars there anytime we were in Navesink Bank.

"And Eamon Awan as your best man?"

"And all the fixers as my groomsman," I agreed.

"Our wedding is going to be ridiculous. Your upper-crust, billionaire acquaintances. My arms-dealing brothers, a team of professional fixers, ex-conwomen..."

"And we will have to find a way to make Leonard our ring bearer."

"Of course we will. Maybe he can ride in on the farm pig," Wasp teased.

But make no mistake, I was taking notes.

And in six month's time, there was going to be an African Gray perched on a saddle attached to a six-hundred-pound farm pig.

I'd always been known for the ridiculous.

Now we both would.

Wasp - 5 years

"Fenway, what the hell are we going to do with a ten-foot-tall giraffe stuffed animal?" I asked as he grabbed it around its middle, groaning a bit when he lifted the massive thing off the floor.

"We are going to put it in the toy room, of course."

"We'd have to anchor it to a wall. It could fall down and crush her."

"She pointed at it," he insisted, shrugging a shoulder.

That was all it took with him.

Our little girl pointing at something.

Then he was going out of his way to acquire it for her.

Once, when she was just ten months old, she had thrown her chubby hand out of the window and pointed a pudgy finger at a massive dog on the street. This big white fluffy thing that likely weighed more than I did. And the only reason she pointed at it was because it looked like the dog in the picture book I read to her before bed.

What did my husband do?

Pulled over the car, hopped out, ran across the street, and tried to offer the owners an untold sum of money—I'd asked, he'd refused to tell me—to sell him their dog. Thankfully, the owners were attached and declined. I had my hands full with a baby and Leonard and, let's face it, my husband. I wasn't ready for a dog that was bigger than all of us.

This giraffe, while not requiring feeding and washing and numerous trips outside, was equally as impractical as that dog had been.

"Darling, this is Hamleys!" Fenway declared, as though that brushed aside my concerns.

For Little Bee's—Beatrice's—third birthday, I had wanted to do something fun, but normal. Like a backyard barbecue with friends and family. Maybe ramp it up a notch with rented bounce houses and cotton candy and popcorn machines.

Of course, Fenway had other plans.

When it came to stubbornness, we were matched.

But when it came to making plans behind the other's back, Fenway was the clear winner.

Before I had even looked at cotton candy machine varieties online, he had somehow managed to get his jet and a hotel lined up, as well as called Hamleys to work out a deal to rent the world's largest and oldest toy store for the entire day.

Now, was the toy store possibly the most epic place in the world for a child? Even I would admit that. It had an actual, working merry-go-round, a tube slide that went down two floors, a two-level fire engine to play in, a candy shop, and every single toy known to mankind.

That said, Bee was three. She wouldn't remember this birthday. I wasn't against it as an idea, but tried to reason that it would be more appropriate for her fifth or sixth birthday. That way, she would remember it.

What was my husband's response, you might be wondering?

"Well, we can do it on her fifth or sixth birthday too."

A part of me was exasperated.

The other part, though, couldn't believe what an amazing father Bee got to have. One who cared about making her birthday the most amazing day in the world. One who stayed up at night researching the latest and greatest gadgets for her to enjoy. One who had gone to seven different stores in town to make sure he got a roll or two of every kind of colorful wrapping paper so that each of her packages at Christmas would be different. One who sat patiently with her on Christmas morning after being up with me all night arranging the tree and put together every last toy she got, played with her until she started to fall asleep sitting up.

I figured that, through Bee, Fenway was getting to experience the joy and wonder of being a new human, something he hadn't been able to have as a child with an overbearing, unfeeling father.

That little girl had him wrapped entirely around her finger.

Extra juice when I had already said it was time to switch to water? Go to Daddy. Ice cream for lunch when I was out running errands? Daddy had her back. Going to the fair every single night of the week for ten days while it was in town? Yep, Daddy made sure of that too.

I had my concerns about what would happen when Bee was older and she realized she could get away with anything when it came to her father.

When I'd expressed those concerns, Fenway had shrugged. He claimed that I had him wrapped around my finger too, and nothing bad had come from that. He'd been so sweet and sincere in the moment that I had forgotten my counterargument. Which was that I was a grown ass woman who had already been through struggles by the time I met him. Bee was a little girl who could very easily become a spoiled adolescent.

But, I figured, I had time to try to curve that before it was too late.

Besides, I learned, being spoiled a little bit was nice.

But the giraffe? That was where I needed to draw the line, right?

I mean, Bee couldn't even actually play with it. It was too big, too clumsy. It was even too high for her to climb on. So having it in the house would just be more of a stupid status symbol that took up far too much space. Besides, we were in London. Getting the damn thing home would be a pain as well. We'd be tripping over it in the jet.

"Okay, let's compromise," I suggested, planting a hand in the center of Fenway's chest, halting him.

"But I don't *wanna* compromise," he said, imitating a child by stomping his foot, then giving me that big, boyish smile I never got sick of seeing. Even when he was being a pain in the ass.

"How about we get her that whole Disney Princess wardrobe set?" I suggested. I had shaken my head at it when he eyed it earlier. The price tag just seemed astronomical for something she would grow out of in less than a year. But if it was between a massive, useless giraffe, or a wardrobe that Bee actually would have fun playing with? I was willing to be a little ridiculous.

"And the dolls to match."

"Fenway."

"Don't make me demand the stuffed animal companions too," he said, eyes dancing.

"Okay. We have a deal," I agreed, offering him my hand.

He took it, and in true Fenway Arlington style, dropped down on his knees to kiss my knuckles while declaring to whomever was behind me, "Excuse me, but have you met the most beautiful *and interesting*," he added, smirking, "woman in the world?"

"Well, seeing as she is my best friend in the whole world, yes," Raven said, and I could hear the smile in her voice. "Bee would like to know if she can have that lobster stuffed animal thing from *The Little Mermaid*."

My stomach, even all these years later, twisted at the mention of lobster. Yes, even a stuffed fictional lobster from a movie.

"Don't even start," I told Fenway, pointing at him. "We had a deal."

"I know. We did. But we forgot to include Bee in the discussion. Which is utterly bad business on our part, don't you think?" he asked, releasing my hand, getting to his feet, and taking Bee out of Raven's hands, raising her above his head until she giggled, then settling her on his hip. "You want all the stuffed animals, don't you, angel?"

"She's going to be a little devil if you keep spoiling her," I called after him as he started to walk away.

"She'll be fine," Raven said, moving in beside me. "Roman spoils the kids too. Which makes me have to be the bad guy at times. And the one to balance out all the crazy. But they have turned out alright so far. Bee will be okay too."

"And if she's not, I can just blame Fenway," I agreed, smiling.

Fenway - 11 years

"Sit down," Alvy demanded, patience wearing thin with my pacing.

"I can't," I said, heart hammering, thoughts swirling.

"Making yourself sick isn't going to help Wasp," they reminded me, ever my voice of reason.

Alvy had long since retired as my personal assistant, taking instead a corporate position in one of the family businesses, where they proved every bit as capable as they had been when they were keeping my messy life from falling apart.

They had still been an ever-present part of our life, though. Babysitting Bee. Coming over for dinner parties.

And, like now, sitting with me when I felt like everything was falling apart.

"I wanted to get rid of that goddamn thing a decade ago," I ranted, raking a hand through my hair, fear a live wire through my system, sparking off of every nerve ending.

"I know you did. But she was attached to it. You know that."

"Yeah," I agreed, jaw ticking. "But I never should have let her take it out."

"Fenway, this is Wasp we are talking about. If you told her she couldn't take Wanda out, she would have suggested kissing her ass. She wanted to take a little weekend trip for old time's sake with her best friend. No one could have predicted the driver of a semi passing out at the wheel," Alvy told me, making my gut twist painfully, the image playing itself out in my head for the millionth time since I'd heard the news.

I'd never known panic like that before in my life.

I'd been frantic when I called her brothers, getting one of their wives to take Bee so I could catch a plane, get to the hospital in North Carolina where they'd been struck.

Roman had been on the same plane with me, both of us rushing into the hospital, begging for updates.

Roman was the lucky one.

Raven had been in the back of the skoolie when they'd been struck head-on, getting only a mild concussion and a couple stitches to her temple from slamming into a cabinet.

Wasp?

Wasp had been right there in the front.

And it was a sad state of affairs when you had to be thankful the truck hit from the passenger side instead of the driver's, or we wouldn't be at the hospital right now. I'd be losing my shit at the morgue.

As it was, she was in surgery. And no one had any updates for me. Not even after I offered to build a whole new children's wing onto their hospital to get some.

"I won't feed you platitudes right now," Alvy said, taking a deep breath. "But I am going to suggest you hold off on losing your mind until you know if you need to or not."

The woman I loved—the only woman I could ever love—was on a cold metal table in a surgery room with parts of her ripped open. I couldn't be fucking calm.

"A new children's ward *and* a new cancer ward," I called to the nurse manning the desk a few feet away from me.

"That won't be necessary, Mr. Arlington," a voice said at my back, making my heart fly up into my throat as I turned, finding a doctor standing there, his mask still hanging off of one ear. "Your wife is out of surgery," he started.

All I could think was: out of surgery meant she was alive still.

I could handle anything if she was still alive.

No arms? I could feed her.

No legs? I could get one of those wheelchairs that damn near did everything for you.

She just had to be *alive*, damnit.

"Tell me," I demanded as Alvy got up, came to stand at my side.

"Your wife endured a blow to the head from hitting the window, a broken arm, and a laceration to her liver."

"Her liver? Does she need a new one? She can have mine. I don't need to drink. Just tell me where to go to get cut open."

"Thankfully, that won't be necessary," the doctor said, calm, professional, but his lips twitched ever so slightly. "The laceration was moderate. We managed to repair the damage. Her arm has pins. She has stitches to her forehead. But we suspect she is going to make a full recovery," he said, clamping a hand on my shoulder.

I was not, almost as a rule, affectionate with male strangers.

But I threw myself at the good doctor, giving him a bear hug.

"Do you have children? I will pay for their college tuitions. Grad school. Med school. Their weddings. You name it," I told him, pulling away, feeling the sting of tears in my eyes the relief was so acute.

"That won't be necessary," he assured me. "I am just doing my job."

"Can I see her?" I asked.

"She is being moved to the ICU. Once she is settled, you can visit with her."

"The ICU doesn't sound like she is fine," Alvy insisted, thinking more clearly than I was at the moment.

"It's standard after a surgery like hers. I suspect she will move onto a main floor before the night is out."

With that, the doctor walked away, leaving me so weak that I collapsed down into a chair, taking my first real breath in half a day.

"Alvy."

"Yes?" they asked, sitting down beside me.

"We need to set up some sort of charity," I decided. "Helping pay for med school."

"I will look into it," they assured me, patting my shoulder. "She's okay," they reminded me.

"She has to be," I told them.

"She is. And you will get to see her in a little bit."

Forty minutes later, I was led into her room, finding her in one of the hospital beds, looking way too small, way too pale, way too weak for the Wasp I knew and loved.

I'd never seen the woman look weak a day in her life.

She'd gone into labor like she was going to war, screaming, cursing, barking orders.

Seeing her look that way made a piercing sensation stab my chest as I moved toward her bedside.

"Oh my God, Fenway. I'm not dead," she grumbled up at me as I sat on the side of her bed, reaching for her hand, feeling the tears that had been in my eyes before break free.

"I worried you might be," I admitted. "I couldn't have lived with that. Not for a minute. You're not allowed to die first, darling. I forbid it."

"I heard you were offering out random organs to save me," she said, giving me a soft smile.

"Not random ones. Just the ones you might need."

"Luckily, that wasn't necessary," she said, sighing. "Wanda is dead. Like dead for real."

"I heard. I'm sorry, darling."

"It feels like the end of an era. Even though I hadn't used her since we got together."

"There were a lot of good memories there," I said, giving her hand a squeeze. We had the pictures on a gallery wall, all her favorites from her adventures with Raven. Across from that were her favorites with me. Then with both of us and Bee.

"How is Raven?"

"Just a little banged up. She's already on her way home. She wanted to stay," I told her. "Roman nearly had to have her sedated to get her to leave you. But her kids were worried."

"Thank God she's alright. The other driver?"

"No injuries."

"Where is Bee?"

"With your sister-in-law. Your brothers are here. But they are downstairs. They couldn't come up to this floor."

"Everyone's all shaken up over a little nothing."

"It's hardly nothing. And, yes, we were all worked up. You have a lot of people who love you, darling," I reminded her.

"What is that smile for?" she asked a moment later. "What's so funny?" she pressed when a chuckle escaped me.

"I was just thinking."

"About what?"

"Your old lady driving. I think it saved your life today."

"So maybe you can stop teasing me about it."

"I guess I can do that."

"Don't look so sad. I'm sure you can find something else to tease me about."

"Like the fact that you're now part cyborg?" I suggested, touching her arm.

"That will do," she agreed, reaching out with her good arm to pat my head.

Wasp - 20 years

"How dare she grow up to be so damn practical," Fenway grumbled, tapping his fingers on the kitchen table beside his coffee cup.

"I know you tried your hardest to make her into a spoiled socialite with cotton candy for brains," I told him, smiling. "Somehow, someone imparted some good sense in her."

"I will never forgive you for it," he told me, giving me small eyes.

Bee was leaving for college.

And Fenway was having separation anxiety about the whole situation.

I couldn't blame him. She'd always been his little baby. And a daddy's girl. The two were as close as could be.

"She is just going away to school," I reminded him, patting his hand.

"She doesn't have to go to school. She could be like one of those people who are famous for no other reason than being rich," he insisted.

"Even if she did want to live the shallow socialite life, Fenway, she would want to leave home. I don't know about you, but I would much rather she go off to school to become a neurosurgeon than party all across the globe, getting up to no good."

Bee had, as it turns out, become nothing like either of us.

She was calm, rational, collected, sure of what she wanted, and dogged in her pursuit of it. She wasn't prone to the outlandish or the reckless. She enjoyed the simpler things in life.

And, now, she wanted to make a living helping people.

I couldn't have been prouder. Even if my heart was breaking a bit too.

"We could cut her off," he suggested, clinging onto straws. "Then she couldn't go."

"She needs to have her own life. We are going to see her all the time."

"I don't know what we will do without her around."

"Well, I sort of had an idea," I suggested, having been pondering it since Bee came to me and asked if she could bring Leonard to her off-campus townhouse with her, giving us even more freedom than we had been anticipating.

"What's that?"

"It's been a really long time since we had an adventure," I told him, watching as his gaze found mine, interest there. "I mean, when was the last time we toured the world? There have to be thousands of new things to be seen. Besides, we have been saying we wanted to take an anniversary trip back down to Bali, to that cave, for old time's sake. Now would be a great time to do that, don't you think?"

"It would be nice," he agreed, still a little hesitant. "If we took the jet. And the yacht."

It was ridiculous.

Over the top.

Just like him.

"I think we can arrange that," I agreed.

"Did I ever tell you how happy I am that you conned me into loving you," he asked, reaching to pull me onto his lap.

He had.

Every single day.

Of every single month.

Of every single year.

And I never got sick of hearing it.

I never would.

DEAR READER

This book is a <u>completely</u> standalone novel.

But once upon a time, a town called Navesink Bank was founded. It was full of outlaw bikers, loan sharks, fixers, hired muscle, and the mob.

All those people do have books.

If you read this book and are intrigued by some of the side characters mentioned here, the team of "fixers" can be read about in my PROFESSIONALS SERIES. The biker brothers are from my HENCHMEN MC SERIES. Eamon Awan and the crew at the casino can be found in my RIVERS BROTHERS series.

On the following pages, you can find a comprehensive list of all my series and standalone books, so you can know where to start :)

<3 Jessica

PLAYLIST

"Hell on Heels" - Pistol Annies
"Wild Child" - Kenny Chesney
"Lady Like" - Ingrid Andress
"I Can Break Hearts Too" - Carter's Chord
"Boy Like Me" - Jessica Harp
"Chasin' Me" - Caroline Jones
"Strong Enough" - Sheryl Crow
"Get Away With It" - Lacy Cavalier
"Eyes On You" - Chase Rice
"I Don't Know About You" - Chris Lane
"All I Need to See" - Mitch Rossell
"Love That About You" - Filmore
"Best Shot" - Jimmie Allen

ALSO BY JESSICA GADZIALA

If you liked this book, check out these other series and titles in the NAVESINK BANK UNIVERSE:

The Henchmen MC
Reign
Cash
Wolf
Repo
Duke
Renny
Lazarus
Pagan
Cyrus
Edison
Reeve
Sugar
The Fall of V
Adler
Roderick
Virgin
Roan

Camden
West

The Savages
Monster
Killer
Savior

Mallick Brothers
For A Good Time, Call
Shane
Ryan
Mark
Eli
Charlie & Helen: Back to the Beginning

Investigators
367 Days
14 Weeks
4 Months

Dark
Dark Mysteries
Dark Secrets
Dark Horse

Professionals
The Fixer
The Ghost
The Messenger
The General
The Babysitter
The Negotiator

Rivers Brothers
Lift You Up
Lock You Down

STANDALONES WITHIN NAVESINK BANK:
Vigilante
Grudge Match
The Rise of Ferryn
Counterfeit Love

OTHER SERIES AND STANDALONES:

Stars Landing
What The Heart Needs
What The Heart Wants
What The Heart Finds
What The Heart Knows
The Stars Landing Deviant
What The Heart Learns

Surrogate
The Sex Surrogate
Dr. Chase Hudson

The Green Series
Into the Green
Escape from the Green

DEBT
Dissent
Stuffed: A Thanksgiving Romance
Unwrapped
Peace, Love, & Macarons

ABOUT THE AUTHOR

Jessica Gadziala is a full-time writer, parrot enthusiast, and coffee drinker who enjoys short rides to the bookstore, sad songs, and cold weather, and who had developed an unhealthy obsession with acquiring houseplants. She lives in New Jersey with her three dogs, seven parrots, and eleven chickens.

She is a strong believer in snark, strong secondary characters, and badass women.

STALK HER!

Connect with Jessica:

Facebook: https://www.facebook.com/JessicaGadziala/
Facebook Group:
https://www.facebook.com/groups/314540025563403/

Goodreads:
https://www.goodreads.com/author/show/13800950.Jessica_Gadziala
Goodreads Group:
https://www.goodreads.com/group/show/177944-jessica-gadziala-books-and-bullsh

Twitter: @JessicaGadziala

JessicaGadziala.com

<3/ Jessica